Praise for Stupid Fast

ALA Best Fiction for Young Adults Selection
YALSA Best Fiction for Young Adults
2011 Cybils Award Winner, Young Adult Fiction
Junior Library Guild Selection
ABA Best Books

"In the tradition of great young adult protagonists like Holden Caulfield and Eric 'Moby' Calhoune comes Felton Reinstein... Surprises abound in this future youth classic...It is difficult to imagine a reader who will not find Felton's tale compelling and highly entertaining."

—*VOYA*

"This story has a little bit of everything: the challenges of growing up, the issues surrounding interracial romance, navigating tough class issues, and a narrator who is one of the most real, honest, and still funny male voices to come around in a while."

—*YALSA*

"Felton's sarcasm, anxiety, self-doubt, thoughtfulness, and compassion carry the day and perfectly capture the voice of his generation."
—*School Library Journal*

"Herbach has created an endearing character coming to terms with his past and present in a small, well-defined Wisconsin town."
—*Booklist*

"Felton's manic, repetitive voice and naive, trusting personality stand out in a field of dude lit populated with posturing tough guys and cynical know-it-alls."

—Kirkus

Praise for *Nothing Special*

"Felton's voice is fresh and believable as a teen on the edge of manhood…Kudos to Herbach for this deep, moving, LOL funny, and completely original story."

—School Library Journal

"Felton and Andrew are both appealing…readers who like their funny stories mixed with sports will root for the siblings' reconciliation."

—Booklist

"Sports abound in the story—track, football, tennis and Frisbee. The writing is particularly fresh in these descriptions, which depict all the internal rhythms, workings and mantras of an athlete in a critical moment."

—The Star Tribune

"Fans of the first book, as well as fans of authors like Chris Crutcher, will enjoy these novels. And—and this is the best part!—recently Sourcebooks (the publisher of the novels) announced that there will be a THIRD Felton book, about his senior year of high school, out in 2013. So even more Felton = awesomeness."

—Dancing Through YA

I'M WITH STUPID

Geoff Herbach

sourcebooks
fire

Published by Sourcebooks Fire, an imprint of Sourcebooks, Inc.
P.O. Box 4410, Naperville, Illinois 60567-4410
(630) 961-3900
Fax: (630) 961-2168
teenfire.sourcebooks.com

Library of Congress Cataloging-in-Publication data is on file with the publisher.

Printed and bound in the United States of America.

VP 10 9 8 7 6 5 4 3 2 1

For Leo and Mira

Early September

The Future, Felton

CHAPTER 1
Who Are You?

I sat at the kitchen table back in early September. Jerri, my mom, sat across from me. She studied a giant accounting book. She wore this business suit because she'd decided not to be in love with anyone but herself, to go back to college, to be a student and learn accounting, and then get a real job and a real career, which I thought was a pretty good idea because she's always seemed a little pathetic. (Working an hour a day as a crossing guard isn't a great career.) She sighed and read. Meanwhile, I studied a bunch of brochures from colleges who were recruiting me to play football.

My brain hurt. All these college brochures listed different majors I could take: agriculture, biology, French, engineering, English, journalism, badminton, bowling, urban geography, female studies, anthropology, ball cell anatomy, the bugle, bun steeling, cat sexuality, business, marketing, mass media, ass scratchology, etc. *What? Ass what?* My eyes hurt.

All the brochures had pictures of students sitting in classrooms smiling and listening to bearded professor dudes who were clearly, energetically imparting some kind of giant, important life lesson about how the world really works. *How?* I wondered. *What?* My head swam.

"Jerri," I said, "I'd like to know how the world really works."

"Shh," Jerri said. "I'm studying."

"But I can't decide. Too many colleges. Too many freaking majors. I can't think."

"Don't think so hard," she said.

"Good one. Thanks."

"Yeah." She didn't look up from her book. "Don't think."

I stared across the table at her. She used to look like a hippie with little jangling bells sewn into her skirts. No more. "Okay. Why'd you go to college here?" I asked. "Back when you decided? Did Bluffton have some good programs?"

Jerri looked up from her book. She squinted. She shook her head, then she talked fast. "My dad was a jerk and I couldn't go anyplace else because he wanted me to stay in town, so I'd keep bartending at his bar on the weekends so he could get drunk."

"Oh," I said.

"Yeah." She nodded. Her face turned red. "Stop, Felton."

"So…" I said, even though I knew I should stop talking. "At least you didn't have to make any big choices that might totally destroy your future if you screwed them up, right?"

"Felton," Jerri said. "Be quiet."

"I'm sorry. I know. You're studying."

"No. Just shut the hell up," Jerri spat. "Okay?" Her face was very red by that point. "I made no choices and then your father and now I'm almost forty and I'm still stuck here."

"Yeah," I said. "You're stuck. With me."

Jerri nodded. Then she looked back down at her accounting book.

I got up, kicked my chair back, and left the table. I went downstairs and out the door into the garage and got on my speedy-ass bike and biked the hell away from my terrible house and my mom, Jerri, who has often made me hate the whole world.

Hi, my name is Felton Reinstein. It's true: I'm stupid fast. It's true: I'm blessed. It's true: I have big problems. It's just true.

I rode through the warm fall night. I buzzed it. Gravel flew when I cranked through the curves. This wasn't a pleasure ride. I felt like I might get sick. Freaking Jerri.

Eventually, I went over to Gus's house.

• • •

Gus has always been my best friend. His dad and my dad were actually good friends way back in the day. We have a giant history filled with lots of sitting around and talking about *The Avengers* and Muppets and also girls, and we also spent time planning for revenge against our enemies at school who were so mean to us. (We never enacted any of our plans. They were pretty elaborate though, like breaking into Ken Johnson's house during summer vacation and crapping in all his socks, which would've been gross and also kind of impossible.)

My absolute earliest memory of Gus is from when we were still crawling. I remember this open-mouthed, drooling kid. (I've remembered lots of weird stuff in the last year.) He drooled a bunch and hugged my head and put his mouth over my nose. I remember his wet little baby tongue licking my face. This is not a memory I've shared with him.

In the fall, Gus still had his punk hair wad, which he'd had since middle school (except for a while, after his grandma made him cut it), which covered his eyes and made him look like an excellent sheepdog.

Later that same night in September, the two of us sat in his kitchen eating Pizza Rolls. He was freaking out about applying to all these prestigious little liberal arts colleges. He was leaning over the table chewing a hot Pizza Roll, so his mouth didn't stay closed. He jabbered fast.

"They all want this personal essay from me saying who the hell I think I am. Who am *I* to actually believe I'm cool enough to go their school? Grades aren't enough! Forensics, National Honor Society, student government...*not enough*! I have to write out my philosophy! Tell them what I really think. Jesus! It takes hours. And I can't write the same essay for all the schools because they all word the question a little differently, so my focus has to be on something a little different, and, dude, it's not like I don't have homework!

"You think I'm going to let Abby Sauter be the valedictorian? Hell no! Abby? Not a chance, man. Victory will be mine. So I can't take a damn break from studying. Plus essays! I'm going crazy!"

"Hmm. Tough," I said, my mouth packed with a Pizza Roll.

"You don't have to do any of this, do you?"

"This? What's this?" I asked.

"You just get by on your fat legs."

"I don't have fat legs."

"Giant man football thighs. I can't believe how easy it is for you. College recruiters busting down your door. Filling out your paperwork."

"What paperwork?" I asked.

"That's what I mean!" Gus shouted.

"Wait. You don't know my pain," I said.

Gus's dad walked into the kitchen carrying a big leather notebook where he keeps lecture notes for teaching. (He's a professor.) He stroked his beard and nodded at me. "What schools are you considering, Felton? Hope you're paying attention to academics and not just athletics," he said.

"I don't know," I said. "There are too many. They call all the time. I just got a text from UNLV."

"Las Vegas?" Gus's dad asked.

"Yeah. I guess."

"I hope Jerri is giving you some advice," he said.

"Uh…sure. Tons," I said.

Gus's dad furrowed his brow. He breathed in and stared down at me. "Well, if you narrow down a list of schools, you can bring it over and I'll tell you what I know about their programs. Would that help?" he asked.

"Yeah. Yes," I said. "Please."

"I don't know anything about football," he said. "But remember. This is a *great* time in your life."

"*The hell it is!*" Gus shouted.

"Calm down, boy. My God." Gus's dad laughed and left the kitchen with a banana.

"I'm in crisis here and Dad's eating a banana," Gus said. He held up his hair wad so I could see his giant, freaked-out eyeballs.

"Calm down, boy," I said. "Your dad is awesome."

"What would you write if you had to justify your whole existence?" he asked.

I put on my best redneck accent. "I play football real good."

"Yeah, funny," Gus said.

I thought it was funny. A few minutes later, I biked home. Jerri was already asleep. The recruiters weren't though. I got a text message about Iowa football at 11:45 on a Saturday night.

Justify your existence, I thought.

• • •

Yes, I'm stupid fast. But I can also be pretty stupid. We all have that ability, I think.

Oh no. You are not alone.

Also this: I have big problems. Seriously.

• • •

At 1 a.m., I texted my girlfriend, Aleah. She had a recital that night in Chicago, where she lived at the time. She's a big-time pianist. The *New York Times* called her the best young African-American pianist in the country. I'm not kidding. Then a whole bunch of people wrote in to tell the *New York Times* that couching their compliment with "African-American" was racist. She's the best young pianist of any race or color or whatever in America. That's what the commenters online said. The *New York Times* apologized. Aleah's so good we never get to see each other.

Go well? I texted.

She didn't answer until the next afternoon.

I wasn't tired. I texted Andrew, my little brother, who had moved to Florida over the summer to be with our grandpa Stan, to play in a Beach Boys cover band with a bunch of old farts who wear Hawaiian shirts, and to go to a private school for very smart kids. (Andrew is, in fact, a very smart kid.)

You awake? I texted.

No, he responded.

What's happening? I asked.

I sat there in bed, waiting for a reply, but I got no reply. Apparently, Andrew really wasn't awake.

Jerri. Aleah. Andrew. Gus freaking out, so all he could do was talk about college applications? I was lonely a lot in the fall.

And I carried this twist in my stomach, this tweak, ever since the summer when I'd met my grandpa (I guess I knew him when I was a little kid, but he hadn't talked to me and Andrew for over a decade and I didn't remember him), which never went away. It was like I had a hole in my gut and I felt lonely even when I was with people. This hole scared me. I lay in bed feeling lonely.

Focus on the good stuff, I told myself. Focus on the good stuff. The great stuff. Football is great stuff! Grandpa told you to love the game. Football! It's great! It's the best! It's awesome! Think about Cody throwing the ball to you or Karpinski catching a screen and you knocking the shit out of some kid who wants to tackle him or Reese, that sweet fat ass, hitting a linebacker and you cut and you see daylight and you explode and the crowd goes wild and you fly down the field in this blur of stadium light and light speed and the end zone comes rushing up so fast in a blur that it doesn't seem possible you run so fast…

I think I fell asleep.

Playing football last fall *was* great. For real. I was ESPN's third-ranked running back in the whole damn nation. Might've been number one, except they said I played against weak competition because Bluffton, Wisconsin, is small and the schools we played were small.

Football is great. When I play football, everything makes sense. There's a goal. *Score a touchdown!* There are rules. *Don't crush anyone after the whistle blows!* There are quarters and halves and time-outs, and at the end of the game, you know if you've won or lost.

Last fall, Bluffton High School never lost. Me and my football pals Cody, Karpinski, and Reese? That was a hell of a way to end a senior year of football, right? State title.

It was perfect.

• • •

I woke up that Sunday morning in September and rolled out of bed worried I'd forgotten something. I've always been pretty good at school for reasons unknown. (I'm naturally sort of distracted.) I opened my school email to see if I'd brought home everything I needed to do my English homework for Monday. There was a message from the guidance counselor. It said:

> Seniors invited to be senior mentors. Help a freshman acclimate
> to high school. Great for college application!

I stared at the email. *Justify your existence,* I thought.

Right then, Andrew texted back.

I'm awake now. Why do you insist on sending messages in the middle of the night? Florida IS an hour later, my brother.

I squinted at the phone. I thought. I wrote.

You ever feel a need to justify your existence?

Andrew answered.

I am a whole human being. I need to justify nothing.

I read. I nodded. I wrote.

oh.

Then I emailed the guidance counselor and said I'd like to be a senior mentor.

Mr. Childers was ecstatic that I volunteered.

FELTON? REALLY? THAT'S FANTASTIC!

"I just want to give back to the community. I've been blessed, you know?" I said to the mirror while I combed my hair.

• • •

Tommy Bode, freshman schlub.

The next morning, Monday, we met. My mentee walked into the classroom in this stumblebum sort of way that made me know

9

he'd been picked on his whole dipshit life. (I understand this—before football, I was a dipshit much like him, except skinny and squirrely instead of chubby and pork faced.) His eyes were nervous and shifty. He had fat, red cheeks. He wore a giant T-shirt with a Bakugan warrior on it.

"Hey there, buddy!" I said. "Nice to meet you!"

"I know you," he said.

"Oh yeah?"

He nodded. His eyes watered. "You're Andrew Reinstein's brother," he said.

Most people in my hometown don't know me as Andrew's brother. Most know me as a football player.

I nodded. I said, "Yeah. That's right. Andrew!"

"I heard Andrew moved. Why didn't you move?" he asked.

"I don't know," I said. I paused and stared at his face. I smiled too big. "I like it here, I guess!"

"Oh. Weird," Tommy said.

We stared at each other for a few seconds.

"What are we supposed to do?" he asked.

"Talk about what it's like to be a student, that kind of thing," I said.

"Do we have to?" he asked.

"I don't know," I said. "Maybe not?" I felt my ears heat up. "Do you want to talk about something else?" I asked.

He sat down at the desk next to me. "Not really," he said. He started doodling in his notebook. He drew a pig with an arrow stuck in its head.

"Whoa," I said. "That's a fine-looking pig!"

"Thanks," he said.

Then I watched him draw for twenty minutes until the bell rang. I felt a cloud of doom around us. I understood Tommy Bode in a weird way, okay?

CHAPTER 2
I Have Some Massive Sacks of Baggage, My Friend

Before we go any further, this is important to establish: I have problems.

Not, *Oh dude, I can't find my wallet! Crap!* (Even though I definitely lose my wallet a lot. I actually don't know where my wallet is right now.)

More like, *Oh dude, my dad killed himself when I was a tyke. Oh shit, I found him hanging and he was twitching, shivering, because he'd just done it, because he thought Jerri had taken me and Andrew to school and daycare.*

I mean, I'm sure Dad didn't want me to find him. I was five years old.

Except I left my snack bag on the floor of the garage. (It was my job to buckle Andrew into his car seat and I often dropped my crap on the floor.) So Jerri yelled at me, turned the car around, drove back down the main road, pulled back up the long driveway, and told me she didn't want to get out to open the "damn garage door"—and she told me to hurry, so I ran in through the front door and through the house and opened the inside door to the garage and I found Dad there.

Shivering. He was twisting a little. The beam with the rope

creaked. Our step stool was knocked over under him. I couldn't move. I can still see how his neck looked smashed sideways. He had to have just done it. A minute before? A couple? What if he saw me? His little boy. The last thing he saw?

And I turned and the air sucked out of me like a backward explosion and I had to scream, but I couldn't, and the walls melted away and the floor rolled and I tried to run but cracked my face against the side of the open door—witch whistles ripping in my ears—and I bled in a heap and up above me, Dad died.

If I'd run right out to Jerri, maybe she could've saved him? Really, probably not.

You know what I remember Jerri saying when she finally came in? "Where did he get that rope?"

This happened. It's the truth. It's part of me like my hair is part of me.

I'm a great football player. I am blessed. I have problems.

CHAPTER 3
Jerri Has Problems

It's important for me to remember that Jerri has problems too. I mean, holy balls, she was nineteen when my dad knocked her up. She was a widow at twenty-five! Poor Jerri! Poor, sad, Jerri!

Except I could've used an actual parent in the house last fall. I needed someone to help me deal with all this crazy stuff that came from being recruited. Recruiting was super intense for me—more than for most players because colleges didn't know who the hell I was until I was already a junior. Most elite players get recruited early and visit schools several times. I only really had time to visit once (which I put off—couldn't make decisions) and just a few places, so it was like a feeding frenzy.

All fall, football programs kept calling me. Many college coaches showed up at my games and at the house. I got constant IMs and texts and Facebook messages and tweets from people all over the country trying to get me to go to whatever university to play football, and I had no idea how to respond, what to do, how to make a choice. *Thanks for calling! What the hell is an Illini?*

Occasionally, a coach or a coach's wife called Jerri to talk to her about the educational culture at whatever school. Jerri would be sitting at that kitchen table, her head buried in some book, the phone would ring, and she'd scream, "Get it!"

I'd pick up and call from the basement, "It's for you, Jerri."

She'd get on the line and say something like, "That's not my business. Felton is the one making a decision. Thanks for your interest." Then she'd hang up.

Downstairs, I'd think: *Help! What am I supposed to do? What the hell is an Illini?*

On Thursday of the week I became Tommy Bode's senior mentor, after it became clear I was shivering in my shorts (I'd forgotten plays in practice on Wednesday), my football coach, Coach Johnson, who is a real adult and a good dad, helped me choose four universities to visit. He tried like a trouper. We sat down in his office after our team's Thursday walk-through to discuss what I wanted.

"What do you want to major in, Felton?" he asked.

"I don't know, Coach," I said. "Probably not agriculture."

"No," he agreed. "What are you interested in?" he asked.

I thought for a few seconds. "Football?"

"Are you saying you want to study football?"

"Not exactly. But I do like football."

"Yeah. That's good," Coach said.

Before my growth spurt, I always wanted to be a comedian, but I hadn't seen "comedy" in any of the college brochures.

"Other things, Felton. Academics."

"Why did your son pick Iowa?" I asked. I was stalling for time.

"It was his only Division I offer. You've got a lot more choices than Ken. What are your interests?"

"I mean, I like Frisbee. I like TV. I like…I like smart comedy." *Shit.*

"Felton," he exhaled. "Come on, son. You're good at school. What's your favorite subject?"

"English, I guess."

"Okay. That's something. How about this? Let's choose three schools with good academic reputations and one school known primarily for football."

We ended up choosing Wisconsin, Northwestern (not smart for me), a School That Shall Not Be Named, and Stanford. Two were close to Bluffton; one was a giant national football powerhouse; and one was near San Francisco, where Aleah might end up.

I went home and told Jerri. She looked up from her accounting book and said, "Northwestern? That's dumb."

"Oh," I said. "Yeah, I guess."

I went downstairs to my bedroom and thought, *Thanks for all your help, Jerri.*

That tweak, that hole in my stomach, opened big. *I am alone in the giant universe of pain!* That's crazy crap. I thought, *You are pretty crazy.* I thought, *Thanks so much, Jerri.*

Granted, Jerri has problems.

CHAPTER 4
Aleah

Late that night, Aleah and I Skyped. Since we first got together, a year and a half earlier when her dad was a visiting poet at the college in Bluffton, we'd barely seen each other at all except for Skype. Those couple of months that she was in town were awesome. They were great. Aleah and I are like one person with two heads and two bodies. We're so in sync when we're together that it's weird. (Like mind-melding aliens.)

We biked together and went to Country Kitchen and laughed through eating sandwiches and made out in her basement and walked through the cow-pie-smelling Bluffton evening holding hands. I was pretty damn sure we'd get married and probably live on the side of some mountain in a giant house with a piano that she'd play and blow me away with, but then she went back to Chicago and we barely saw each other and we broke up once (over the prior summer). When we're apart, we're not so good.

It was a little past midnight. Our Skype connected. Aleah was lit only by her computer. She wore white flannel pj's. She sat on her bed. She whispered because I assume her dad, Ronald, was asleep in the room next to hers. "Hi there," she said.

"Hey. Big news. I have my college visits set up." I whispered too, even though Jerri sleeps like a brick.

"Oh," she said, nodding. She didn't look happy. "Good?"

"I'll be at Northwestern in a few weeks!"

She perked up. "Can we see each other?"

"I think! Why not? I'm staying in a hotel! Can you stay with me?"

"I'm going to stay with you even if I can't!" she said.

"Yes!" My heart began to beat. I thought of Aleah stretched out on a bed next to me. That's good. That's not lonely. "It's going to be awesome to kiss you."

She nodded and smiled.

"I'm visiting Stanford too. Any chance you can go? Maybe visit that school you liked out there?"

Aleah didn't say anything. She just stared at her screen.

"Hello?"

"Maybe," she said.

Here's the thing: the only reason I chose to visit Stanford was because a few weeks earlier, Aleah had said she'd researched good football schools near San Francisco because there's some conservatory in San Francisco that teaches composition (I thought she meant paper writing, which confused me, but she meant music writing) and Stanford seemed like a good place for me. So...

Here's the other thing: Aleah doesn't have to go to college if she doesn't want to. She was paid professional money to play in Germany over the summer. She had constant, growing offers. I knew this. But I hoped. Back when we were sixteen, we said we'd go to college in the same place.

"Are you okay?" I asked. "What's wrong?"

"Daddy's angry at Jerri," Aleah whispered. "She has a bunch of his books and she won't respond to him, but he needs his books back."

Here's one other thing: Jerri and Aleah's dad dated over the summer. Jerri broke up with him because she wants to focus on school. (Jerri developed a bad habit of dating my friends' dads, by the way.)

"What books? Maybe I can find them," I said.

"Dang it," Aleah whispered. "Daddy's awake. I have to go."

"Oh. Okay," I said. "Okay, I love…"

Aleah was gone. The Skype window closed.

I sat in the light of my laptop. Alone again. I had to go to sleep. We had a game the next night and I play better if I'm rested (although I'm never exactly rested). The house was dark. I lived in the basement. The basement is a door away from the garage where my dad died. This didn't ever bother me when I was younger. Why didn't it bother me?

My stomach tweaked. The hole got big. I texted Andrew: *You awake?*

No, he replied.

I have a hole, I texted.

Are you being gross? Or trying to be profound? Andrew texted.

I feel weird, I texted.

Let's talk tomorrow, brother. We should talk, he replied.

We didn't talk because I had a football game against River Valley and I scored three touchdowns and ran for 228 yards and then I went for pizza with Cody, Karpinski, Abby Sauter, and Jess Withrow.

It was a great night.

Accelerating Fall

Recruiting, Mumble Mouth,
Justify Your Existence, Pig Boy,
The End

CHAPTER 5
Barfed Upon in Madison

I made two recruiting visits during football season—Wisconsin and Northwestern—and two right after the season—the School That Shall Not Be Named and Stanford—because they're not so close to Bluffton and I needed time to travel.

I went to these schools to see if I liked them, to see if I wanted to move to one of these foreign places where I would be part of a football program, be part of a "culture." (That's what the coaches called life in the program—a "culture.")

Not enjoyable for me. I didn't really know what I was looking for, so I didn't ask questions. Plus, I didn't like most of the football coaches—didn't like the way they talked, the way they moved, the way they smelled. Didn't like their haircuts or their clothes or their big-knuckled hands. These dudes make me jumpy, squirrely. The football players, for the most part, seemed like young versions of these big-knuckled, powerful old dudes.

I didn't know how to talk to them.

I didn't want to talk to them.

What a dork!

They didn't like me either. In the end, at the end of my visits,

I think most of the coaches and players wanted to punch me in the face.

At least no one actually punched me. That would be bad press for the program for sure.

Headline: *Coach Punches Top Recruit's Dumbass Face!*

• • •

Wisconsin Visit

Before visiting Madison, Wisconsin, home of the University of Wisconsin, I sort of figured I'd end up a Wisconsin Badger. Especially if Aleah didn't go to college. Everyone else thought I'd be a Badger too. The university is close to Bluffton (only like an hour away). Madison is a cool town. I'd have some friends there. (Abby Sauter, who is a great friend, the best, is going to Wisconsin.) I was excited to make this trip.

Because I'm from Wisconsin, the Wisconsin coaches set me up to hang out with another Wisconsin "product." (Players from a state are considered "products" of the state. Other Wisconsin products include cheese, sausage, beer, and also lawn mowers.) The dude they set me up with is named Bart Kunzel. He's a giant lineman from a town called Hartland (near Milwaukee). He'll be a senior next year, and if he doesn't break a leg or get his knee ripped in half, he'll definitely play in the NFL.

He was okay. Fine. I just didn't have much to say to him. I stuttered a lot. Mumbled. I asked him if he'd ever visited the Milwaukee Zoo. He said no. Then I asked him if he ever saw the famous shit-throwing gorilla at the Milwaukee Zoo. He said, "How would I see the gorilla if I never went to the zoo?"

Good point.

He squinted at me.

On Saturday evening, after their game against Illinois (an Illini is some kind of Native American, I found out), Bart picked me up at my hotel. He limped because his knees hurt. Then he took me to this giant beer party crushed wall to wall with people who smelled like they'd had whole bottles of body spray blasted all over them (like there's some body spray car wash near campus and everybody walked through it on the way). Still, riding just underneath the sweet chemical fragrance, you could smell a horse-butt, monkey-donkey animal smell in that packed house.

I stood smashed in a corner for an hour trying not to smell anything and then this girl stumbled out of nowhere and puked on my foot. "Ha, ha, ha!" everyone laughed.

"Ha, ha," I said.

After I spent ten minutes trying to wipe the barf off my shoe onto the little bit of grass that wasn't trampled dead in the front yard, we went back to a dorm and played video games with a bunch of other giant football players.

The dorm room smelled of ass, Doritos, and chew. (The farm boys in Bluffton dip tobacco constantly—I recognized that odor.)

Have I mentioned that I'm kind of a super smeller? Smells kill me. Very intense. It's a damn curse. I can smell squirrels that have bad breath way up in the trees. You might think I'm joking. (I'm sort of joking but not really.)

While in that dorm, my ability to not be freaky exited my body. These football guys all barked like my friend Karpinski.

"AAAHHHH. BAAHHH. DUUUDDE. BAHHH." Back home, there's only one Karpinski, not seven screaming, "AAAAAAHHH. BAAAAAH." I began to get twitchy and I blinked a lot and I stared at dudes' foreheads, which is a bad habit, and my adrenaline began flowing.

I asked Bart to take me back to the hotel at midnight because my muscles were getting so wound I thought I might punch a wall.

Bart said, "You sure? You want to hook up with some girls or something?"

"No, thank you," I said.

At the hotel, I showered for an hour and did jumping jacks and push-ups and stretched my hamstrings, which are naturally tight. Then I stared at the damn wall for like three hours before I fell asleep. (The remote control didn't work and I didn't feel like getting out of bed at that point.)

What is wrong with you? I wondered.

You're a damn dipshit! I answered.

Okay, maybe. But you're disappointed too. Isn't college about reading big books in an ancient library?

I found out later that there are good libraries at Wisconsin, but I didn't ask questions while I was there because I was unable to justify my existence to myself.

The next day was a little better. Me and Bart stood on the actual field at Camp Randall (the football stadium), at the 50-yard line on the W in the middle, and he said, "Pretty awesome, huh?" And I said yeah because it did look really cool. (I'd seen it on TV—but this was such a different view.) I imagined cutting on that turf, running like a gorilla, bursting through a seam. I imagined fans doing "Jump Around" in the stands. (YouTube it!) I liked that.

Then we met with the strength and conditioning coach who showed me these different workouts they do, including carrying bags of cement up the stairs, all the way up to the top of the stadium. Yes. I love working out. Carrying bags of cement sounded fantastic, I must say.

Then Bart took me upstairs to the football offices, which are fancy (they were all fancy everywhere I went), and the offensive coordinator, a big-knuckled, slick-haired mofo, told me I might play some tight end at Wisconsin.

"What?" I asked.

Then he asked if I had a good time at the party the night before while he slapped me on the back too hard, which made my neck tense.

I said, "This girl barfed in my shoe."

"Barfed?" the coach asked.

"Well, a little barf," Bart said. "Not really *in* his shoe. *On* his shoe."

"Tight end?" I asked.

The coach refocused on me. His big face nodded. He said, "You have good hands." He said, "You're a big target and you're as fast as they come. Think of the mismatches, Felton. Could a linebacker cover you? No."

I thought about catching passes. I like catching passes. I liked being a running back a lot though, and I think they should've told me about this tight end thing before I showed up on their campus to be barfed on.

"We want to get you on the field next year too, which isn't going to be easy because of the players we have returning."

I nodded. This I already knew: Wisconsin is wealthy in talent. They have two returning 1,000-yard running backs (very good running backs—uncommon).

Here's the truth: I probably could deal with tight end. I'd had other coaches tell me I'd make a better pro prospect as a tight end. (Not that I'd thought much about pro football—I could barely imagine the next day at that point.) Tight end didn't matter.

Here's what did matter: I didn't like the culture. Big-head coaches. Barf. Ass. Chew. Body spray car washes. Remote controls that don't work in hotels. When Jerri picked me up, I felt pretty crappy, sort of terrified because before that, I thought I'd just go be a Badger, you know?

"Have fun?" she asked when I climbed in the car.

"Great!" I said.

"Great!" she said.

Here's what I was really thinking: Jesus, I don't think I can do it. Jesus, where am I going to go college? Northwestern, Dad?

Bart Kunzel IM'd me when I got home and said he was sorry about that stupid-ass barfing girl. No biggie, I replied. Then he said I should let him know if I had questions.

I didn't send him a single text or Facebook message after that.

Wisconsin still checked in with me constantly, which I sort of ignored because I was Mr. Bernard Dickman.

• • •

The next week in school, everyone—all of them smiling too hard and red in the face—asked me how my visit to Madison went. I told them, "Pretty good."

Then they smiled like their faces would break and they nodded like bobbleheads.

Wisconsinites really like Wisconsin. Cheeseheads. I like Wisconsin too, but I didn't back then in the fall.

"Pretty nice place," I told everyone.

Only Tommy Bode, my freshman mentee, saw through me. We met in the morning on Tuesday after my visit. I told him I'd been in Madison for the weekend. (He seemed to have no idea about my football situation.) He asked if I liked Madison.

I said, "Great town."

He said, "My mom's neck turns red when she lies."

I said, "That's weird."

He said, "Your neck is red, you liar."

"Hey!" I shouted.

"I'm not joking," he said.

"I know," I said.

Then I watched him draw pictures of guns.

CHAPTER 6
The Blood of My Foes Makes Me Happy

The next weekend, we beat Cuba City by 40 points. It was a blast. I scored five touchdowns in the second quarter, which tied a state record. After the game, I got so many texts from coaches that I decided to turn my phone off for a couple of days (after texting Aleah that she should call our landline if she needed me). Then me, Abby Sauter, Cody, Karpinski, and a bunch of others did what we always did after games: hit Steve's Pizza, where I ate a whole large sausage and mushroom pizza by myself. I fell into bed in love with the world.

Saturday morning, I went over to Gus's because he had an idea for a series of videos about dudes in pajamas fighting each other with different kinds of small stuff (pipes, pencils, sewing needles, etc.). Tiny shit fighters.

I rode my bike to his place wearing my pajamas. On the way, Karpinski's dad sped by me on his scooter. He beeped, slowed down, and said, "Victory grows from hard work, am I right?"

"Hard work," I nodded.

"Why are you wearing your pj's?" he asked. "You look fruity. Have a little pride, Reinstein."

Then he buzzed off.

Mr. Karpinski wore short shorts, even though it was only like 60 degrees. Who was he to talk?

When I got to Gus's house, Gus said, "Look at your happy face. Killing kids on the field makes you happy?"

"Yeah," I said. "It does."

"Spoils of war."

"I love the blood best of all."

"Hmm. Questionable, morally speaking."

We sat down at his kitchen table, which had become our meeting place (used to be the corduroy beanbag chairs in the basement).

"I agree," I said. "I try not to think too much about my essential bloody nature."

Gus lifted his wad and looked at me. "Maybe you should think," he whispered.

"I was joking."

"And I'm saying you should think," Gus said.

"Jerri tells me not to think," I said.

"Too bad you're not a regular person," he said.

"Why?"

"So you'd have to write college essays because having written several of my own, I feel I understand myself better and will be a better person in the future."

"Really?" I asked. I wondered if I should write an essay.

"Yes. No. Sort of. I'm half bullshitting."

"Oh," I said.

"Only half, man."

I thought for a second. *Essay? I should write an essay?* I got confused. *About what?* "What are we talking about?" I asked.

"I don't know," Gus said. "You want some cereal?"

After I ate, Gus and I made a hilarious movie of us dressed in pajamas, holding tobacco pipes. (His dad used to smoke a pipe.) Gus filmed me wielding the tiny pipe from all kinds of angles. I filmed him taking mighty pipe blows to the forehead, temple, and cheeks. He edited the crap out of it, and we looked like we were expert pajama kung fu pipe fighters. Most of it was sped way up or in slow motion. Awesome.

That night, though, I worried about my existence.

Beating up other football players makes you happy?

CHAPTER 7
Ghost of a Great Athlete Past

The next weekend, we played an away game at the Richland Center. It was another beautiful slaughter, which, yes, made me happy. I woke up early on Saturday morning and packed my overnight bag. This wasn't the best time to go on a visit because Northwestern had a bye that week, so I couldn't see them play. Didn't matter because I wasn't really going to Northwestern to visit the school. Aleah would meet me at the hotel.

Right before I got in Jerri's car (no, she didn't actually visit a single school with me, which Coach Johnson told me was abnormal), my grandpa Stan called my cell, which was out of the ordinary. He said, "Northwestern today, right, Felton?"

"Yes. Weird, huh?"

"It's a fine school. I'm not sure...I'm not sure it's the best place for you, of course. I don't know."

"Well, I really want to see Aleah."

"She'll be there?" he asked.

"Yeah."

"Good. Good. I almost flew up to be with you there myself. But next week, you know?"

He and Andrew were coming up to Bluffton for the home-coming game.

"Don't worry," I said.

"Good," he said. "Make sure you have them tell you about their academic programs. Northwestern is a very good school."

He should know. He sent my dead dad there.

"I will," I said.

"Good. Good," he said.

I appreciated someone in my family actually caring about my college career. Jerri drove me to Janesville, put me on a bus, and said, "Have fun."

The bus trip was pretty short, just a couple of hours. Two college kids sitting next to me drank straight out of little vodka bottles, then started making out.

"Get a room!"

I didn't actually say that. I wished I was with someone making out.

• • •

Northwestern Visit

Okay, there's a kind of older football coach who isn't like the big-head, slick-haired coaches. This older coach talks fast and mumbles and says weird stuff like, "Get me a bottle of that Gatorade, you boob. Who am I? Your old forgotten granny? Show a little class." Totally incomprehensible but kind of funny. I tend to like these coaches better than the younger ones. My track coach, Coach Knautz, is sort of like this.

So was Northwestern's coach.

When I got to campus, the weird old dude flat out told me,

mumbling fast, "You aren't going to come here, Mr. Fancy Pants Big League Reinstein. I appreciate you making a visit to our humble little backwater school though." When he said that, I thought, *Oh yeah? Then I will come here!*

I think he was using reverse psychology on me. When I was a kid, Jerri would get me to eat fish by serving it to Andrew and telling me I wasn't allowed to have any, which made me beg her for fish, even though I hate fish. Then I'd eat it, gagging and choking.

Nice try, Northwestern coach. I will not eat your fish. Recruiter people are tricky.

It's not because I didn't like him though. I did.

And I liked visiting Northwestern.

Within ten minutes of me being dropped off at the hotel, Aleah was in my room. She did stay overnight. Good times in the hotel.

The host football dude, Antwan Jackson (another Wisconsin product but a Northwestern player), invited us to a party. He walked Aleah and me there, talking about how cool the football players are at Northwestern, what good students most of them are. "It's a different kind of thing here. A different kind of culture." That's what he said.

Aleah nodded and smiled. (Normal football culture confuses her.)

While he talked, I stared at Antwan's ear because it looked like it had been torn half off by a tiger or something.

Not so different…

We were at the party for like ten minutes when two large dudes who smelled like the body spray car wash started shoving each other, crushing into people, beer spilling, everybody screaming, and Aleah said, "Get me out."

We walked back down this street across from the campus. Aleah said, "I thought Northwestern was a smart school."

"Are football players everywhere just assholes?" I asked.

"Maybe," Aleah said. "You're not really a football player though."

I stopped. "No," I said. "I really am. I play football."

"Yes. But you're not the same as those boys, right?"

I didn't answer.

We walked to the hotel in silence. We ordered room service twice. We messed around in bed in between. There were some awesome french fries at this place.

At 7 a.m., she was gone because she had to play with some ensemble at a park downtown. "Bye, Felton. Bye. I love you. Okay? Bye," she said. She put her hand on the side of my head and stared at me hard. "Remember I love you, okay? Remember this?"

I nodded. My heart sank. She got on a bus and was gone, and I was alone.

I didn't hate touring the campus. Not exactly.

Northwestern is nice. (College campuses are often nice, I guess.) Unfortunately, it hit me about halfway through the tour, while passing a set of dorms, that I'd seen a picture of that very place in a photo album at Grandpa's house, that Dad lived in those dorms, that Dad had friends who lived in those dorms, that Dad stayed up all night in those dorms talking or studying or eating pizzas or something.

I don't know my dad at all. What did he do? I pictured him with his ghostly Jewfro head (like mine when my hair's not super short) walking on those sidewalks, laughing, carrying a backpack, thinking about poetry. (He was a "jock" and a poetry student…that's all I really know—he eventually got his PhD in modern poetry from Indiana University.)

He's dead…He's dead…He's gone forever…

Thoughts like that can still crush me like boulders.

At one point, we visited an athletic facility with this glass case at the front that contained a giant picture of my dad—giant black hair bursting from his head—crushing a tennis ball. He was a national champion in tennis. The big-knuckled running backs coach barked, "You're a legacy, Felton. Wouldn't it be excellent to grow the Reinstein legend right here where it started?"

I'm not going to Northwestern, I thought. The Reinstein legend includes dangling from your neck in a garage.

My poor dad. My poor grandpa. Poor Jerri. My poor little brother.

Sad Felton too. That Sunday was the last time I saw Aleah for nine months.

CHAPTER 8
University of Sexpot

Over the course of the next month, I barely thought about recruiting (although recruiters thought about me—I got dozens of texts a day and Jerri screamed and yanked the phone out of the wall once because the constant ringing apparently made studying accounting very difficult).

There was homecoming, which Grandpa Stan and Andrew came up for. I didn't go to the dance because Aleah had another damn recital that night in Chicago, plus she was acting weird, plus I'd never been to a school dance and I didn't feel like treading those waters, even though Cody said I might be named homecoming king (I wasn't even on homecoming court), plus Andrew wanted to go to Steve's Pizza with Bony Emily, his best friend, and I like pizza, so I went with them and they talked about stuff I didn't know anything about, but I ate a lot so I was happy…plus…whatever. We destroyed Prairie du Chien in the game. Killed. I killed them, which apparently made Grandpa Stan weird out.

Sunday morning, sitting at Country Kitchen, Grandpa Stan stared at me. "You doing okay, my friend?" he asked.

I stared back. Andrew stared at the side of my head. Lots of staring. "Sure. Pretty great."

"You ever feel sad? Maybe it's hard that Andrew moved to live with me?"

I stared some more. Andrew's stare made my ear feel itchy. "Me?"

"You? Sad?" Grandpa said.

"Sad. Sure. Who doesn't feel sad?"

"I don't," Andrew said.

A year and a half earlier, Andrew had refused to come into the house. He'd burned all his clothes and shaved his head. He lived like a caveman in the freaking garden. "I witnessed your total breakdown," I said, turning to him. Staring at him.

"That was then. This is now," Andrew said.

"Back to you, Felton. You all right?" Grandpa asked.

"I…I think so?" I said.

"You sure loved stomping on your opponents in the game the other night."

"That's my job," I said. "Destroy."

"I'd like you to think about that some," Grandpa said.

"Think?" I asked.

"Meditate on it," he said.

"How do I do that?" I asked.

"Think. We'll talk some more when you come down for the holidays," he said.

"Tovi's coming down for winter break too," Andrew said.

At that moment, my Farmers Breakfast was delivered in a sizzling cast iron skillet! Delicious.

We had a nice weekend.

• • •

And then another conference game and then three playoff games in two weeks, which culminated in the state championship game against Ashwaubenon, which was a struggle into the third quarter before Cody, Karpinski, and Kirk Johnson blew it open with passing, so we won big.

For three days after the game, it felt like the whole school celebrated, the whole town really. There were banners on Main Street and we all rode on top of a fire truck and the marching band played and the city manager, Tim Krueger, gave a speech about Bluffton values. (We value winning apparently.) It was on fire! November heat, baby! So much fun.

And then, the Wednesday after our victory, I felt that hole in my stomach and I slept in my basement bedroom one door away from where Dad killed himself. The recruiters texted and Facebooked, and I didn't want to go to Wisconsin and I couldn't go to Northwestern because of my dead dad, and ESPN had me announcing my college choice live on TV in a couple months (seriously) and so I had better damn well pay attention to what the hell was going on and so…Sexpot U.

● ● ●

The School That Shall Not Be Named
No ancient libraries and big books.

Talk about culture.

First, at this not-named school, I was offered pot by a linebacker. He said, "You smoke up, man?"

I said, "Cigarettes? My friend Gus used to."

He said, "Herb, dude. Helps with the pain. You want to chill?"

I had only heard rumors of weed up in Bluffton. Burner rumors about one-hitters and Dumpsters, and I didn't know what the hell and I got real jumpy. Before I flew down there, Abby Sauter told me people in the South are polite, so I said, "Oh jeez! Heck! Wow! Jeez! No thank you, sir!"

Duh. I'm a dipshit.

I'm sure he wanted to punch my dumbass face.

Second, they had a girl (blond girl who said she was a former pole vaulter) give me the school tour. The first thing she said to me was, "Wow, you're bigger than I dreamed."

How am I supposed to respond to that? I said, "Why, thank you, ma'am."

Then she grabbed my hand like five times while we walked around, and she put her hand on my thigh while we sat on this bench next to the administration building. And finally—I'm completely serious—while we ate a damn cheeseburger in the student union, she laughed and leaned back, then leaned forward and reached her hand pretty much directly into my freaking groin, which I found way too exciting. *For real*—I jumped like a monkey on a hot stove—"*Wow! Whoa! Heck!*" And then I thought about Aleah and asked to go back to the hotel.

The girl looked really hurt. "Are you sure?" she asked.

"I'm sorry. I'm sorry," I said. And I felt bad. But, Aleah. She was on my mind because, as I mentioned, she'd been acting weird. And, really, what should I have done? Do players really end up *doing it* to random pole vaulters on recruiting visits?

I didn't sleep a wink.

The remote control worked very well in the hotel, which was nice.

Then Saturday, I got to be on the sideline for the big game!

Third problem, the Unnamed team lost by three points to its rival and the jerk players yelled at each other and a couple shoved each other and they spat on the ground and swore a lot and pointed fingers in each other's faces. (I don't respect players yelling at each other for messing up.)

I can't tell you how bad that sideline smelled. Southern heat. All that anger. All that steaming football gear. Disgusting.

Then I refused to go on the football facilities tour. The shit on the sideline got into my body and I worried I might fight someone because I can sort of lose my head and go nuts and I was especially jumpy back then.

The running backs coach was very confused by my decision. He actually said, "Are you kidding me?"

"No, sir. I'm tired," I said. (I think I sounded like a robot.)

"Really? You're not messing around?"

"No," I said.

"Suit yourself," he said, giving me that *punch your face* look.

You know what? Of course people want to punch my face. What football recruit accepts a visit invitation, then refuses to visit the football facilities?

Me.

Fourth, the next day, Sunday, the head coach came over to the hotel and took me on a walk around campus (which I'd already seen with the groin-grabber girl) and talked to me about his beliefs in Jesus, which is fine, except my dad was Jewish and Jerri is like a weird mixed bag of hippie goddess accounting worship, and then he took me up to his office, which looks like a glass castle, and told me I could start in the backfield the next year.

I told him I didn't feel like I fit in. "It's the culture," I told him.

He squinted at me. He ran his hand over his short-cropped, hair-gelled head. He asked me if I like music.

I said I did.

He put this slow-ass Motley Crue hair-band metal song on the sound system ("Home Sweet Home!") and showed me slow-motion football highlights. And he looked kind of emotional, like he was going to cry. And I said, "Holy shit." I felt like I was living a scene from a Will Farrell movie ("Home Sweet Home!"). I sort of laughed. (Along with being a dipshit, I can also be a pecker.)

At the end, I could tell the coach wanted to punch my face very badly. He didn't try to shake my hand or anything, which I didn't mind because shaking hands with these dudes was awkward for me. He barely looked at me as he handed me off to the groin-grabber girl, who took me to the airport. She barely talked to me either.

You know what? That coach is a pecker, not me. Why would I be interested in the crap he tried to sell?

Sex and drugs and God and 1980s music. That's me? I don't think so.

I'm not going to name that school. And I'm definitely not going to college there.

Here's what I maintain: that place is a shit sandwich.

● ● ●

After the School That Shall Not Be Named

Even though the Not Named people seemed to hate me, I kept getting messages from the groin-grabber girl, calling me hot and from the coaches telling me we'd compete for a national championship together. Meanwhile, other schools called me and called Jerri on the landline (she would hang up) and Facebooked and tweeted and texted me, all trying to tell me how I fit in their program and that their culture was so good and I thought, *What am I going to do? I hate college football culture.*

At that point, I really wanted to stay in high school. *Just stay home…*

But Gus was going away to Dartmouth, Swarthmore, or Amherst College. Cody and Reese, my football pals, had already decided to go to UW-La Crosse to play Division III football. Abby Sauter would be at Madison. Only Karpinski would be left (going to college in town), and as much as I like Karpinski, he's not home to me.

He's the dude who babbled about girls' asses and shot food out of his mouth while we ate at Taco Bell and drove around firing popcorn seeds out of straws at pedestrians. And this: I could never completely trust him. He bullied the shit out of me when I was a small, weak squirrel boy. *I don't want to hang out with Karpinski every weekend! Home will not be home…*

The football season had been ecstasy. I got to kill people in a societally appropriate way. But high school football was done. I felt done. What was I supposed to do with myself?

In mid-November, Tommy Bode, my freshman mentee said, "Why did you stop being so happy? Do you miss your brother?"

"Yes," I said.

"I do too. I miss Andrew," Tommy said. "He's the only nice person I know."

I squinted at Tommy. "Really?" I asked. Tommy had never mentioned that he and Andrew were friends. Andrew had never mentioned Tommy at all as far as I could remember.

"I don't want to talk about it," Tommy said.

Depression filled our hearts.

And a few days later, I got the worst phone call ever.

CHAPTER 9
Aleah Bails

When I visited Northwestern, while we lay next to each other in the big hotel bed, Aleah said, "I like you too much, Felton. It's no good."

I smiled and took that as a compliment and it gave me hope that we might work something out.

What Aleah actually meant when she said "I like you too much" and "no good" came to me in a phone call the week after the Not Named visit. (She'd said similar crap and had gotten weirder and weirder on Skype ever since Northwestern.)

My phone buzzed at 11 p.m. I was lying in bed, trying to read *Waiting for Godot*, which Mr. Linder, my AP English teacher, had assigned.

I answered. "Hey, baby. No Skype?"

Aleah said, "Felton, I can't see your face."

"Then Skype," I laughed.

"No," she said, "I mean, I don't want to see your face."

"You don't like my face?"

"Felton, I'm sorry I'm doing this on the phone, but I don't know when I'm going to see you again and this can't go on."

"What?" My heart pumped funny. "What can't go on?" I wheezed.

"I have two offers in Europe, Felton. I'm sorry."

"No," I said. "It's okay. It's fine. Europe is good," I said. Upstairs, I could hear Jerri doing sit-ups. The floorboards squeaked. Jerri did sit-ups like two hours a day during the fall. Part of her "I'm a new human being" routine. My heart began to pound in my throat.

"No," Aleah said. "I get an offer and I get sad because all I do is think about you and I'm not making any choices and I'm only seventeen and we don't know what's going to happen and I can't sit around my bedroom thinking about how great everything is going to be when we're married…"

"Let's just get married," I blurted. "We can. Next summer!"

"No, Felton," Aleah whispered. She took a deep breath.

"Please," I said. "No."

Aleah went into a rehearsed speech. "I like you very much. You are a sweet, wonderful person, Felton. Unfortunately, we're too young to be making decisions based on our potential lives together. I can't spend any more time wondering where you'll be, wondering if we'll be close. My life is taking me far away and I don't…"

"Don't," I said. "This is just your break-up speech from last year. We aren't breaking up. It didn't work last time. We're not going to break up, okay?"

"I can't think about you anymore," Aleah said. "This is the last time I'm going to talk to you. I'm sorry, but I…" Aleah exhaled hard. "But I hope you'll be happy. I want you to be happy. You have so much to look forward to and so do I. I hope you understand."

"I don't understand," I said.

"Please," Aleah cried.

My gut filled with poison. My muscles all tensed. I said some bad stuff while I kicked the shit out of my room.

"I'm sorry," Aleah whispered. Then she hung up.

I totally cried like a small, weak, dipshit kid.

Upstairs, Jerri did her squeaky sit-ups. The floor creaked above. I knew she could hear me when I yelled on the phone. I knew she knew how broken up and stupid I was down there alone in the basement.

A million fire ants bit me in my guts.

"Why are you such a psycho?" I screamed at the ceiling.

Jerri paused for a moment. Then the floor began to creak again.

I felt like I'd blow away.

CHAPTER 10
Mr. Hair Trigger

The next day, while I shuffled alone and sick and defeated through the peach hallways of Bluffton High, I saw Nolan Sauter, Abby's little brother, knock Tommy Bode's books out of his hands and onto the floor. When Tommy bent down to pick them up, Nolan kicked him in the side and Tommy slid down, face to the floor.

Without a thought, in a blink, I smashed the back of Nolan's head against a locker. I held him by his throat and stared at his stupid face. Then I let go and walked away.

"What the hell, Felton?" he called after me.

I know now that Nolan was roughed up because of his mom and dad's divorce. His dad is a giant asswipe. That's true. But you can't go around kicking the crap out of little fat boys because your parents are getting divorced. That's not right.

Somehow—I don't remember walking there—I ended up at my next class, a lame social studies class called Current Events. All the senior jocks take it. I sat down between Abby and Cody. Cody said, "Your hand is bleeding."

I looked over at Abby. "Your brother is a dick."

She stared at me. "I know," she said.

I held up my bleeding hand. "I got cut when I smashed him against a locker."

"Dude, Jesus," Cody said.

"Are you kidding?" Abby asked.

Then class started.

Even though I'd wanted to, I'd never gone after someone the way I went after Nolan. I sort of trembled and I felt a little like crying.

Also this: It felt good to crush him. I admit it.

Hi, my name is Felton Reinstein, and I'm scary.

CHAPTER 11
Ultimate Stanford

The following Friday, I was scheduled to fly out to California to visit Stanford. The only reason I chose to do this visit in the first place, of course, was because Aleah said she might end up in San Francisco to study music composition.

Oh holy balls, I didn't want to go. I'd already seen enough college football crap. Plus, I'd texted Aleah a thousand times telling her I was still going to visit Stanford and she should still look at that school for composing because it might really be the perfect fit for her and really good for her future and if that meant it was good for our future too, then that's great! But that's not why I was texting her, I wrote. I said I just loved her and just wanted her to be okay and to succeed in life…(ugh). And she hadn't returned a single one and I felt so sick in my guts and I couldn't eat and I slept only in ten-minute stretches and I was dizzy and heavy and the corner of my right eyelid started twitching really badly, which made me think maybe I was having a stroke and I'd die, which I didn't mind.

The only person I told about Aleah was Gus. I told him in the lunchroom.

"She did it. She let me go. She's gone," I whispered.

"Saw that coming," he said.

I put my head on the grimy table where we sat.

"You'll be fine. There will be other girls, man."

"Why didn't I have sex with that pole vaulter while I ate that cheeseburger?"

"I don't know, dude. You should have done it."

"Shit. Shit. I don't want to go to Stanford, man."

"Why?"

"I hate these recruiting visits. I can barely speak."

"Why?"

"All these people just remind me of middle school. They all stick out their chests and grunt and crap. Aleah said I'm not even a football player. She was right. She knows me."

"You are. You play football. You sure look like a football player."

"That's what I told her," I said, lifting my head up and nodding. "I am a football player."

"Yes."

"Oh shit. Why didn't I grow into a little violin-squeaking geek?"

"Stop, dude. Don't deny what you love."

"I'm not."

"Why don't you try to have fun when you visit Stanford? Pressure's off, man. You can just go to Wisconsin if Stanford sucks. Everybody wants you to go to Wisconsin. Enjoy whatever's offered. Aleah's done with your sorry ass anyway."

"Thanks."

"Who cares? It's about time you guys break up."

I looked down at the stupid high school lunchroom floor.

"Come on, Felton. Just go and have a good time. This is a free trip to California, man. Check the place out. Maybe some blond pole vaulter will grab your wang."

I nodded. I agreed.

"I bet if your eyes are open, you'll see stuff you really like," Gus said. Then Gus, eighteen-year-old boy wonder, gave me some tips on how to behave. He did the job Mother Jerri hadn't.

• • •

Stanford Visit

Okay. This is true:

It is really, really beautiful in California. Hugely. That's good.

First, the driver took me around San Francisco. I'd asked to fly in there instead of Palo Alto when we'd made the visit plans because I'd hoped Aleah would go with me.

San Francisco.

Hills and old homes and big pointy parks in the middle of these awesome neighborhoods. I got an iced tea in this coffee shop with giant old-fashioned movie posters on the wall. I think the coffee girl was actually a little man in a dress. I'd never seen anything like it.

Second, this fog rolled in while we drove to Palo Alto. I watched it curl around giant hills.

Third, Stanford. What a place.

On the campus tour, when the tour guide talked, I nodded and listened. She didn't try to grab my business. (She was very cute, but I respect the fact she didn't try to grab my business.) She took me into this giant reading room in the library, where there were old books and leather chairs. That's what I wanted to see.

When the coaches knocked on my room's door, I looked them in the eye (Gus told me to) and shook their hands. (Thanks, Gus.) This worked. They didn't squint at me. This is what I should've done at the other schools (except Not to be Named maybe).

And, yes, I went to a party with players. It was right after their game with Cal-Berkeley, and they'd won and people were pretty psyched. There was a lot of high-fiving and fist-bumping, which I enjoyed. We had a lot of beer. Actually, they had a lot of beer. I had a little, which I hadn't done at the other schools. It tasted terrible, but it definitely calmed me down a lot immediately (unwound me), which turns out not to be a good thing for me to know about beer. And when I talked about stuff I like, I found some people.

A few players didn't just fist-bump me but had actual things to say. I got into a long conversation about comedy and Louis C.K. with the second-string kicker, Sean McDermott. He said the show *Louie* on FX is an anti-narrative version of *Seinfeld*.

Here's my brain: *Whuh? Anti-narrative? WHUT THUH FUG?* But I nodded and thought, *Smarty pants like Gus. This guy is the man.*

And then there's completely awesome: the next morning, I played Frisbee with a couple of real students on this big green lawn. I'd asked to stay on campus (again, Gus's suggestion—"No hotel TV, dickhead") instead of in a hotel, and I stayed in this ivy-covered guest house and the Sunday morning was blue-skied and beautiful and I wandered out onto the grounds, which were awesome… And the Frisbee dudes! Incredible! They did these wicked, jumping catches, and they told me that there were three different Ultimate Frisbee leagues on campus.

Then, after they told me I'm awesome (I am a good Frisbee thrower and catcher, and I have a great deal of speed, of course), they said they were going to have some beers and lie out in the sun and asked me to come with, which I couldn't do because I had some more meetings. But, man, I liked these guys. I love Ultimate Frisbee. These dudes hugged me when they took off. I seriously thought I'd cry tears of happiness, but I didn't, which is probably good because that would've been weird.

I love the Stanford campus. It was really, really good.

Okay, yes, in the afternoon, I met with the running back coach, who looked a lot like the other coaches at other schools because he wore those gut-buster coach shorts pulled halfway up his stomach and a white polo shirt with a Stanford tree on his boob and he asked me about my football goals.

"Do you want to play pro ball?" he asked.

I shrugged and I could tell he was sort of confused by me, but I don't think he wanted to punch my face.

Several people, including the cute tour guide (who showed up wearing these big, plastic smart-girl glasses) and Sean McDermott and the head coach, were there when the driver picked me up for the airport. They all shook hands with me.

Sean said, "Total pleasure to meet you, man." I believed him.

"Yeah. Awesome to meet you. Awesome. Thank you," I said.

Leaving campus in the cab, I felt so light and excellent and I could breathe and there was no tweak in my stomach. *Oh balls. Yes.* I could picture my future away from high school for the first time.

No Aleah thoughts. No basement bed. Beautiful Frisbees. Blue skies and mountains.

Off we rolled. The buildings at Stanford are this white brick and they have these Spanish red roofs that I really like (mostly from seeing them on *COPS*). And I thought about that Frisbee and smart people and green, green lawns, and you know what? The beer was pretty tasty if you like goat pee that makes you relax—because holy balls, the only way I can usually relax is to run my ass off for like an hour straight.

I called Gus from the airport.

"Good times?" he asked.

"Shit, man," I said. "Thanks for the help."

"I'm your top advisor. Remember that when you get your NFL contract. I want a full-length leather coat to wear in your entourage."

"Maybe some big gold chains?"

"Yes," Gus said. "Old school bling please. A bejeweled grill."

"Okay," I said. I meant it. I would get him those things if I ever could. And I would make him wear them.

• • •

But I couldn't tell anyone (other than Gus, of course). I had to wait until February 1, even though I made my decision that day in November.

Why wait?

This had seemed like sort of a cool deal early in the fall, when everything was easy and sweet and I imagined Aleah there smiling behind me. A producer from ESPN asked me to make my college announcement live on National Signing Day. Part of the deal was that I had to keep it secret. "You can tell no one. Do you understand?" the producer said. "We'll break the news."

"Awesome," I said.

Awesome? Really? Not for a dumbass like me.

Back home, I texted Aleah: *I won't even tell you I'm going to Stanford.*

She didn't text back.

CHAPTER 12
Justify Your Decision

Stanford.

The secret lodged itself in my chest like a fat chicken.

The following week was short due to Thanksgiving. Instead of going to school, I got the flu (might have been psychosomatic—caused by the fat chicken).

Colleges called me. My Facebook and Twitter bubbled with recruitment. I watched TV and thought about Frisbees and mountains. *I am in love with California!*

• • •

For Thanksgiving, Jerri and I ate grilled cheese sandwiches (burnt). Then she studied and I watched football on TV alone. Green Bay Packers.

The fat chicken pecked my lungs all Sunday. *Want to celebrate good things! Why can't I just celebrate this?*

• • •

I couldn't stay home the next week.

"You like California, man?" Cody asked by my locker Monday morning.

The fat chicken choked, scratched. I blinked at him.

"Pretty cool?" he asked.

I pressed my forehead against the cold metal. "Yeah…yeah, it was pretty okay," I said. My face got hot.

"What's wrong?" he asked. "Did it go bad?"

"Not great," I said.

"Screw Stanford, man. We want you in the Midwest."

"Thanks," I said. Here's what I wanted to say: Stanford is the most beautiful place in the world because there are bridges that disappear into the sky and old houses that look like they're made out of freaking candy, and did you know there are foggy mountains out there in the world, not just on TV, and little dudes in dresses who smile and say, "You're welcome," when you order iced tea?

In Current Events class, while Mr. Farber warbled on about labor unions and corporate greed and crap, Karpinski leaned over and asked if the California bikini chicks were hot. *You don't know what hot means because it's not bikinis—it's library girls in plastic glasses who smile when you make jokes!*

I whispered, "Not at all."

"Madison girls are totally hot," Karpinski said, nodding.

"Karpinski, care to share?" Farber asked.

"*Madison girls are totally hot!*" Karpinski shouted.

"True enough," Farber said.

My English teacher, Mr. Linder, who is not a football fan, stopped me after class and said, "Great writers at Stanford. You could learn from the best."

"I don't know," I said. "I'm not much of a writer." *I would write love poems to Frisbees!*

"Bullshit," Linder said.

"California has earthquakes," I said. I made a face.

Then Coach Johnson, Coach Knautz, Abby Sauter, Jess Withrow, Mrs. Callahan, Ms. Rory, etc., etc., etc., all pulled me aside to talk in private, to get the lowdown. Everyone wanted to know about Stanford.

While I thought, *I'm in love with library couches and red roofs and fist-bumping second-string kickers who talk smart about Louis C.K.*, I told them all, no, it wasn't that cool, which seemed like what I should say—I was doing my duty to God and ESPN, keeping my secret—except Gus cornered me after he heard me tell Abby Sauter that Madison is prettier than Palo Alto (where Stanford is located).

"Felton. Shit," he whispered.

"What?" I whispered back.

"Follow me. Now," he said.

I followed him into the faculty bathroom, which was right across the hall from where Abby and I had been talking. Going in that bathroom made me totally nervous. (Gus does what he wants.)

"Jesus. It's clean in here," I said, looking around.

He turned to me, lifted his hair wad, and said, "They are going to *kill* you."

"Who?" I asked.

"You're telling people that Stanford wasn't cool?"

"I have to keep the secret for ESPN," I said. "It's my job."

"But you're building expectations. You're making everybody think you'll be at Wisconsin. These are Wisconsinites, man! You know how pissed they're going to be if you dupe them like that?"

"Dupe?" Slowly his words sunk into my brain. "Oh."

"Yeah," Gus nodded at me. "Jesus. Just don't say anything. Just keep it to yourself. Can't you just hold it in a little? Can't you just be calm and in control?"

I swallowed. I thought. "No. That's not me."

"Really? And who are you?" Gus asked. "Why does everything rattle you? You're rattled about liking Stanford, aren't you?"

I thought about it. "Well. Yeah. Sort of. I have a chicken…"

"What chicken?"

"Never mind."

"Where are you heading in life?"

I began to get a little hot, a little mad. "Why does that matter?"

Gus looked around, then whispered, "Stanford. It's great, right?"

"Yeah."

"If you understood why Stanford's the best choice for you, if it was part of the larger plan, wouldn't you be calm?"

Larger plan. *Justify your existence.* "Maybe."

"As it stands, even this good news shakes the shit out of you and you walk around lying to people, acting like an idiot, causing trouble for your future because you know you'll have to justify your decision when you announce it and you *can't* justify it because you have no idea why you make any decision." Gus's face had turned totally red.

I whispered, "Oh." I sort of hated it when Gus acted like my dad, but he was generally right.

"Go home and write a list of the reasons why you like…" Gus looked around the empty bathroom and whispered, "Stanford."

"Yeah. Okay," I mumbled.

"And then, when it comes time to make your announcement, you can earnestly tell the State of Wisconsin why you're destroying their dreams of Cheesehead Heaven, okay?"

I nodded.

Gus nodded. He dropped his hair wad and walked out of the bathroom.

I stood there and breathed for a moment. Then Mr. Linder entered.

"Hi-ya, Felton! Great to see you! Get the hell out of here!"

"Sorry," I said and bolted.

• • •

My reasons for liking Stanford seemed ridiculous when I wrote them out instead of repeating them in my head.

1. Dude in dress served me iced tea.
2. Cute guide didn't try to grab my wang.
3. Library had leather couches.
4. Kicker discussed Louis C.K.
5. Frisbee players were very good.
6. Fog on mountains.

I looked at the list and thought, *Maybe I'm gay. Is that why I'm so confused at this tender time in my life? Is that why my stomach hurts?* Then I thought about Aleah and knew I definitely wasn't gay, unless Aleah was a dude, which she wasn't.

An hour later, I noticed I was watching *Storage Wars* on TV.

An hour after that I went for a run, a hard run, and I felt better because running calms me down.

Then I did multiple sets of sit-ups and push-ups. Better.

Then I went to bed, but I couldn't sleep. My heart went back to racing. My stomach tweaked. I thought: Just tell them all Stanford was okay, okay? They're going to be so pissed. Cheesehead Heaven destroyed?

• • •

In the middle of the night, I got out of bed and emailed my list to Gus. I had to get it off my chest.

I saw him in the hall the next morning.

"Are you kidding?" he asked. "Are you having some kind of problem with your sexuality or something?"

"No."

"It's cool if you're gay, I mean. That would explain some of your confusion, right?"

"No. I love Aleah. She's not a dude."

"Enough about her," he said. "Get over it. You're seventeen. You're not going to marry her." He turned and left.

• • •

Between Thanksgiving and Christmas, I struggled all night long, every night, to get anchored, to be calm while the recruiters kept calling, and Bluffton kept nodding and winking and acting like it was all done and I'd play for Wisconsin, and Aleah didn't return my texts.

Eventually, not even working out helped to calm me.

I began to wonder if I should just make my Stanford announcement, just post it on Facebook, call ESPN and cancel.

Would ESPN sue me?

I had good news! Stanford was good news! Why couldn't I just love it and be cool? Instead of being happy, I felt like crap. Miserable about my full-ride scholarship to Stanford. Worried that I didn't know how to explain it without falsely implying I'd come out of the closet. Worried that everybody had abandoned me.

CHAPTER 13
Sidekick

You know who didn't care about my worries?

Tommy Bode. He had no clue.

In our final senior mentor meeting before winter break, Tommy said, "You look like a superhero."

"Oh yeah?" I mumbled, looking out the window.

"Definitely," he said.

We met alone in Tommy's homeroom before school. We hadn't talked a single time about what high school was like or if he had questions. I never asked him about his classes. He never asked how to do anything. Pretty much he said weird crap and I watched him draw and then I told him, "Good job," which he seemed to like.

"You have the muscle," he told me.

"Yeah. Thanks," I said. Outside, the first snow of the year fell.

"You looked like Batman when you hit Nolan Sauter on the neck against the locker that one time. I've been practicing that move on my brother. I can hit him against the wall and he doesn't even bounce off. I just stick him there and choke him."

I turned to Tommy. "Choke? Doesn't your mom get mad? You can't just beat the living crap out of your brother, man."

"Curtis doesn't care. He wants to take karate, but Grandma won't pay. He wants to death-chop everybody."

"What about your mom?"

Tommy stared at me. He shook his head. "Why don't you ask me about my dad?" Tommy asked.

"What about him?"

"He's a bigger bully than Nolan," Tommy said. "You should choke my dad."

"Do you live with him?" I asked.

"Him and Grandma. Mom moved out two years ago. She works in Dubuque."

"Oh." I looked at Tommy, which I didn't like doing because looking at him made me sad. "Hey. Why does Nolan Sauter want to kick your ass?" I asked.

"Because," Tommy said.

"Did you do something to him?"

"No. I'm fat. A fat ass little pig."

"That's not true," I said.

"You want to look at my ass?"

I couldn't help it. I laughed. "Uh. No."

"Good because if you looked at it, you'd want to kick it."

I stopped laughing. "No," I said.

"But don't worry." Tommy cocked his head down and whispered in this deep gravelly voice, "I will get my revenge on all of you."

I stared at his fat-cheeked face. Patches of red grew under his eyes, on his neck. He blinked.

"So…What are you drawing today?" I asked, trying to change the subject.

"Can I be your sidekick? Nobody would mess with your sidekick."

"What do you mean?"

"Like Robin, you know? Superhero sidekick."

"No," I said. "I'm not a superhero. Not at all."

"Please?" Tommy said. He chewed on his cheek. He wrinkled his nose. "Come on!"

"Hey, I have to talk to Coach Knautz about track this morning. I have to cut off our meeting a little early. Sorry about that," I said.

"Yeah," he said. "Okay." He stared down at his backpack for a second. Red flooded his face, then he pulled out his notebook and began sketching.

"Okay," I said. "I'm gonna run."

He didn't say anything.

• • •

Two hours later, between second and third hour, I saw this sophomore jackwad (Ben Fiedler) slap Tommy Bode in the back of the head. I lost my breath for a second. I turned around and walked the other way and my stomach tightened, my chest tightened. I couldn't breathe.

I turned back and waded into that crew of sophomores. Tommy wasn't in there anymore.

Jackwad Fiedler was though. I grabbed him by the collar and spun him around.

He said, "Oh shit."

I said, "Don't ever touch Bode again." I poked the poor kid in the forehead and his face lost all color. He might've shit his pants. "Asshole," I hissed.

A whole crowd of frightened sophomores glued themselves to the wall around us.

I let him go and walked away. Adrenaline poured through me. I trembled.

• • •

I only saw Tommy once the rest of that week. I'd just spent the first half of my study hall sitting in the locker room bathroom sending Aleah text after text.

We can take a break for a few years. Just not date others. Then? After that? Right? When we're adults?

Please? Shit! This is stupid! I don't want you to go.

Are you with somebody else? Is there someone, Aleah?

Why?!!!!

She didn't respond. I pictured Aleah walking, holding hands with some really good-looking twenty-five-year-old dude with glasses on because he's probably a lot smarter and more bookish and more adult than me, and I started sweating.

I jogged out of there and decided to lift weights to get the bad energy out. I got a pass from Coach Knautz.

On my way back to the locker room, I saw Tommy in the commons. He smiled and waved to me. I shook my head *No*, like *I'm not talking to you*...and his face collapsed and he looked down at the ground, and my stomach ached and didn't stop hurting all the way through my workout and into the evening. I didn't think of Aleah, but I felt sad like I did about Aleah.

Why are you so messed up about Tommy? I asked myself, and then I thought about Andrew when he was little and me and Gus and Peter Yang, an old friend, when he was little, and Andrew's friend Bony Emily's little wrists and how fragile everything in the whole world is, and that's when something dawned on me in this flash of light. I recognize Tommy because he's me. I was him. In some ways, I'll always be that kid. I still am. We all are. *What if you're supposed to protect that kid? All those kids? What if you are meant to be a superhero?*

I called Gus. He answered. "I want to protect dipshits," I said.

"Good for you. I'm studying."

"I mean, seriously protect them, man."

"For your life? Like your life's work?"

"Maybe?"

"As what? A teacher or something?"

"Or...or something."

"What?"

"Maybe a teacher eventually."

"Good. After your pro football career, you can be a teacher."

"I'm going to act on this now," I said.

"Oh. Okay?" he said.

I hung up.

I looked up Tommy's home phone number. Nervous as hell, I called.

Some kid picked up the phone. I guess that was Curtis, Tommy's brother. "What?" the kid mumbled. In the background, I could hear a man shouting like he was going to kill someone.

"Tommy. Get me Tommy," I said.

"Okay," the kid whispered.

The man in the background kept yelling for the minute I waited. (Yes, I wanted to hang up—I was sort of trembling because the guy was so whacked out.) He clearly believed something wasn't right in his house because he kept screaming, "That shit's not happening in my house. Not in my house. My house, my house, my house…"

Finally, Tommy got to the phone.

"Who is this?" he said.

"Felton," I said, nervous and fast. "Listen, Tommy. You're my sidekick, okay?"

There was silence (except for the screaming in the background).

"You there?" I asked.

"Yeah," Tommy whispered.

I began to lose air, lose my breath because of the screaming. "Did you hear what I said?" I asked.

"Okay. Okay. Good choice. You won't be sorry, okay?" Tommy said.

"Is that your dad screaming?"

"He'll go to sleep pretty soon," Tommy whispered.

"Okay," I said.

"Okay," Tommy said. He hung up.

Holy shit. Poor Tommy.

But something felt right. *Protect the dipshits.* I sat down in my desk chair and grabbed a piece of computer paper. I wrote:

Felton Reinstein will justify his existence by:
  Protecting dipshits.

Those kids deserve something from me because I'm so lucky (athletics-wise).

I wish I could say I spent the rest of my senior year being a big hero, but while I'm lucky, I also have problems. Serious problems.

• • •

At least in the short term (very short term because I'm not, in fact, a superhero who can adequately protect the weak), it worked for Tommy. Pig Boy.

I actually didn't see him for a few days, but the day before winter break, Tommy entered the senior hall, which takes a lot of guts.

I stood with Gus, ass against my locker, discussing Gus's upcoming nightmare trip to Venezuela to visit his long-dying grandma. He was flying out with his parents that night.

"We're going to be traveling for like three days and we're only going to be there for four days, man. What's the point? Why would they…" Gus said.

Out of the mob of seniors, Tommy emerged. He wobbled up to us. My classmates stared at him, confused that he had wandered into their domain. He wore a T-shirt with a Sharpie drawing of a pig on it. (The drawing was pretty awesome.) The pig wore a cape and held a crossbow. The words "BULLY ME" were written above the pig. The words "PIG BOY" were written below the drawing.

Gus stopped in mid-sentence and took in Tommy's odd presence. "Can I help you?" Gus asked.

Tommy didn't look at Gus. He addressed me. "It's working," he said.

"It is?" I asked.

"Nobody's dicked me over all week. They're running scared."

"Who are you?" Gus asked.

"Pig Boy," Tommy said. "I'm Felton's sidekick."

I nodded. I'd slept better since I told Tommy he could be my sidekick. "Gus," I said. "Meet Tommy. He's my…"

"Sidekick," Tommy repeated.

"And mentee," I said.

"Wow," Gus said.

Tommy nodded solemnly. "Running scared," he repeated. Then he turned and wobbled back down the hall. My football number, 34, was drawn on his back. He knew more about me than I thought.

Gus turned to me. "You're protecting him?"

"Yes."

"That's pretty cool," he said.

CHAPTER 14
The End of the Fall

School ended for two weeks. Winter break. I'd be leaving town to visit Andrew and Grandpa Stan and Tovi, my cousin, which I was psyched about because college questions would go away and I'd be with family in a not-empty house.

And Tommy's Pig Boy thing had calmed me down. He'd given me a purpose! So before leaving for Florida the next morning, I agreed to be social. (I hadn't done anything with anybody since Thanksgiving.)

I went to Dubuque, Iowa, to walk around the mall there with Abby Sauter and Karpinski. Karpinski drove. I sat in the back.

On the way, Abby turned to me and said, "My little brother told me you're protecting some kid in his class."

"Me?" I asked. "Or do you mean Karpinski?"

"Ha!" Abby laughed.

"I don't do shit for children," Karpinski said. "I don't like children. They're really dirty, have you noticed? Dirty hands and shit."

"That's nice of you, Felton," Abby said. "Keeping a young man safe from terror in the halls of Bluffton High."

"Yes," I said. "It's my duty."

"What kid?" Karpinski asked.

"That pig kid," Abby said.

"Little fat ass?" Karpinski asked.

"No," I said. "Tommy Bode. He's not a little fat ass."

"He's pretty fat," Karpinski said.

"Nolan doesn't like him," Abby said.

"No shit. Nolan kicked him in the stomach," I said. "I saw him do it."

"Nolan has problems," Abby said. "That's when your hand bled?" she asked.

I nodded. "He pissed me off."

"Yeah, Nolan's not doing so well," Abby said. "He's not so…" Abby trailed off.

"Why? What's wrong with Nolan?" I asked. What did Nolan have to worry about?

"I'd probably kick that little fat ass in the stomach," Karpinski said. "I'm a dick."

I looked at Karpinski. His jock eyes twinkled.

"It's my job," Karpinski said. "I have to keep the dipshits in line."

"It's my job to protect them."

"There's gonna be some trouble, man. We're going to have to fight!" Karpinski laughed.

"You're a dick," I said.

"Always have been, always will be," Karpinski said.

"You just figure that out, Felton?" Abby smiled.

"No," I whispered.

"Abby, you drinking peach schnapps or something?" Karpinski asked. "What's that smell?"

"I don't know," Abby mumbled.

Karpinski had moved on from the conversation, but my hands were balled into fists. I was pretty close to crushing Karpinski. Here's what I thought: Why don't you bully me, you dick? I'm a dipshit. Bully me, okay?

In Dubuque, I didn't have a lot to say.

"Come on, man, lighten up," Karpinski said. "I was just joking. I wouldn't kick that fat pig kid. He's beneath me, man," Karpinski said as we waited for Abby outside PacSun, where she bought clothes that made her look like a beach volleyball player. (She was an All-Conference volleyball player after all.)

I just nodded at Karpinski.

"You think Abby's drunk?" he asked.

"I protect the dipshits, man," I said.

"Ooh, I'm scared," Karpinski laughed.

• • •

Jerri took me to the airport in Madison the next morning. "Have fun!" she said dropping me off.

She didn't say, "I'll miss you."

Back in Bluffton, Jerri disappeared into the arms of a dude named Terry Sauter. (Is that last name familiar to you?)

Winter Break

Am I Brutal Like My Dead Dad?

CHAPTER 15
Grandpa Stan Thinks I'm Dad's Clone

My grandpa Stan sipped an iced tea on the side of his back-yard pool. It wasn't too warm outside, maybe mid-70s, but Andrew and Tovi were swimming around, splashing each other. The sky above was winter Florida blue. Grandpa's little palm trees blew around in a breeze. I lay on a deck chair next to him.

"Why do you play such a brutal game?" he asked.

"Football?" I asked.

"What other game do you play?" he asked.

Tovi had told us earlier in the morning that she'd accepted a tennis scholarship to the University of Georgia. Andrew and I were like, "That's amazing! That's so cool!"

Grandpa Stan said, "Are you sure, sweetheart? You don't have to play if you don't want to."

Up until my grandma Rose's death a year ago and Andrew's entry into his life, Grandpa Stan only cared about tennis. That's what Tovi told me. I wouldn't know because Grandpa wouldn't talk to us back then. He pushed Tovi to play like he pushed my dad when he was a teen. Tovi said, "He just yelled at me to work harder and run harder, and he shouted at me about scholarships all the time."

But that morning in Florida, he said to her, "Maybe you should stop the competitions and start having a little fun."

"What the hell?" was Tovi's response.

So…

"Why do you play such a brutal game?" Grandpa Stan asked me.

"It's fun."

"Fun? Murder is fun?" he asked.

"It's not murder," I said.

"Slaughter? Is that a better word?" he asked.

Remember, Grandpa had been at Bluffton's homecoming game in the fall. We played Prairie du Chien and I destroyed them. Coach Johnson took me out midway through the third quarter because we were ahead by a lot and the Prairie players were diving on the ground instead of hitting me because I'd crushed so many of them that they'd gotten scared. (I like that feeling, knowing they're scared of me. I look to hit them instead of running toward open field.) Recruiters said I run angry.

"I don't slaughter anybody. It's a game. I score touchdowns."

"You could play golf. Have you ever played golf?" Grandpa asked. "It's very relaxing."

"I'm one of the best football players in the country. I don't want to play golf."

"How can that be fun? Breaking people's backs?"

"I get out my frustration…It makes me feel normal."

"Okay, okay." Grandpa Stan waved his hand, dismissing the conversation.

Tovi and Andrew splashed around. I rolled off the chair, stretched in the sun, then cherry-bombed the hell out of them.

• • •

NCAA rules forbid schools from contacting recruits between Christmas and New Year's. I didn't get a single call. Facebook was still going. (Unofficial representatives—girls and alumni—posted on my page.) I received direct messages on Twitter. But if I turned notifications off on my phone, I didn't see any of them. For the first time in several months, I was sort of free.

Free.

Except that Andrew asked me about Aleah the third day while we ate some cardboard toaster waffles. "How is she?" he asked.

The waffle caught in my throat. "Gone" is all I said.

"Okay," he said, nodding. "It's okay," he said, like he expected the break-up.

My chest hurt.

• • •

When I stay in Florida, I stay in the room where my dad used to sleep when he visited years ago.

I don't necessarily believe in ghosts. Not real ghosts, spirits floating around and saying "Boo!" and crap, but maybe I did back then, back on winter break.

Dad's room doesn't have much in the way of pictures or posters or stuff from when he was a kid, except one framed poster of Bill Murray, totally cross-eyed, from the movie *Caddyshack* with "The Wisdom of the Lama" written on it (*Gunga Galunga…Gunga Gunga Galunga*). It's pretty funny. "Your father made me move this poster all the way to Florida—he loved Bill Murray that much," Grandpa said.

I can appreciate that Dad loved Bill Murray. Was Dad a comedian wannabe like me? Maybe.

There are no boxes filled with papers or books in the closet. There are no boxes of old cassettes or records. There are no tennis trophies or medals or ribbons. I actually sort of figured that Andrew, because he's constantly on the lookout, would find some awesome treasure trove of Dad information: diaries, letters, musings, crap like that, which would say, *Felton Reinstein…this was your father who gave unto you your hair and manly life…*

He left behind a Bill Murray poster and some clothes.

A couple pairs of his shoes sit on the closet floor. They fit me perfectly. (I took a pair last year.) A few dress shirts hang on the bar. One drawer is filled with T-shirts and shorts. The shirts smell like my dad, which you wouldn't think I'd remember, but I do.

That smell made me feel close to him. Over break, late at night, I'd ask questions to the air. "Did you feel better when you crushed a tennis ball?"

I don't know that I believed in ghosts exactly, but I'd feel air move when I asked a question. It felt like Dad was saying, "Yes."

• • •

"Papa's worried that you're too much like your dad," Tovi said. Tovi calls Grandpa "Papa."

Me, Andrew, and Tovi walked down Fort Myers Beach. Grandpa Stan had stayed behind at the house because he wasn't feeling well. (Turns out he had an ulcer and a hernia!) We'd driven out there because Andrew plays with that old-fart Beach Boys cover band called The Golden Rods. He had a practice a little later at the White Shells Hotel.

"He's worried you're too much like our dad too," Andrew said to Tovi.

"I'm not anything like him. I don't get why all you other Reinsteins are so angsty. Life is great," Tovi said.

"I agree," Andrew said.

"Yeah, well…" I said. "There's a lot of bad shit in the world, you know?"

"So?" Tovi asked. "There has always been bad shit and there always will be bad shit. Why worry about it?"

"You sound like Karpinski," I said.

"Who?" she asked.

Pelicans crashed into the water near us, scooping up fish in their big rubber beaks.

"Papa asked me last night if I thought you'd be offended if he sent you to a psychologist," Tovi said.

"Me?" I asked.

"She's not talking about me," Andrew said. "I'm my own psychologist."

Tovi laughed.

"Yeah, good luck to you, brother," I said. We walked for a minute or two, then I said, "Do you think I'm really like Dad?"

"I do," Tovi said. "Totally."

"Why? How exactly?" I asked. I knew I looked like him and we were good at sports and crap. But Jerri had told me that we weren't alike otherwise.

"You have a killer instinct," Tovi said.

"All great competitors have a killer instinct," I said.

"I mean…I mean…" Tovi paused.

Andrew stopped walking. He grabbed her wrist. "What?" he asked.

Tovi spoke to Andrew, which I guess was easier than speaking to me. "Felton just has this vibe. It's like this coiled thing. It's like if the wind blows the wrong way, he might destroy somebody's face."

"Oh," Andrew said, nodding. He looked up at me. "Remember when you kicked the doorframe by the bathroom and the lights went out and that picture of me, you, and Jerri fell off the wall upstairs?" Andrew asked.

I sort of heard him, but I wasn't thinking about my door kick. I was thinking how fast I pinned Nolan Sauter's neck to a locker and how good that felt. I was thinking about how close I was to killing Karpinski because he got away with bullying little schmucks, which sucks, which made me want to destroy (and if I was going to protect dipshits, wasn't that a good thing?).

"That's life. That's who I am," I said.

"That's exactly who your dad was too. Wound tight, man."

"Are you scared of me?" I asked Tovi.

"Me? Hell no. You're not going to mess me up. I actually feel awesome when we're together because I know you could kill just about everybody."

Andrew nodded thoughtfully. "That's why Tommy Bode likes you so much. He's your Pig Boy."

I shook my head. "What? How do you know about that?" I asked.

"I'm not dead," Andrew said. "I'm in Florida, but I have a cell phone and email and friends. Bony Emily tells me everything."

"Okay," I said. "Well, I'm proud of protecting the little people."

"You're protecting a pig boy? Do people want to make him into bacon?" Tovi asked.

"No. They're just mean to him."

"You're nice, man," Tovi said.

"Are you going to hurt others to protect him?" Andrew asked.

"I don't know. I don't think I have to really. Nobody messes with me, Andrew."

"But…but…but…" Andrew stuttered.

"What, man? Get it out," Tovi said.

"Aren't you just pouring more mean into the world?" Andrew asked.

"No," I said. "No. I'm not doing anything. Just keeping Tommy Bode from getting his ass kicked all the time."

"Seriously. That sounds awesome," Tovi said.

"Yeah. I suppose," Andrew said.

• • •

New Year's Eve, Tovi's mom, Evith, came down from Atlanta and we all went out to a giant buffet at the club in Grandpa Stan's golf community. This was something I was looking forward to. Growing up with hippie Jerri, I didn't have the opportunity to attend many buffets.

Last fall, I went to an "all you can eat" buffet with Cody Frederick and his dad and it was maybe the best day I've ever had in my entire life. I probably ate ten pounds.

During the New Year's Eve dinner, I became vaguely aware that Evith and Grandpa were staring at me. I had ham in my mouth and I was cutting a piece of prime rib and my plate (third plate) had maybe three pounds of mashed potatoes piled on it. I looked up (felt the stares). Evith and Grandpa stared back.

"Whuh?" I said, mouth full of ham.

Evith shook her head. "Like seeing a ghost," she said.

"This is what I'm saying," Grandpa said to her.

"Felton is sitting at the table, duh," Tovi said. "He can hear you."

I swallowed the ham, then looked back and forth between them. "Tovi's right. I can totally hear you," I said.

"You just look so much like your dad," Evith said.

"I know, I know," I said. "I've heard it all before."

"Not just look," Grandpa Stan said. "You act. You are. You eat like Steven."

"I eat like my dad?" It sounded so ridiculous. My head buzzed a little. "Everybody eats, Grandpa. You eat like Dad too. So does Tovi."

"No," he said. "Nobody eats like Steven but you."

I pushed my chair back and stood up. "Well, I'll stop then. Don't mean to bother you."

"No, honey…" Evith said.

"Sit down, Felton. Grandpa doesn't mean anything bad," Andrew said.

"I mean, I want to help you," Grandpa said, his face flushing. His tufty white hair stood on end. "Have you ever tried meditating?"

This made Tovi burst out laughing. "You guys are so nuts!"

"*Not nuts!*" Grandpa shouted. "*My son is dead!*"

People at tables around us paused. They stared at us.

"Sorry," Tovi said.

What's weird is that I'd already sat back down and I was already eating again. Jesus balls, I love me a buffet.

• • •

One of Dad's T-shirts from the drawer has a picture of hand on it pointing to the left. Above it, in these blocky 1980s letters, are the words, "I'm with Stupid." There's a picture in a family album of Dad, maybe seventeen, arm around Evith, maybe fourteen, wearing this shirt. "I'm with Stupid"—arrow pointing at Evith. It totally killed me. I thought it was hilarious.

I'd pulled the shirt out of the drawer several times during the week. I showed it to Evith on New Year's and she said, "God, I hated that shirt. Your dad tortured me with that. I was always stupid." She kind of laughed. Tovi laughed. Andrew stared at it.

Grandpa said glumly, "Your father's favorite shirt."

That night, I asked, "Can I take this?"

Air moved in the room. "Yes," it said.

I packed the shirt in my suitcase. I was leaving in the morning.

• • •

I woke up before almost everybody. I climbed down the stairs and found Grandpa Stan alone, sitting at the kitchen counter, drinking an orange juice.

I poured a glass for myself and sat down next to him.

"Have you made your college choice?" he asked.

It was nice to have someone ask oddly. As much as I hated all the people up in Bluffton constantly being in my business about college, I felt sort of bad that no one in my family had asked.

(I know now they were trying not to pressure me, that Andrew had actually told Tovi and Grandpa to lay off.)

"I think so," I said.

"Not Northwestern?" he asked.

"No," I said. "Definitely not."

"Good," he nodded. "Wisconsin?" he asked.

I exhaled. "Can you keep a secret?"

"Who am I going to tell?"

"Stanford," I said.

"Yes!" he said. He pumped his fist. "Very good school. Very good choice!"

"Thanks," I said.

"I'll pay for it," he said.

"What?"

"If you don't want to play games, if you want to study and forget athletics, I'll pay for Stanford. That's a fine school."

"Grandpa," I said, "I love football. You even told me to love it last summer."

Grandpa nodded. He looked down at his hands. "I know. And it feels good to run people over. Okay, fine. I want you to love what you do."

"It's sort of what my body was built to do," I said.

"Yeah?" he asked.

"Yeah," I said.

"Stay here." Grandpa stood and shuffled to his study, where he listens to music and pays bills. A couple of minutes later, he shuffled back. "Found it." He placed a folder in front of me.

"What's this?"

"Open it. Your father's poem from high school."

I swallowed hard. Something real? Something from my dad? A real document? I opened the folder. Made me so nervous.

There was just a wrinkled piece of dirty notebook paper inside with "Steven W. Reinstein" written on the top. This is what the poem said:

I will break the mold.
I will start to stop now.
I'm a Flying Wallenda between two clouds.
I am not what I do.
I am not what I will be.
I will stop and let go, balanced between two clouds.
I will break this mold.

"Hmm," I said. "He wants to break the mold."

"See?" Grandpa said. "That's your poem now. Take it."

I put the poem in the folder and held on to it. "See what?" I asked.

"Your father's body played tennis, but he had other ideas."

"I don't see that in this poem," I said. "I don't think he had any idea what he wanted to do but wished he did."

"Oh?" Grandpa asked.

"I get it," I said.

Grandpa paused. He breathed. He nodded. "And you? Might you like something else? Maybe sitting on a mountainside like a swami? Meditate like an old holy man?"

"Yeah, that's me."

"You might like to grow a long beard?" He smiled.

"Maybe," I said. I sort of smiled. "I'm a fan of loincloths."

"Me too," he said. "I like air on my boys."

I laughed a little. Then I said, "I'm going to play football."

"I've just been thinking…you know, worrying, as I get to know you more."

"Don't worry," I said.

"Good." He smiled. "Fine. Go play your game. If it doesn't work out, you have other options. Sports aren't everything. You understand?"

"Okay," I said. Then I paused, thought. "Hey. What's a Flying Wallenda?"

"They were tightrope walkers who crossed spectacular divides and used no nets. Very risky. Sometimes, they fell and died."

"Wait. That's what Dad wanted to be?"

"Maybe it isn't such a good poem." Grandpa's face lost color. "Give it back to me."

"No. I want it," I said.

• • •

An hour later, I said good-bye to Grandpa and Evith in the kitchen. Two hours later, I hugged Andrew and Tovi at airport security. Three hours later, I was on my way home to Bluffton, the "I'm with Stupid" T-shirt folded perfectly in my bag. By mid-afternoon, Jerri had pulled up in front of the Dane County Airport in her crappy Hyundai.

• • •

On the way home from the airport, rolling through the mucky hills of a forty-degree Wisconsin January (too warm, by the way), Jerri said, "You'll never guess who I spent New Year's Eve with!"

No, I would never have guessed.

Abby and Nolan's parents divorced in September. Terry Sauter is an orthodontist. He wears a shiny brown leather jacket and he smiles too damn hard.

I didn't really care. Sure, Jerri had said she couldn't be with Aleah's dad and be a student at the same time. Sure, I thought she was contradicting herself. So what? I came home ready to get on with it. I wrote this on a piece of loose-leaf notebook paper:

1. One more high school sports season. Run. Stretch. Get ready for Roy Ngelale. Win at least one state track championship. Maybe three?
2. Figure out good words to say about Stanford. When announcement comes, you'll show the choice was right one.
3. Be nice to Pig Boy. Bring him some new drawing pens?
4. Wear "I'm with Stupid" T-shirt? Looks like something Gus would wear. Hilarious.
5. Graduate. Have fun. Leave.
6. This is going to happen whether you like it or not, dickweed.

See? I was ready to go!

But…

Buried/Unburied

CHAPTER 16
The Death of Curtis Bode

I've thought a lot about this. Would I have crashed if Tommy Bode hadn't been my mentee-sidekick? Maybe not right away. Would I have screwed up my college announcement if Curtis Bode had stayed at school that day in early January? Maybe. Would I have crashed if I wasn't a jock, if I was just a normal dude who didn't have colleges texting every minute? At some point, yes. Definitely.

I have a big problem in my past. I'll never actually be a normal dude.

· · ·

Bad. Okay.

Tommy Bode's dumbass, drunken, shouting dad kept guns in the house. Do I look like a hunter? You're right. If my hair grows out, it's a Jewfro. I'm not a hunter, so I don't know anything about gun safety, but I'll tell you this: I'm pretty sure you're not supposed to keep a loaded handgun under your pillow, which is what Tommy's dad did because he's a psycho.

(I only know this because Tommy told me later. He didn't tell anyone else because he thought the cops would come and arrest his dad, which is probably the damn truth—and maybe would've been good.)

On January 3, the first day after winter break, after a rough morning, Tommy's little brother, Curtis Bode, left Bluffton Middle School. He walked home, walked into his dad's bedroom, picked up the pillow, lifted the handgun, turned it on his own chest, and shot himself in the heart.

He was fourteen and in eighth grade, okay?

• • •

I didn't see Tommy that morning. I'd looked for him a little in the commons when I got to school because I wanted to show him my "I'm with Stupid" T-shirt. (I wore it.) It just seemed like something he'd find funny. On my way into choir, filled with forty-four singing dorks, an announcement buzzed on the intercom. "Tommy Bode to the principal's office immediately."

My knees went weak and my heart accelerated. I don't know why I knew.

I knew something.

Curtis Bode died on the floor, his grandma next to him, crying and screaming at a 911 operator. That's what Tommy said.

• • •

Bluffton is a small town. Everyone knows everyone, which can suck (and sometimes not suck). We haven't had a lot of suicides. I remember Jerri crying when I was ten because the brother of one of her high school friends shot himself in the woods by Belmont Tower. Other than that, I can't remember any suicides other than my dad and Curtis Bode.

Some places have suicides all the time. Some schools. It's old hat. It isn't. I'm sure. I know. I hate this.

The news ripped through the choir (and the school). Kit Hinkins had texts from his cousin within a few minutes. Ms. Rory had to stop class because everyone started buzzing. Kayla Zielsdorf's brother is an EMT. Ms. Rory let her call him. He confirmed that it was Tommy's brother. He said it was a gunshot. He did not call it a suicide, but everyone sort of knew.

Ms. Rory leaned back on the piano and covered her mouth. My classmates muttered back and forth. They all covered their mouths. I sat crumpled in a folding chair, my head in my hands. Gus sat behind me on a riser. He leaned over and whispered, "Is that Pig Boy's little brother?" I nodded. He said, "Oh, man. I'm so sorry."

"Don't be sorry for me," I said.

"Okay. It's okay, man," Gus said.

"What's okay?" I spat.

"Nothing," Gus said.

• • •

An hour after lunch, the whole Bluffton school district closed down. Cody asked me if I wanted to go out to the big M, my favorite hill near town, which would be muddy and cold as crap in the crap January weather. "Me, Reese, and Karpinski are going out there."

The last thing I wanted to do was to sit around talking about "life" and bullshit with a crew of jocks who had it totally easy all the time. (Including one who bullied the shit out of me when I was a broken kid, who thought "keeping the dipshits in line" was funny.)

Gus asked if I wanted to drive around with him and his sophomore punk rock girlfriend, Maddie O'Neill. "We're just going to cruise, maybe over to the Mississippi." I didn't want to talk about life with them either. Her especially. Maddie likes horror movies and her bedroom is painted black. It's like death is her style. This did not appeal to me.

"No thanks."

I walked home in this January soup air (a couple miles of muck on the streets). My eyes burned. I thought of Tommy pinning his brother, Curtis, against a wall, choking him the way I did Nolan Sauter.

• • •

Speaking of Sauters.

When I got home, Jerri wasn't at school. Jerri was in the house with Nolan's dad, Terry. His giant Cadillac Escalade blocked the garage door, so I had to climb up the stairs and go in the front, which caused me to catch them making out on the couch.

"Whoa, ho, ho!" Terry said when I entered.

"What are you doing home?" Jerri barked.

"Kid died. They let school out. Can I speak to you, Jerri?"

"Kid died?" Terry asked, sitting up. "High school?"

"No. Middle school," I said.

"Oh good," Terry said.

I stared him down. His kids were both in high school. I guess I understand why he'd say, "Good." Still, it was a shitty thing to say.

"Do you two know each other?" Jerri asked.

"I used to see Mr. Sauter when he lived in Abby's house," I said. "Can I speak to you, Jerri?" I asked.

"Yeah, Felton. Of course."

She got up and followed me into the hallway.

"Jerri," I whispered. "An eighth grader killed himself today."

"Oh God. Oh shit," she said. "Do you know who?"

"Curtis Bode," I said.

She nodded. "I was in school with Doug," she whispered. Jerri graduated from Bluffton High. "That's his dad," she said. "Doug."

"I heard him shouting on the phone one time," I said.

"You? What? You called that kid? Do you have something to do with this? Why would you call an eighth grader?" Even in the dark hall, I could see color rising in her face.

Did I have something to do with this? Did Tommy smash Curtis into a wall so much he decided to die?

"No. I'm his brother's...I'm Tommy Bode's senior mentor at school. I just called because I wanted to tell Tommy something, and his dad was screaming in the background. Sounded like a psycho, okay?"

Jerri swallowed. She nodded. "In art class, Doug could draw any car you could name with perfect detail. Any car."

"Tommy draws pigs. Good ones."

"What the hell happens to people?" Jerri asked.

"Hey," I said. "Could we go to a movie in Dubuque tonight? I don't want to...I don't want to see my friends and I don't want to be alone and I...I'd like to see a movie."

"Oh shit," Jerri exhaled. "My first Accounting II class is tonight. It's a new semester...I want to get off on the right foot, you know?"

I nodded. "What happens to people?" I asked.

"I don't know," Jerri said, like nothing had ever happened to her, like she hadn't gone through a hundred crazy changes. "I just don't know," she said.

• • •

Thank God for Andrew. An hour later, he got a text about Curtis and called me. Then we played *Minecraft* (him on a school computer in Florida, me in my bedroom) for a long time.

Jerri and Terry left the house while we played. Andrew missed his bus home, and Grandpa had to drive to pick him up.

Later, Andrew and I talked again, which was good. Something had been bothering me and I didn't know who I could ask, other than Tommy himself, and I definitely didn't have the guts to just call over there.

I sprawled across my bed, staring at the ceiling, phone pressed to my ear. "Was Curtis pushed around?" I asked Andrew.

"I don't really know him," Andrew said. "I suppose. Probably. He's a year younger than me, so I don't know for certain."

"But do you know someone who would push him around?"

"Sure. Ryan Bennett is in his grade and he's a very bad egg," Andrew said. "When he was in sixth grade, he'd spit on dorky people's faces, even if they were eighth grade."

"I know who he is. His sister is Carly, that sophomore girl, right?" I asked.

"Yes. Are you going to hunt Ryan down and murder him?" Andrew asked. "So you can keep protecting Tommy Bode?"

"Maybe," I said. I was sort of serious.

"Don't, Felton. You can't…you can't just…Plus, Ryan will grow up and just be a sad person," Andrew said. "You don't have to hurt him. Time will take care of this business."

"You think, huh?"

"I'm positive," Andrew said.

"You're smart for a dipshit," I mumbled.

"I am, Felton," Andrew said.

Then we played *Minecraft* late into the night.

CHAPTER 17
Brains Are Weird

I decided not to go to the funeral. I never knew Curtis. *I'm just going to show up now? That wouldn't be respectful...*

Respectful, my ass. Is this the choice a "superhero" trying to take care of the weak would make? Avoid tough parts?

No. I was too scared to go. I felt guilty as hell because I knew I was too scared to go.

On Thursday, a couple of school buses lined up in front of the high school and a large part of the freshman class actually went, including Nolan Sauter. They were dressed just like they would be for school. They stood there in the commons like they were waiting to go on a field trip.

I couldn't hold steady. I felt dizzy.

Karpinski, who stood next to me, said, "*Now* these little peckers give a shit. They probably all took shots at that kid, and now that he's dead, they're all going to go cry about it."

I turned to Karpinski. "You fuck off, man."

"What?" he barked. "Truth hurt?"

Cody said, "Have some damn respect, you idiot."

"Maybe they should've had some respect when the kid wasn't dead," Karpinski said.

I spun and walked away fast. I thought of Nolan Sauter. I thought, *Karpinski's right.* That didn't make me like Karpinski any better. He was the same guy who said a few weeks earlier that it was his job to kick Tommy Bode.

• • •

Really, maybe I didn't need to go to the funeral. I lived funeral.

In the couple of days after Curtis killed himself, I remembered Dad hanging in the garage. Before Curtis, I knew it had happened and where, but I couldn't remember the details. Jesus, did I remember the details now. I woke up choking, the whole freaking thing in my brain, stuck in the back of my throat, ringing in my ears. I asked Jerri about the snack bag on the floor: "Did I forget it so we went back to the house?" She nodded.

I remembered Dad's funeral for the first time. Me, Andrew, and Jerri rode in the back of Grandma Berba's car. (That's Jerri's mom— she lives in Arizona now.) We all wore black (little black pants and a white shirt—that's what Andrew wore). Grandma kept changing the radio station in the car until Jerri yelled at her. At the service, these tall men read poetry. Who were these men? Dad's friends?

Evith sobbed. She gulped for air.

There was a dog loose in the cemetery. It galloped down a hill and around the burial people. The dog scared me. I grabbed Jerri's arm. She pulled her arm away. I looked up and her chin shook. She shook her head like someone trying to clear the cobwebs after getting hit on the football field.

"Mommy?" I asked because I called her Mommy back then, not Jerri.

"No," she whispered. "No."

This was in Chicago. I remember seeing tall buildings from the back of Grandma Berba's car.

I remember Grandma Rose, Dad's mom, hugging me, telling me she loved me. I remember there were little green leaves on this skinny tree. I climbed on that tree and someone pulled me down. Another tall man. I remember Grandpa Stan, how he'd been so funny before, how he once called me a little pistol because I tore through their house so fast. At the funeral, he wouldn't even look at me. I remember Tovi hanging in the folds of Evith's dress, just one eye uncovered staring out at me.

Before Curtis killed himself, I had no memory of this at all.

You know what? Before last year, I didn't remember Grandpa Stan. I didn't remember Grandma Rose existed at all. I didn't even know I had a cousin.

Brains are damn weird beasts. A few months ago, I read about post traumatic stress disorder on the Internet. Guess what? I've got it. Apparently, we weak-ass, trembling little human beings make bad memories disappear. This is weird, right? I had suppressed memories.

"Suppressed" means they were always there though. Just hiding. They were in me and I didn't know about them. Back in the fall, Gus told me I didn't know myself well enough. How could I justify my existence? Clearly, he was right. Jesus. Whole important people had disappeared from my memory.

During that part of January, I spoke at length to Gus only one time. I told him about the memories. He said, "This is probably normal for a dude like you."

Normal? Paranormal? Alien inside me? Who am I?

"That's good," I mumbled.

For weeks after Curtis's funeral, the memories just blossomed in my brain like gross flowers trembling awake in time lapse on PBS, and I could barely think about anything else, definitely not the phone calls from recruiters and the coming ESPN announcement (how dumb and useless). I'd sit in class, barely able to breathe, seeing dirt on the cuff of Grandpa Stan's pants after he shoveled a little dirt on my dad's coffin in the ground. (I think this is a Jewish thing.)

Space case. Mr. Linder said stuff like, "You in there, Felton?" when I didn't hear him to answer a question he asked during class.

"What?" I asked, shaking my head. "What?"

"Never mind," he said, looking concerned.

In the halls, people kept getting in my face.

"You okay?" Gus asked.

"You okay?" Cody asked.

"You okay?" Abby Sauter asked.

"I'm okay," I told them all. *Filled with buried treasure.*

Occasionally, my phone buzzed. Aleah texts. Out of the blue. After she tortured me with silence. *You okay? I'm thinking of you.*

I wouldn't respond to her. No more. She'd hurt me enough.

One time, she texted: *I'm writing a lot of music, Felton. You're the inspiration.*

I wouldn't respond.

Days and nights sort of blended together. I remembered the ambulance in front of our house. I saw my dad in a damn bag being pulled out of the garage on a gurney. I heard Jerri sobbing in the bedroom. I saw Andrew coloring in a Mickey Mouse coloring book. He turns to me and says, "Daddy's dead. That means he won't come home."

No shit, little guy.

I'd climb out of bed and hold my phone, thinking about Tommy Bode. I wanted to call, to ask Tommy if he was okay. I worried so much about that little pig boy and his crazy dad. I wanted to tell him to come over to my house. To get out of there. But I never called. I was too wussy to call.

Tommy didn't come back to school in January. He was out all four weeks.

Sometimes, awake in the middle of the night after suffering through all these new memories, I'd ask the air, "Are you there, Dad? Please?" I didn't hear, "Yes," like I did in Florida.

Aleah texted once: *I know about the boy from Andrew, okay? We can talk. I'm here.*

I didn't text back.

No Aleah, no Cody, no Karpinski. I didn't want to talk to anyone. I didn't even want to hang out with Gus really.

You there? I only wanted my dad, so long ago dead. *You there?*

I read and reread that high school poem of his.

I will break the mold.
I will start to stop now.
I'm a Flying Wallenda between two clouds.
I am not what I do.

I am not what I will be.
I will stop and let go, balanced between two clouds.
I will break this mold.

I thought: Why did you want to be dangerous? Why didn't you want a safety net? Why did you want to break stuff?

I got no answer. There were these blinding moments when I thought I should break stuff.

It's freaking weird. The death of Pig Boy's brother made me miss my dad like I'd never missed him before. Uncovered. Pig Boy's brother made me remember my dead dad like never before.

I was not in great shape.

And in January, I stopped running, stopped working out, stopped functioning.

(Track season? What's track?)

(School? Never heard of it.)

CHAPTER 18
Andrew Thinks I'm on the Cusp of Recovery (Uncovering Causes Recovery?)

When Andrew first left for Florida, he said that of me, him, and Jerri, he was the only one who had managed to grieve for Dad appropriately.

"I figured out what happened. I figured out how old Jerri was when she got pregnant. I figured out that Dad was angry and mean and that he slept with other women. I sat in the garden eating pukey tomatoes and crying. That was what I needed to do to make peace with our father's demise."

"You burned your clothes and shaved off your hair," I told him. "You didn't shower for like two months. I'd say you went nuts."

"No, I went sane," Andrew said. "You started running like a scared ostrich so you could bury your head someplace else, and Jerri started taking antidepressants so she could see straight enough to buy new clothes. You're both in trouble still. But I want you to know I still respect you and will be here for you when you break."

"Oh, thanks a lot, you little asswipe." That's what I said to him back then.

• • •

One night during January, while I was totally suffering my Curtis-Bode-induced Dad memories, I called Andrew. Andrew said,

"You're doing it, Felton. You're dealing with it. Maybe you should see a counselor or something? Someone who could help you make some sense."

"You didn't see a counselor," I said.

"I've read a lot of philosophy and religion, you know?"

"I know, Andrew. I know." Even though I like books, I used to make fun of him for his reading habits. He read the complete works of Spinoza last summer for Christ's sake. What kid does that? (I don't really know who Spinoza is, by the way, other than that he's some philosopher.)

"I made the decision to move on in my life in a certain way. And I'm very healthy, emotionally speaking. I'm my own counselor," Andrew told me.

"You're fifteen, Andrew."

"I'm timeless," he said. He didn't sound like he was joking.

"Okay...okay," I said. "I'm not timeless and I can't be my own counselor. After this ESPN announcement, I'm going to get some help. I'm so tired of this shit. I have to get out. I'm dying, man."

"I'll help," Andrew said. "I'll research psychologists who accept Jerri's insurance."

"Okay. I'm going to do this," I said.

When I was little, Jerri did send me to therapists and I had a really bad time. Terrible time. The therapists made it all worse, I swear to God. I didn't want to go back to that...

But this Dad stuff. Seeing him hanging. Missing him. Talking to him. Seeing his funeral in my brain. Not being able to study or sleep or think really...I knew this shit could take me down for real. I felt it. (Andrew told me I had a healthy response in that I understood the danger.)

But.

You know what dudes like me love? A good excuse not to deal. I created a huge one too. Nationally televised.

Some part of my messed-up brain decided to screw up bad so I wouldn't have to deal. Really.

I'm weak and weird and scary.

I'm also normal.

You are not alone.

CHAPTER 19
The Badger Baiter

I knew it was coming. Those football programs, especially the four I'd visited, texted and texted. Called and called. I didn't respond to any of them, not even Stanford, but I knew it was coming.

Early in the afternoon of January 31, Mrs. Duensing, the assistant principal, got on the intercom and announced that second-hour classes the next day should go to the gym instead of meeting in their rooms because the whole school was invited to see my ESPN announcement live. "We could all use a reason to celebrate," she said. "Let's show our school spirit! Everybody wear school colors!"

My classmates were pretty psyched to get out of an hour of school. Jess Withrow actually hugged me because my ESPN thing delayed her chemistry exam.

Here's what I thought: *Are you shitting me? A reason to celebrate? Curtis Bode is dead, Duensing.*

The ESPN producer called me in the evening and told me all I had to do was show up. "Your family can come out on the floor with you, and we've already talked to your coach. Just relax and get ready to make a little history. Sound good?"

"Uh-huh," I mumbled.

"Bring your A game," he said.

"Uh-huh."

I didn't ask Jerri to go with me. I barely slept. I saw Dad hanging in the garage.

Then, that morning, after I got out of the shower (after I listened to messages from coaches at the four schools…"We look forward to watching the broadcast!" they all said), I checked email and saw I had a new message from Tommy Bode. (He hadn't been in school that whole time.)

Oh shit…Oh shit…

I swallowed hard and opened the message.

Here's all it said:

I know who killed Curtis.

"Jesus Christ," I shouted. "Curtis killed freaking Curtis!"

I leaned back in my chair and stared at the ceiling, the inside of my head crackling.

Why the hell did you decide to be a senior mentor? I asked myself.

You want to be a good person, I answered.

Yeah, good luck, idiot! I shouted (in my head).

Are you going to protect the weak? I shouted back.

Stop. Ask Jerri to go with you. Stop. Please.

I slapped my computer shut, dressed, climbed up the stairs, and found Jerri dressed up, ready to go. "You're coming with me?" I asked.

"Of course," Jerri said.

"Thank you," I said, nodding.

"Terry's going to drive us in the Cadillac," she said.

"Who?"

"Terry?" Jerri said, squinting at me.

"Oh. I don't care," I said.

I cared that Terry drove when we got to the school and Abby was in the parking lot. She stared at us as we rolled into a spot.

When I got out of the car, I sort of waved. Terry smiled big and stupid and waved. Abby stared for a second longer, then turned and walked fast (half ran) into the school.

Turns out brave Terry Sauter hadn't told his kids that he was dating anybody. Turns out he didn't really talk to them at all. I never mentioned him to Abby because why the hell would I want to talk to her about our gross parents making out? Plus, I was quietly going psycho all January. Plus, I figured she knew anyway.

No.

Anyway, she was quietly going psycho too.

• • •

Okay.

How can I communicate the intensity of the next hour or so? They stuck a mic pack in my pants and clipped a mic to my shirt. Jerri and I got very sweaty while people told us how to sit, stand, where to look, and the gym filled up, up, up…

Not good enough.

Okay, imagine this:

I am thinking about my dad hanging. I sit behind a table on the floor of the gym. I am surrounded by TV lights and a TV crew and there's a camera pointed at me. The stands are filled with people not just from the school but from all over the state of Wisconsin. I'm serious. Maybe from the whole damn world. *Who are all these people?*

I'm shaking in my boxer shorts. I think of my dad in a body bag.

Coach Johnson sits next to me. He keeps patting me on the shoulder. "Good stuff, my boy. You earned this," he says.

Jerri stands behind me. She's a little twitchy. "Wow," she keeps saying.

Boom...Boom...Boom. (That's my heart pounding.)

"Looking cool, my man. Use this towel to wipe your forehead, all right?" An ESPN guy hands me a towel.

"Uhh..." I say, taking the towel.

"You're fine, man. You're fine."

"Uhh..."

9:14 a.m. The crowd gets louder. They're really packed in.

I find Gus. He sits next to punk girl Maddie. Her bleached hair explodes off the top of her head like a big white chicken. Her black eyeliner makes her eyes look like bat caves. She gives me the finger, laughs.

Jerri sees. Jerri says, "Nice manners."

I wonder if my dad made an official announcement when he decided to go to Northwestern, when he was alive, when his body wasn't dangling from the ceiling of the garage.

Karpinski, Abby, Cody, Jess, and Reese sit twenty feet away from Gus and Maddie. They're all clean shaven and dressed in their Bluffton black and gold. They're all laughing and joking, except Abby, who stares off into space. Her face is hot. She's blinking. I can tell her face is on fire, even from the gym floor.

And then a crew of freshmen comes in. At the back of that line, wearing his BULLY ME, PIG BOY T-shirt, is Tommy Bode. He's back. He's here. He looks skinnier. He looks confused. My number, 34, is on his back. He squints to the front of the gym and sees me. His mouth hangs open.

I nod. My heart pounds. His brother, Curtis, is buried in the ground. His brother, Curtis, is decomposing. *Don't think what he looks like in that coffin. Don't think...*

Tommy nods back. He gives me a slow thumbs-up.

"Who is that?" Jerri asks.

"Dead kid's brother," I whisper.

"He's staring at you weird," Jerri says.

"I know."

Coach Johnson leans over to me. "Are you friends with him?"

"I'm his protector," I say. "I'm not a great protector."

"Oh?" Coach Johnson squints at me. "You okay, buddy?"

"Fine," I nod. I see Dad's zombie body in the ground, his neck cracked to the side.

Pig Boy. *Friends?* Abby. *What am I doing here? Pointless shit.*

The ESPN guy points at me. He nods. It's 9:15 a.m. and the TV lights come on for real. It's so damn bright I can't see the people in the stands. I can't see anything.

Coach Johnson says, "Get ready."

My heart pounds in my throat.

The ESPN guy says, "Here we go. Nick's going to ask you a few questions, then you'll make your announcement."

I nod. My throat is dry leaves scratching. I cough.

There are baseball hats from the four schools sitting on the table in front of me: the Not to Be Named, Wisconsin, Stanford, and Northwestern. I'm supposed to put the baseball hat on my head from the school I chose when I make my announcement.

"We're live," says the ESPN man.

The whole gym explodes in shouts and cheers. Kids chorus, *Bluff-ton High-School!* Clapping and repeating. *Bluff-ton High-School!*

A voice comes over the sound system, a voice from back in the ESPN studio.

"Felton Reinstein," says the sportscaster. "Good to see you, buddy. Nick Clemmons here."

"Yeah. Uh-huh. Yeah," I say to the air. "Hello, sir." Lights so bright they're burning my face.

"Looks like you have a full house out there in Wisconsin."

"Big," I say.

"Well, there's a lot of excitement in the studio too. How are you feeling about your choice?"

"I don't know," I say. I blink into the lights. I feel sweat roll down my forehead. *Where's that towel?*

"Your mom happy? She sure looks proud."

I feel Jerri move. She puts her hands on my shoulders. She squeezes.

The whole thing is only supposed to take a couple minutes. ESPN will cut to another recruit in just a few minutes.

"So let's get to business. Felton Reinstein is rated the number three running back prospect in the country by…"

And then I think: *Dad was a national champion…*I picture him crushing a tennis ball, exploding across the court, crushing another, which I've seen on fuzzy VHS video at Grandpa Stan's house.

Nick Clemmons keeps talking. But I don't listen. I think: Dad. I think: Dad ran across the court. Dad crushed the ball. Dad didn't move when he was zipped into a bag. Dad. Where did that energy go? Where did his life go? Where? Are you there, Dad? No. You're dead with Curtis, but Pig Boy is here and Abby is here and Terry is up there in the stands staring down at Jerri and probably thinking he'd like to be making out with her on our damn couch because his marriage is done and Jerri's been done with it all forever because Dad, you're dead and gone forever...I see him crushing a tennis ball. Exploding across the court...*I can't take this anymore.*

And then Nick Clemmons says, "It's time, buddy. Are you still in deliberations?"

I hear him. I jerk to attention. "No. Sorry."

"Where you heading next year?"

I look at the hats. I see them, see the insignias. (I'm not blind.) I reach and pick up the Wisconsin hat. The crowd completely erupts. There are huge cheers, like screams of joy. I say, "Shit," on national television. I shake my head. I say, "No." I put the hat down and pick up the Stanford hat.

"Ouch. Harsh, my man," laughs Nick Clemmons from the ESPN studio.

I hold my breath. I know what I've done. *Intentional.* "No. That was...I'm going to Stanford," I mumble.

Then there's this giant hiss—the whispering of a thousand confused Wisconsinites.

"We wish you best of luck, Felton. Enjoy California, buddy," says Nick Clemmons.

"Thanks. Okay," I say.

The TV lights go off. Jerri says, "Wow, Stanford. Didn't see that coming. That's wonderful."

The gym is so quiet. People murmur. Confused.

The gym is so quiet.

Then Karpinski yells, "Good one, Rein Stone."

Coach Johnson says, "I'm surprised. It's a good school. Good for you. I'm very surprised. We looked forward to seeing you up in Madison."

"I'm not going to Wisconsin," I say.

"No. I see that," Coach Johnson says. His face is red. I've embarrassed him. The crowd hisses.

I decide right then I'm taking the rest of the week off. "I need to leave, Jerri," I say.

She nods.

I pull the mic pack out of my pants, unclip the other part from my collar, hand it to the ESPN guy.

"Congratulations, man," he says.

While kids flow out of the gym into the commons, Jerri and I leave by the side door. We don't go through the school. People from the town and the state and wherever else are in the parking lot. A few say, "Good school." But they're quiet. They're mad. Of course. I picked up the Wisconsin hat.

Terry Sauter meets us in the parking lot. He says, "Was that hat thing a joke?"

"No," I say.

His face is red. "Good. Crappy joke. Wow," he says. Terry Sauter drives me and Jerri home.

Holy shit. I saw the insignias. I saw my hand reaching for the Badger hat. Holy shit. *Why did you do that?*

Wisconsin doesn't call. Northwestern doesn't call. Not to Be Named doesn't call. Stanford leaves a message and tells me to call back that afternoon. "So excited," the coach says. "Good times coming."

Tovi texts: *STANFORD!*

Cody texts: *congrats.*

Abby texts: *is my dad screwing your mom?*

At home, after ten minutes of looking at the Internet in my bedroom, I hold my head in my hands. I sort of laugh. *This what you wanted?* The State of Wisconsin hates me. Wisconsin wants me dead. You should see some of those messages…

• • •

Okay.

A couple hours after I held my head in my hands, I called up the Stanford coaching staff—not to get the letter-signing crap set up, the administrative stuff (we did deal with that), but so I could hear these people who were happy, who didn't care that I was an asshole. The running back coach said, "Can't wait to get you out to Palo Alto, buddy!"

"Can't wait to be there," I said.

"Talk soon."

I needed that. I didn't like being hated, even if I'd caused it, even if part of me wanted it. *Why?*

I think I know why.

Hate causes hate. My Badger hat grab worked. For days after the grab, I stopped seeing my dad hanging. I stopped seeing him buried in the ground. I stopped trembling all the time. I had a new battle. Against the State of Wisconsin.

Uncovering stopped. Covering up started.

Rebury the dead.

Guys like me don't want to deal because dealing is goddamn hard. Dealing is torture. Living the hell again and again. Who wants to do that? Do you understand? Fighting with the State of Wisconsin is easier, even though it's stupid and useless.

I still feel like a prick.

Launching Stupid Chickens

CHAPTER 20
No Thanks, Andrew

On the night of the announcement, Andrew called. He said, "Congratulations. I've never been to Stanford, but I understand it's a beautiful school."

I'd begun stewing. "No shit, you've never been to Stanford," I said.

"No shit?" he asked. "Grandpa said he already knew you were going there."

"I told him."

"You didn't tell me," Andrew said.

"You weren't interested," I said.

"Of course I was interested," he said.

"I have to go. I'm cooking a frozen pizza," I said.

"Wait. I just emailed you a list of therapists, along with some thoughts on each of them. Just wanted to give you warning. I'm glad you're going to…"

"Not now," I hissed.

"What do you mean?" Andrew asked.

The landline rang. I was in the kitchen, so I could see the caller ID. The caller was from northern Wisconsin, the 715 area code.

"You there?" Andrew asked.

"Just a second," I said and waited to hear the message because people were leaving some badass messages.

The caller hung up.

"Nobody home," I said.

"What?" Andrew asked. "Are you talking about your brain because you're acting so weird?"

"No. That's the past. I'm done with the past. I'm moving on," I said.

"Felton. I just thought. I thought you were…"

"I'm tired," I said. The oven alarm started beeping. "Gotta go. Pizza," I said.

"Felton?" Andrew asked.

I hung up. I ate pizza. I read mean things about me on the Internet while I ate pizza.

Andrew called back. I didn't answer. He left a simple message: "Check your email, you ass face."

The landline rang again. Same 715 number. No message.

I checked my email, but only to read mean messages Wisconsin people sent me.

Wisconsinite:

YOU ARE A TRAITOR!

Oh yeah? Come here and say that. Come on…

CHAPTER 21
Rebellious

By the time I talked to anyone (other than Jerri) again, I'd been locked up in the house for the better part of three days. I'd only left twice to run. Although I was sort of out of shape because I hadn't worked out in January, I ran really hard and right into the middle of town, and I ran into the street when cars were coming, which is bad. I flipped off an old man who honked at me at an intersection. (I'm sure he knew who I am too—little Bluffton.)

I was pissed.

Here's the shit:

After my announcement, Wisconsin fans caught fire. Journalists were on fire. Bloggers and Facebook members—all on fire. They were totally united in their hatred of me. They called me traitor and classless and an asshole and a bad citizen and selfish and lots of four-letter words I don't care to repeat. Jerri screamed because we got calls every five minutes, all day, all night—people breathing, hanging up, or shouting profanity. We could see their damn numbers. These people weren't even anonymous.

Worst thing I saw? Some asswipe kids from Appleton in front of their ranch house rapping in a video called "Homo Reinstein" where they rhymed "Reinstein" with "Vi Queen" (I think in reference to the Minnesota Vikings) and replayed over and over me picking up and putting down the Badger hat, eventually putting on some kind of red filter like there was blood covering me. They acted all gangster or whatever. *I could take you. I could wipe that driveway up with your stupid faces.*

People left comments cheering them on.

I read Facebook again and again. I watched the tweets pile on me. I watched the "rap" video again and again.

Why?

I guess I was happy to be pissed (instead of depressed). I thought I understood Dad's poem. I wanted to be fearless, like a Wallenda who worked without a safety net. *I'll break the mold.* Being pissed gave me the courage of my fake convictions (that all Wisconsin people were assholes). It felt so much better to be pissed than incapacitated. I felt like I had a reason, a mission. *Show them you don't care if they live or die.*

The more shit I got, the less sorry I felt for picking up the Wisconsin hat. These people wanted me to crumble on the damn floor because I'd made a mistake? (I convinced myself it was a mistake.) I'd rather set fire to the whole damn Dairy State than crumble on the floor. *I don't back down. I'd pick up the Wisconsin hat again, idiots. I backed down when I was a squirrel nut, bullied kid. Not now. No more.*

• • •

On Friday, I wanted to talk about it. (Jerri didn't want to talk about it.) I called Gus to bitch at him about Wisconsin football fans.

"It's just a damn game," I said. "I'm the one who plays the game. What's wrong with all these people? They're pissed at me? They should go play their own game."

"Mob mentality, man. They like being on a team, and if you mess with their team, they want to kill you. People are brutal," Gus said.

"It's not their team. They watch the freaking Badgers on TV. Idiots should die," I said.

"Uh…You okay?" Gus asked.

"I'm mad, man!"

"Okay."

"Stupid!"

"Um…" Gus was quiet for a second. "Okay. My parents are going to Milwaukee for an art show tomorrow," Gus said. "How about you come over and we have some beer? We'll put down a six-pack, man. Relax and reflect. I've got some big news."

I didn't even think for a second about the alcohol policy at school or the track season or anything (or about "big news" for that matter). "That's what I'm talking about," I said.

"Cool," Gus said.

"I'll break the mold."

"What?" Gus asked.

"I will toast the fire that consumes Wisconsin."

Gus paused. "Dude, calm down."

"I don't think so," I said.

"I have to call Maddie so she can get beer," Gus said.

"Have you heard of the Flying Wallendas?" I asked.

Gus was already gone, calling Maddie. She baby-sits for her older brothers and sisters. They give her beer and wine and everything else as long as she keeps baby-sitting for them.

My anger kept me from thinking about Pig Boy for a couple days.

He'd sent me that weird email about who killed Curtis. He sent me other emails, which I didn't open. I forgot about him and roasted my nuts on an open fire instead.

After talking to Gus, I ran the hill on the main road for an hour. It was a killer workout, but I had to do it.

My plan: Explode all over Wisconsin during track season. Defeat Roy Ngelale (a Wisconsin recruit). I would destroy the rest of their sons in the long jump pit.

Nice plan.

Except something drenched the anger. Drunk.

CHAPTER 22
Mr. Dipshit's Love Day

Here's why alcohol is dangerous for some people: it totally seems to work at first. Unfortunately, "at first" is the end of "work" and the beginning of Shit River.

Gus texted me at midnight: *be here at 8:30.*

Normally, that might seem a little early for a Saturday morning. But I was psyched to get going.

At 8:20, after checking the Facebook taunts, I climbed upstairs to get a lighter coat because February had turned weird warm, like 50 degrees. Jerri and Terry were sitting on the couch. I didn't even know he was at the house.

"What are you doing awake?" Jerri asked.

"Did he stay over?" I asked, pointing at Terry.

"I did, buddy," Terry said. He smiled. Shit-eating smile.

"Great," I said. "I'm going over to Gus's. I think I'm going to stay over there tonight."

"Good! Glad you're reengaging, Felton!" Jerri said.

"Uh-huh," I said. "Reengage this, jerks," I said under my breath.

"What?" Jerri asked.

"Nothing," I said. I got my coat and my stocking cap, got my bike, and hit the road.

When I arrived, Gus greeted me wearing a blue robe and chewing on his dad's old pipe (same pipe he used in our karate video back in the innocent fall). And something bad. He'd gotten a haircut. No more hair wad. To me, this wad was Gus.

"*What the hell did you do?*" I shouted.

"Big news! I'm going to Amherst College. I got in and I'm going. I marked the occasion with a new hairdo," he said.

"Aw, shit. Stupid," I said. "You look like a lawyer. Do lawyers go to Amherst? Are you going to be a lawyer?"

"Jesus, Felton. Relax. I'm not the enemy, man."

"I know."

"I'm really happy about this, okay? Life is change."

I exhaled. "Okay. Why do you have a pipe?" I asked.

"Feels right. Anyway, I'm in the process of preparing us a breakfast for the kings of ass-kicking," he said.

"Cereal?" I asked, walking in.

"Bacon and eggs, mother boy," he said.

In a few minutes, Gus had placed a far better looking breakfast in front of me than anything Jerri had cooked since she had her first freak-out a couple of years ago. (Jerri has been institutionalized once.) There was actual cheese and salt and pepper in the scrambled eggs. The bacon was not burnt to black dust. Along with the eggs and bacon, Gus put two cans of Hamm's Beer on the table.

"I'm told that this beer comes from the land of sky-blue water," Gus said. "It also cost me nine dollars for a twelve-pack, which is affordable on my budget."

"Good. That's a lot of beer, man," I said. I stared at his haircut and my jaw clenched, but I didn't say anything.

"Maddie assured me that twelve would be the minimum we'd need for a day of relaxation and beer drinking. She knows these kinds of things. I trust her."

"Good." One beer at Stanford had made me loose. What would happen with six? Would I rip off my clothes and run out into the street? *So be it.*

"A toast," Gus said. He popped his beer, which spewed some foam on his eggs. "To the end of the world as we know it."

"Yes please," I said. "Blow it up."

"I don't want to blow anything up," Gus said.

"To each his own," I said.

"Okay."

Then I popped my beer can, which spewed some foam. We clapped our aluminum cans together, which spilled beer on the table. Then we sucked down our first sip.

I gagged. My nose burned. I swallowed so I wouldn't spit it out. I exhaled and looked at the ceiling. "Wow," I said. I took another sip. Then a longer drink. *Good. Very good.* Within about a minute, I felt looser. And here's what's really weird: within about two minutes, my anger began draining in a stream from my fingers. (I let my arms hang down at my sides and I felt the draining.) I took another deep breath. I shut my eyes. I swallowed. I opened my eyes and I saw Gus and all he was to me: the greatest damn mother on the face of the whole planet. The *best.*

This chemical. That fast. I'm serious.

Beer is dangerous for me.

"This tastes like urine, right?" Gus said.

"I think I love it. You know what? You're a good man. Amherst College, huh? That's awesome."

"Thanks."

"You're the best, man. Amherst? That's a good one. You're my best man."

"You've experienced an attitude change," Gus said.

"Have I? I guess. Good. Life is hard."

"Indeed, my brother," Gus said, raising his can and taking another sip and making a face.

"You do look like a lawyer," I said, smiling.

"I'm aware of that," Gus said.

"I like it," I said.

I sucked down about ten gulps, and the saintly tears of a million smiling Christmas angels swept down my stairs. My chest expanded with love. My heart slowed. My face smiled.

• • •

I think we were only two beers into our day when Gus put a record on his dad's record player. "'O-o-h Child.' The Five Stairsteps," he said. "You know this song?"

I didn't. It's all these people singing, "O-o-h, child," and telling that child that things are going to get easier and that things are going to get brighter. I had to drink my smelly beer very fast because it was all too much, this song and the nice people on the record. Way too much. Not like the angry Badger fans who wanted to kill me. All these people singing sweet, gentle words of hope to this poor kid, who probably had lots of sad problems but was still alive and still had hope, telling that kid that things are going to get easier and brighter.

"This song's from the '70s, man. I sometimes wish I was a hippie," Gus said. "You know, like dancing naked on a VW van?"

"It's the most beautiful thing I've ever heard, man," I said. The song's sweetness opened up a space for Tommy. "Pig Boy should hear this."

"No. Please don't bring over Pig Boy," Gus said.

"Really?" I asked.

"Seriously."

"Okay. I won't. But you'd really like him."

"I need to play the song again."

"Uh-huh," I said.

He stood up. I could tell he was a little wobbly. He swept himself, robe billowing behind, to the turntable.

We listened to the song about ten times and I was so warm and I knew things would be both brighter and easier... How could the world be so wrong if people with big Afros (serious Afros on the cover) made such nice music?

By like 10 a.m., I'd already had my best day since Curtis Bode shot his own heart.

Gus saves.

Beer saves.

Someday, we'll walk in the rays of a beautiful sun...

(That line is from that song.)

• • •

Outside, the sun poked through the February gloom. After some debate about pizza delivery (it was still morning), we understood that we had to take a walk because Gus wanted a frozen pizza. We each put a can of beer in our coat pocket (Gus wore a red-and-black plaid wool coat over his robe, which looked hilarious), and we walked out into a sun that was not cold.

"I'm going to grow your hair wad on my head to honor your past," I said to Gus, pulling my stocking cap off.

"That's a good idea. That would make me happy," he said.

"I'm going to make a painting of me and Andrew swimming in a fish tank," I said. I pictured this giant mural painted on the side of our house. "People stare, you know? They stare at us. But I need to learn how to paint," I said.

"That's good," Gus said. "You should do that."

"Pig Boy is a good artist. He can help me."

"Where are the womens?" Gus asked.

It seemed like a really important question.

Then we got to the Kwik Trip on Highway 81. There, we were very thirsty from not drinking, so we crouched behind a Dumpster on the side of the store and popped our beers while a cool wind blew and Gus called Maddie.

Then this girl, Robin Tesdell, walked around the Dumpster. She's sort of a burner. She graduated last year. She works at the Kwik Trip. She said, "Look at you two alkies."

I dropped my beer.

Gus said, "Don't do that."

I picked it up and sucked the foam off the top.

She lit a cigarette.

"Can I have one of those?" Gus asked.

Robin tapped a cigarette out of her pack. "You dudes know it's like ten in the morning?" she asked. "What are you doing?"

"Looking for womens," I said.

"And a pizza," Gus said.

Maddie shouted from his phone, "Who are you talking to?"

"Just come over to my damn house!" Gus shouted back.

"I'm still asleep," I heard her shout.

"I didn't figure you for a drinker," Robin said to me. "You feeling good?"

"I am good. I am filled with angels' tears," I told her, nodding.

"Awesome," she said.

We left our beers by Robin (Gus gave her back her cigarette, which she threw in the dirt) and went in and bought three pizzas.

• • •

When we got back to Gus's, it was eleven in the morning. Maddie was there.

"Oh, no," Gus said to me. "You don't have a woman."

"My woman left me," I said. My chest filled with sadness, the angel tears like old car oil gumming up my warm engine.

"Don't you like other girls?" Maddie asked.

"No," I said. "No love."

"Come on," Maddie said. "There must be some other hot chica you've had your eye on."

"No. I love Aleah, but I won't talk to her."

"Why?" Maddie asked.

"She broke up with me too much," I said.

"Oh."

"Abby Sauter," Gus said.

"Abby?" I asked.

"*No!*" Maddie shouted.

"Abby Sauter." Gus nodded. "You love her."

"I do?" I asked.

"Yes," Gus said.

"I should call her?" I asked.

"Oh hell no," Maddie said. "Do not invite that priss over here."

"Do it!" Gus shouted. "I need to speak to her!"

"You do?" I asked.

"Yes!" Gus shouted.

I was already calling Abby.

Abby! Of course!

I felt great! In love!

Abby didn't answer. So I called again. She didn't answer. So I called again and left a message. "Call me, Abby. It's important."

I sat and stared at Gus, who was doing a sexy dance in front of Maddie. She smiled up at him.

"No woman," I said.

Then my phone buzzed.

"Whoa." Then my breath died inside me and, shaking a bit, I answered, "Abby?"

"What's important, Felton?" she asked. "Is your mom going down on my dad?"

"You're mad at me," I said.

"No."

"You are."

"No. My dad's an asshole," she said.

"Okay. Jerri's an asshole too," I said. "But I miss you."

Abby paused. "What are you doing, Felton?" she asked.

"Oh. I'm not sure, baby," I said.

"What the hell?" she asked.

"I don't know for real." Here's the thing: Me and Abby have a long history. After Gus, she's the first person I remember in school. In first grade, she told me to stop staring at her. I couldn't help it. I stared at her one time during lunch and she slapped me. In fifth grade, out of no place, she told me she was my girlfriend. (Nobody liked me then—but me and Abby walked home together every day.)

In seventh grade, she shoved me against a locker. In ninth grade, she and Jess Withrow made fun of me mercilessly. But she was also the first person to apologize, the first after sophomore year to say how awful she felt for the way they all treated me.

Then, last summer, in the middle of the night, I got a text from her that said:

me and jess drunk she says I like you so call me

The text sent shocks through my body, but I was in Florida dealing with Andrew and I loved Aleah, so I didn't call. I couldn't call. I just pretended it never happened and Abby never mentioned it again—maybe she thought I didn't get it?

"What do you mean by 'baby'?" she asked.

"Babe," I answered.

"Where are you?" Abby asked.

"Gus's house. He says I like you."

"What did I say?" Gus asked.

"Are you drinking?" Abby asked.

"I don't know," I said.

"What do you want, Felton?" Abby said.

"I want you to be here," I said.

"*Are you effing kidding me?*" Abby shouted. "So we can be together like our asshole parents?"

I heard Nolan tell her to shut up in the background.

"No," I said. "I like you, that's all."

"Okay," Abby said. "Shit." Silence.

"Abby, baby?" I asked.

"I'll be there in a little bit," she said.

I clicked End on the call and looked up at Gus.

He stared at me. "Is Abby Sauter coming over to my house?" he asked.

I nodded.

"I don't want the prom king in my house!" Maddie shouted.

"Prom queen," Gus said. "And furthermore, this isn't your house."

"You don't think I know that?" Maddie spat.

"And furthermore, Abby would've been the valedictorian of our class if she hadn't screwed up last semester. She's not dumb."

"She's a bitch," Maddie said.

"Abby screwed up last semester?" I asked.

"Straight As all through school, then doesn't show up on the honor roll?" Gus asked.

"Whoa," I said. "I never check the honor roll."

"Just in the paper yesterday, man," Gus said.

"She's a jerk," Maddie said. She poured a bunch of beer in her mouth, then burped really loud.

"I love you," Gus said.

• • •

While Gus and Maddie ate frozen pizza, I sat on the couch staring at the door, waiting for Abby. I stared for a half hour maybe, without any beer, because I felt all floppy and nervous.

The doorbell rang.

"Oh my shit," I said.

Gus and Maddie stared at the door.

Maddie said, "Here comes the prom king."

I stood, walked slowly to the door, opened it. Abby wore a hoodie and sweatpants. She nodded at me. She said, "Give me a drink."

Gus leapt off the couch and grabbed our last can of Hamm's out of the box. He held it up and smiled.

"Do you have anything else?" Abby asked.

"I can get anything," Maddie said. "Anything you want."

• • •

Ten minutes later, we rolled south of Bluffton. Abby drove her giant brown turd of a Buick that belches smoke, and I sat in the seat next to her. Gus and Maddie made out in the backseat.

Abby turned back and looked at them. She shook her head. I could tell she blushed a little. I stared at her like I did in first grade because Abby is a thing of rare freaking beauty and she always has been, to the point that no one will ask her out except Karpinski because she's just too damn much. Karpinski tried to kiss her at homecoming in the fall and she shoved him away, laughing. She also pointed in his face. "Not ever," she told him.

Abby Sauter turned again. This time, she looked at me. She half smiled. "Staring, Reinstein."

I nodded.

"You have something you need to say to me?" she asked. "You like me or something?"

My heart pounded in my throat. I wished I had another goat-piss beer. "I'm sorry Jerri and Terry are an item," I said.

"Oh," Abby nodded. "Don't worry about it," she said.

We drove on.

. . .

"Here! Turn here!" Maddie shouted.

Abby's car slid onto a gravel road. We rolled into a valley near Big Patch. I'd never been there. I thought I knew every place around Bluffton.

"It's about a mile," Maddie said.

The bluffs around us were steep. The road was muddy. Deep, dark country. Maddie's brother Cal lives in an old schoolhouse in the middle of absolute nowhere.

Abby's crappy car radio kept fuzzing out, so we couldn't hear the music.

"Can't even get Dubuque," Abby said.

"Good. You listen to shit," Maddie barked.

"Really?" Abby asked. "Why?"

"KLYV is just a bunch of packaged plastic. There's no lyrical depth. No real emotion," Gus said.

"Nothing except pulsing groinage," Maddie said.

"What's wrong with that?" Abby asked.

"Good point!" Gus said. He reached over the car seat and slapped me on the back of my head.

"I like groins," I said.

"Here!" Maddie shouted. "This driveway! Right! Right!"

Abby fishtailed onto an even smaller drive.

"Where are we?" Abby whispered.

"I don't know."

"What's with your face?" she asked.

"Nothing," I said. My face burned though. Blushing about groins.

• • •

A few football fields into the woods, we came to the old schoolhouse. There were old pieces of cars lying around and a red tractor parked on a concrete slab.

When we parked, Maddie said, "My brother Cal is a weird dude, but he's nice. Just enjoy, because you won't meet dudes like this on your planet."

"My planet?" I asked.

"She's talking to me," Abby said.

"And your boyfriend," Maddie said.

"Felton isn't my boyfriend," Abby said.

"That's not what he told me," Maddie said.

"Shut up, Maddie," I said.

"Hey, hey, hey," Gus said. "Somebody needs a drink."

• • •

Maddie didn't even knock. She walked right in. We all followed her. Inside, a balding 30-year-old with a big blond beard sat at the kitchen table working a drill. He wore a dirty A Tribe Called Quest T-shirt. He squinted down at his hands. He screwed two large pieces of metal together.

"Excuse me, sir," Maddie barked.

Cal looked up, startled. He stopped the drill. "Why are you here, baby girl? The kids are with their mom this weekend. I don't need you."

"We're here for the bar, Cal."

Cal's eyes exploded out of his head. "*Holy shit!*" he shouted. "Mr. Traitor Footballs and Junior Miss McBluffton? What the hell are you two doing at my house?"

He was referring to me and Abby.

"Just with Maddie," I said.

"Dude, that was hardcore what you did on the TV. Woo!" he started laughing his ass off. "Picking up that Badger hat. Man! You've got a couple of pumpkins for testicles, dude."

"It was an accident," I mumbled.

"Bull. Shit. I was watching. That was a badass joke. Seriously."

"I wish it was a joke. Stupid cheeseheads," I said.

"Right on, man," Cal said.

"How the hell do you know about Felton and Abby?" Maddie shouted at him. "You like keeping up with the popular kids, you pervert?"

"I get the *Bluffton Journal*. I have a TV. I want to know what I'm missing. Otherwise, what's the point of hiding out?" Cal said.

"Junior Miss what?" I whispered to Abby.

"Nothing. I won a scholarship last fall, that's all."

"Bar's in the barn, dudes. Head on back. Maybe I'll see you in a little bit. I've got to get some work done first," Cal said.

"Hey, man," Gus said, going past.

"Nice haircut. Good to see you, brother." Cal fist-bumped him.

"What's he working on?" I asked as we climbed through a dark little hall filled with stripped motorcycle frames and buckets of screws.

"He's building an airplane," Maddie said. "He's going to fly to Mexico."

Abby pinched my arm. She smiled huge.

• • •

The house was an explosion of metal and tools. The yard was a freaking scrap heap with piles of old bikes and toy trucks, toy bulldozers, and other assorted crap. The "barn" (more like a big shed), though, was totally clean and beautiful. There was a full bar with stools and neon lights and a giant moose head hung on the wall. (Maddie later told me it was a deer head, but it looked like a moose head to me.) Christmas lights were strung all over the walls. A little heater pumped out heat. There were shelves and shelves of old records along one end of the room and a turntable hooked up to a giant sound system.

"Wow," Abby said.

"Pretty awesome, right?" Gus said.

"You can tell what Cal loves most, huh? Not his kids. Not his airplane. Booze," Maddie said. "Let's do some shots."

Gus and Maddie went behind the bar and started arguing about what liquor we should drink.

"Uh, really, I don't like to drink," Abby said.

"I remember one time," I said without thinking.

"You do?" she asked.

"Yeah…yeah…" *Just say it.* "I, uh, got this text from you."

"Oh," Abby said. "That was dumb. That's why I don't like Jess that much." She walked away from me and sat down on this giant beanbag chair in the corner.

"That thing is called a Love Sac," Gus shouted to her.

"Great," Abby said.

• • •

An hour later, Maddie was on fire. She was telling Abby about all the people she considers to be bitches and asswipes. Drunkass Abby would sort of protest or whatever, but really, Maddie just wanted to shout.

"No. Carly Bennett is a bitch," Maddie said. "She calls me Zitty Cat."

"That's very dumb," Abby said.

"I had a zit one time. A big one on my nose," Maddie said.

"That happens." Abby nodded.

"It's never happened to you," Maddie said.

"No," said Abby.

"Carly's brother is worse. Ryan Bennett punched Felton's brother in the chest so hard, Andrew couldn't breathe."

"*He did?*" I shouted. "Ryan? When?" Ryan was the kid Andrew mentioned when I asked him who might've bullied Curtis Bode.

"When Andrew was in seventh grade," Maddie said, shaking her head.

"I should kill Ryan Bennett," I said.

"Nolan hangs out with him. He's been at my house a lot," Abby said.

"Nolan is a total dick too. You know that, right?" Maddie said. "Your brother is the worst jerk in the freshman class."

"He's mad at my dad. That's what our therapist says," Abby said.

"I'm mad at my dad, but I don't knock anyone's head on the ground," Maddie barked.

"No, I mean really sad because Dad barely talks to us. Dad doesn't like us."

"Oh," Maddie said, nodding. "I get it."

"It's very bad," Abby said. "Things are bad."

"Is that why you blew your grade point?" Gus asked.

"I'm not going to graduate first in class. You are," Abby said, nodding.

"Are you okay?" Gus asked.

Abby set her drink down on the bar. She shook her head. "Dude," she said. She pointed in Gus's face. "You're the first person to ask. Jess hasn't asked," she slurred. "Cody hasn't asked." She pointed over at me. "Felton is in his weird Felton bubble all the time," Abby said. "But I'm not okay. I don't know what's wrong with me," she said.

"I'm sorry," Maddie said, "But if you people weren't so mean to everyone all the time, maybe we'd care, maybe we'd give Nolan a hug instead of wishing he'd die."

"You people?" Abby asked.

"You and all your people." Maddie nodded.

"How are they my people?"

"You're all brutal. Plus, you volleyball girls all look alike," Maddie said.

"Racist," Abby whispered.

"Against asshole jocks?" Maddie shouted.

"Apparently," Abby said, nodding.

• • •

Ten minutes later, Maddie and Abby were hugging and crying. I'm not kidding. Gus and I sat on the Love Sac, watching their exchange and listening to music—some dude named Perry Como singing 1950s Christmas songs. *It's beginning to look a lot like Christmas!*

"What if they start making out?" Gus asked. "I don't know how I'd feel about that."

"I really like them both," I said. "Those are two good women."

"Here's to that. I need to make a toast," Gus said. He stood up and lifted a bottle of beer over his head. "*You! All of you,*" he shouted. "A toast."

Maddie and Abby let go of each other and turned toward him.

"I love you," Gus slurred. "Maddie, you are the best girlfriend who has lived in this place. In this world. Abby. Felton has loved you since before you were born to the local orthodontist."

"How embarrassing," Maddie said. "He's never said anything?"

Abby shook her head.

"To both of you," Gus cried.

"Cheers," Abby said. Then she sucked down more of that black liquid.

It's true. That Abby is top notch. A top-notch lady.

I rolled off the Love Sac and walked up to the bar. I grabbed Abby around the waist and pulled her up to me. Our faces were inches apart. I had to close my left eye not to go cross-eyed and lose my balance. I could feel Abby's heart banging against my chest through her sweatshirt.

"I've never kissed anybody," Abby whispered.

"Oh my God!" Maddie screamed. "Are you made of plastic?"

"I don't think so," Abby said. "Just…never happened."

"Okay," I said. "I have loved you since before your dad ever fixed a tooth. I do. Do you understand?"

"Yes." Abby breathed out slow, the sweet smell of her breath made my damn legs weak. "Okay. Good. I want you to kiss me," Abby said.

We kissed. It was okay. I'd only kissed Aleah before (and I loved that). Abby felt different. She felt cool. She tasted sort of like licorice and ice cream.

We kissed more.

"Woo!" Gus and Maddie cried.

"That's okay. That's not too bad," Abby said. "Right?"

"Yeah. I liked it," I said.

• • •

"You used to call Felton a fur ball!" Gus shouted at Abby.

"No. Jess did," Abby said. "I called him other stuff."

We all leaned on the bar. We drained that black liquid from

the bottle. The floor moved underneath my feet. The Christmas lights blazed in my eyeballs. Perry Como sang about Santa Claus.

"Pig Boy has it worse. Don't you understand? I'm lucky. It's bullshit, mothers. Pig Boy is never going to turn out to be big," I shouted.

"Stop talking about him. He's not the only one in the world," Gus said.

"His brother shot himself," I barked.

"I know, I know," Gus said.

"Wait. Shh. Before I pissed off the State of Wisconsin, Pig Boy emailed me to tell me that he knows who killed his brother," I said.

"Someone killed Curtis?" Maddie asked, her eyes wide. "Curtis didn't kill Curtis?"

"That's what Pig Boy said."

"Oh shit, I hope it wasn't Nolan," Abby said.

"Jocks think they can just slam everyone's body around and it won't hurt." I slammed my hand on the bar. The bottles and glasses jumped. "It's like everyone is just a damn beach ball to kick," I said.

"You're a jock," Abby said. "You're the biggest jock in the world."

"No he's not," Gus said. "Felton is a geek in jock pants."

"The football players at the colleges I visited wanted to kick me like a beach ball," I said, nodding.

"They pushed you around?" Abby asked.

"They better not," I said. "They wouldn't mess with me."

"Oh my God. We shouldn't let it happen," Abby said. "What's wrong with us? We need to stop them."

"You want to stop Karpinski?" I asked. "You want to tell him what you really think?"

Abby paused.

"Karpinski's the worst," Gus said. "He mooned me in Walmart and gave me the finger. Just last week. It never ends with that guy." Gus shook his head.

"Why are people so mean?" Abby asked. "I used to think it was so funny. I used to think everyone was a beach ball."

"I'm not a beach ball," Maddie said. "I'm really not, okay?"

"I'm sorry. I'm so sorry," Abby said.

• • •

Abby, all almost six feet of her, lay on top of me on the Love Sac.

"Why we never do this before?" I asked.

"I know! I love drinking!"

"Not just drink. You know, hang together, baby."

"I don't know," Abby said. "I had soooo much business to take care of."

"Buying and selling business?"

"School and volleyball, and I don't like all these boys breathing on me. They're gross."

"I'm not gross."

"Not that gross. I like you best," Abby said.

"I like you best too. Better than Karpinski," I said.

"This is the best night I ever had," she said.

"I think it's like dinnertime," I said. "We have just begun…"

"Oh shit! We have to eat!" she said.

Then Gus shouted from the records, "Five Stairsteps! Holy shit!" He held up the album with the people and their giant Afros. "Let's hear it!"

"Not again, man," Maddie said. Gus had played it at his house another five times when Maddie got there.

"Oh yes," he said.

He played "O-o-h Child," and within about a minute, Abby was totally bawling. Her tears coated my face.

"The singers are so nice," she said. "We should be so nice."

"Safe," I said.

"My parents aren't even my parents anymore," she cried.

"I know," I said. "Where are the adults?"

"They don't exist," Abby cried.

• • •

Maybe an hour later, Cal showed up in the barn. He had two bags filled with sub sandwiches from Pickle Barrel Subs, which had to be like a forty-minute round-trip drive. "Sammies!" he shouted.

"Awesome, man!" Maddie said.

"You dudes are eating and staying. Nobody is going to drive any place, you got that? Eat up!"

"He's an adult," Abby said.

"He's building an airplane," I said.

"I want to go to Mexico," Abby said.

"With me?" I asked.

"Okay," Abby said. "Let's totally do it."

"Hey, Cal, can we come with you to Mexico?" I asked.

Cal cocked his head at me. He put the bags of subs on the bar. "Hell no, man. You're exactly what I want to get away from."

"Me?" That hurt my feelings.

"Can we at least visit sometime?" Abby asked.

Cal thought for a second. "Sure. Why not?"

"Thanks, man!" Abby said.

• • •

My last memory of the night is so blurry. Abby snored on my shoulder. We stretched on the Love Sac. Gus, Maddie, and Cal all had cigarettes in their mouths. Cal played an electric guitar (pretty loud), and Maddie and Gus pounded on bongos. Every now and then, Cal would scream, "Rock it, mother scratchers!" and Maddie would call back, "We rock it!"

How did I fall asleep during that?

Really, it was only like nine at night.

Booze.

• • •

I woke up spooning Abby. Morning light came in through small windows high up on the barn's walls. The world smelled like sweet, rotten alcohol. We were covered with a dirty bedspread. Abby turned her cheek to my mouth. She whispered, "Are you really my friend?"

"Yeah," I said. "I'm here."

My mouth tasted so gross. "I think mice slept in my mouth," I said.

"Yeah. You get sort of used to it," Abby said.

"You have a lot of experience with this?" I asked.

"No," Abby said.

Before we left, Cal made us all bacon, egg, and cheese sandwiches. He gave us Advil. He said, "Now don't make it a habit of coming out here. You got it? There's no open invitation. I might chase you out next time. I have guns. Lots of them."

"Shut up, Cal," Maddie said.

"I'm serious, baby girl," Cal said.

"Really, really serious?" Maddie asked.

"Very, very serious." He pointed at each one of our faces.

• • •

On the drive back, Gus said, "Hope there isn't trouble. Hope we're okay. I think I left a note for my parents. I did, right? I said I was staying over at your place, Felton. Did you call Jerri?"

"No," I said.

"Are you worried? Are you in trouble?"

"No," I said.

"I'm not either. My mom doesn't get mad at me for bad shit I do," Maddie said. "She gets mad at me when her life sucks."

"My mom probably didn't notice I was gone," Abby said. "She goes to bed at like eight."

"Great," Gus said. "My parents give a shit, so I'm the one who'll get in trouble. What a deal."

Nobody said anything.

Abby dropped me at Gus's so I could pick up my bike. She grabbed my hand as I got out and pulled me toward her. She squinted at my face. She said, "Talk later?"

"Yeah. Of course."

CHAPTER 23
We Love Our Little Boy Soooo Much!

As I unlocked my bike from a street sign in Gus's front yard, he stood staring up the street.

"Hey," he said, "Would you come inside for a minute? I don't want to face Teresa alone." Teresa is Gus's mom.

"I'm sort of tired."

"Good. I'll make you some coffee."

"I don't drink coffee."

"You'll want to drink coffee in college."

Clearly Gus wasn't going to let me go. Why did I have to face Teresa?

Life is change. Gus's parents have always been pretty strict, and they totally love punishing and grounding Gus and calling Jerri to tell her the crap we've done. That morning, we found his parents reading the newspaper in the living room. Did they yell and scream? Did they ask where the hell we were?

No.

"Look what the cat dragged in," Gus's dad said.

"You boys have a fun night?" Gus's mom asked.

"Pretty great," Gus said.

"You hear the big news, Felton?" Gus's dad asked.

"Maybe?" I said.

"Amherst! Top-ranked liberal arts college in the nation!" Gus's mom said.

"Well, one of the top," Gus said.

"Number one most years," Gus's dad said.

"Awesome," I said.

"Oh…" Gus's mom said. "My boy worked so hard and look what he did." She sort of teared up. "I'm so proud. I'm so proud…"

"Jesus, Mom," Gus said. "Get a grip."

His parents totally beamed at him.

"I'm going to make some coffee. You guys want any?" Gus asked.

My body felt like lead pajamas. My stomach knotted up.

"I have to run," I said.

"Stanford is a heck of a school too, Felton," his dad said as I stumbled out the door.

Biking was hard.

CHAPTER 24
Lead Pajamas

I stumbled in the door from the garage. My guts burned and my hands trembled. I thought I might puke. I thought of that black liquid we were drinking the night before, and I had to run into the bathroom. I didn't barf. In the mirror, my face stared back at me. My Jewfro hadn't been shorn since right before I went to Florida. (Before that, I went to the barber every other week.) It stuck up all over. There were dark circles under my eyes. Seemed like I should probably shave.

The phone rang. The machine beeped. Someone said: "You're a fucker, Reinstein." They hung up. Wisconsin.

"No. Shut up. Please," I said out loud. My drunkenness didn't make Wisconsin go away.

I stumbled out. On the floor in front of my bedroom, I found a piece of paper.

Jerri had left a note for me.

F,
I'm at Terry's tonight. I'd like to unplug the phone. The calls are terrible. I'm sorry, honey. Are you okay with me unplugging the phone?
Love,
J.

Yes, I was ready to unplug the phone. No, I didn't like Jerri.

She was with Terry. Terry Sauter, a man who stopped speaking to his kids just because of a divorce.

A minute later, I fell into bed. An hour later, I woke up. Dad had been in my dreams. *No. Please.* Dead Dad hanging from the rafters. *No…*

I don't want to go back here. Please.

Dad wasn't buried.

I tried watching the Homo Reinstein rap to get angry again, but I didn't get angry. My stomach hurt. It hurt my feelings. I walked through the house and unplugged the three landlines. Jerri had said to. I couldn't hear another bad message.

I lay down in bed, so sick, and dreamed of Aleah and me biking, delivering newspapers, like we did during our summer together. I woke, turned over, grabbed my phone, and I texted her: *I'm with Abby S now. I'm sorry.*

Aleah responded immediately. *Why do you want to hurt me?*

My response? *Because you did this to me.*

Aleah: *Do you want to talk?*

Me: *No.*

Then I literally fell on my face on the floor. Then I got up and tried to run. I put on workout clothes: a jacket, sweats. Headed out the door. Ran about two hundred yards down the driveway and onto the main road. Then I barfed in the ditch.

Oh shit. This is bad shit. This is the worst. Okay. Okay. Andrew?

I hobbled back up to the house. Grabbed my phone to call Andrew. Found a text from Abby: *Feel like crap. You want to come over?*

Yes, I did.

Dudes like me want to be normal.

Just going to run over to my new girlfriend's house! No time for your doctor, Andrew!

CHAPTER 25
Drunken Abby and a Plan

I did notice when I ran to the road and barfed that February had gotten more February-like. Didn't think to dress more warmly. I left too fast to think.

I biked to Abby's freezing my ass off, the wind cutting through the light jacket I'd worn the day before. (It smelled like Cal's cigarettes from the barn.) I shivered. My teeth chattered. I groaned.

In sixth grade, Abby had moved from my neighborhood by the golf course to a brand-new giant house on the west edge of town (with big, fake-looking pillars). Terry wanted to show off, I guess. He showed Bluffton how much he made straightening out all the kids' ugly teeth. It was a three-mile ride through freezing.

I breathed hard. I felt tired in my legs. My muscles burned. When I'm myself, it takes forever for me to get tired.

At least I didn't puke again.

I rolled up Abby's big drive, panting, gulping for air. I dropped my bike on the ground and bent over, trying to catch my breath (my breath rising in clouds around me).

Nolan answered the door when I rang the bell. Even though he's just a freshman, he's a pretty big kid. He's a jock, of course, just like his sister.

He glared at me. He said, "What do you want?"

"Abby."

"Take her," he said. He left the door open but walked away into the house. I didn't hear him call for Abby or anything.

I stood for a while longer (I imagined throwing Nolan off a bridge), then rang the bell again.

A few seconds later, Abby showed up in a robe with a towel around her head. She was just showered and I could smell all that soap and lotion and my heart beat funny. "Hey, Rein Stone," she said.

I followed Abby through the house. I hadn't spent any time inside it since the Sauter divorce. Before the divorce, Abby's mom cleaned constantly, like a jumpy rabbit. Terry would show up on occasion and crack jokes and call Abby "Princess" and crap (which she clearly liked). Even while me and my friends were there, eating pizza or whatever, Abby's mom was bustling around us, picking up napkins, wiping pop drips off the counter. Sort of sad and annoying.

The house in February? Messy. Empty feeling. Trashed. There were dishes on the coffee table and side table and winter coats lay piled on the floor. A vacuum sat plugged into the wall on the side of the living room. Looked like it had been sitting there for a long time because there were tortilla chip crumbs on the floor right in front of it (next to a bowl of half-eaten chips).

Piles of dirty clothes lined the hall heading to Abby's room.

"Wow," I said.

"I should be cleaning. I can't do it," Abby whispered. "I have to wash my own clothes, but I don't touch anything else."

"Where's your mom?" I asked.

"She's shut in her room. She's shut in there all the time," Abby said.

"Sounds familiar." Jerri had done pretty much the same exact thing a couple of years earlier. I recognized the state of affairs. Of course, my house is a lot smaller and shittier in the first place, so the change wasn't as noticeable.

Abby's place was a freaking disaster. Seriously.

But not her bedroom. It was clean. Super clean.

Abby led me to her bed. We sat down. "I'm glad you're here."

"Me too," I mumbled.

"You don't seem okay," she said. "Are you okay? Are you mad at me?"

"No. Why would I be mad at you?"

"I don't know. People get mad at me."

"I'm having a bad month, I guess."

Abby nodded. "I'm with you, man. My life's been terrible since volleyball."

"Divorce stuff?"

"I don't know. Yeah. Probably. I can't concentrate."

"You should've told me before because then we could hang out and not concentrate together," I said.

"Yeah." Abby smiled. "Hey. Have you ever had a fuzzy navel?" Abby asked.

"What?" Was she talking about her own belly button? Did she want me to have her navel somehow? "I…I have some hair around my belly button," I said.

"No." Abby laughed. She lifted up a plastic cup from her bedside table filled with what looked like orange juice. "Fuzzy navel. Orange juice and peach schnapps, man. It's delicious."

"What is schnapps?"

"Sweet liquor. My mom drinks it all the time. She has like a hundred bottles. You want one?"

Somewhere deep in my head, I heard the voice of my little brother Andrew saying, *Think before you act, Felton.* Then I thought of Pig Boy and my dad and the State of Wisconsin, and even though I'd puked from alcohol and my stomach still ached in a weird way, I said, "Yeah, I'd like to try."

• • •

An hour later, everything was totally great. Abby put on the country music station, and we tried out the swing dancing that we learned in seventh grade. She shoved me when I stepped on her foot and I fell through her closet door and we laughed really hard.

Then we sat in the closet on the floor holding hands.

"I can't believe I didn't drink before now! I should've been drinking fuzzy navels since I was born!" I shouted.

"I know! Can you believe we let Cody tell us to not drink for like our whole adult lives?" Abby said.

"Cody doesn't have problems. He doesn't need the navel, man."

"He doesn't understand us," Abby said. "Plus, he's always so worried about you, but he never asks me if I have problems."

"Why's he worried about me?" I asked. "I'm a champion."

"Because you have a crazy mom and your dad and you're jumpy and you help him win and I don't matter. I'm just nobody," Abby said.

"No. You're everybody. You're the best student."

"Second best now. Gus beat me because I can't concentrate."

"He's smart."

"I'm a better student. I work harder. I used to work…"

It's true. Abby took AP English as a junior and quit track so she could take all this advanced science at the college. She was the most motivated student in the world. "You are better. Gus is just a super genius."

"But Felton…shh." She put her hand on my mouth. "I have to turn in my grades at the end of the year. The only way I can do college without Dad…the only way I can go to Madison is with the Regents Scholarship."

"You already got that," I said. She did too. They awarded it in November.

"I have to turn in my grades and I can't concentrate and the professor told me to drop cell biology on Friday. He said I'm not ready for college."

"No," I said.

"You want some spaghetti?" she asked.

"Yes."

Then we stood in her kitchen, which was spinning around because I was pretty drunk and also pretty happy because Abby was cooking me some spaghetti, which I love, and I knew we belonged together and I knew we were soul mates and would probably get married in the next few months and we'd have some kids and live on an island where we'd drink in a hot tub.

Then Abby sat at the table in her robe. I could still smell her lotion and it made me thirsty. I wanted to drink her in my cup. Her shoulder kept slipping out of the robe and she has a really pretty shoulder. Nolan was nowhere to be found. "In the basement," Abby told me. I could hear the TV on in her mom's room. "She has a bathroom in there. I see her like once a day," Abby said. "Dad's really mean to her, so she sleeps all the time. She's never had a job, you know?"

"Your dad's nice to Jerri."

"He used to be nice to me," Abby said. "He used to sing me songs when I was a little kid. I don't understand what happened." She spun spaghetti noodles around her fork. "He's really, really mean."

"Yeah?" I asked.

"What are we going to do? What's wrong with us?" Abby asked, her face hot.

This fuzzy navel oozed warmth through my body. Abby's face. You have to see Abby's beautiful face. "You want to make out or something?"

"Probably." Abby nodded. "But have you ever been happy?" she asked.

"No. Except I like playing football."

"I used to like everything. I wanted to be a doctor in Africa or Mexico to help the kids."

"I was happy when I helped Pig Boy."

"*See!*" Abby shouted. "But now I can't do anything. I don't know why. And I don't have any friends, Felton."

"Me."

"But Jess and Cody are glued together like Ken and Barbie, and Jess doesn't care that I'm...I'm..."

"Maybe we need to be a team, Abby. Like Cody and Jess."

"Me and you. Ken and Barbie?" Abby asked.

I tried to picture Ken but instead pictured the offensive coordinator at Wisconsin, with his slick hair, and my throat tightened and I grabbed my fuzzy navel and took a big swig. "Listen, Abby, I don't want to be like that asswipe Ken," I said.

"Yeah. Ken is an asswipe. So is Barbie. She's a bitch and she doesn't even return my texts like half the time and she knows that my life is hell and Dad is mean and Mom is a total basket case."

"Are you talking about Jess?"

"I want to be the opposite of that! What's the opposite of Barbie?"

I knew in a flash. "We need to protect dipshits," I said. "Ken and Barbie are mean to dipshits!"

"Cody's not mean to dipshits."

"Karpinski says he needs to keep the dipshits in line," I said.

"So we stop him? Like you protected the pig kid? How do we do that?"

I thought of those Northwestern football players shoving each other. I thought of Karpinski. "We should be mean to mean people," I said. "Right? Wouldn't that blow their minds if we just did mean stuff to them? A little reverse medicine for those doctors of mean shit?"

"Mean to mean people," Abby said.

"Yeah." I nodded.

"I'm good at being mean."

"I know."

"It makes me feel bad."

"But if you're on the good team?"

Abby squinted at me. She pursed her lips in a sexy fashion. "Can our team get drunk and study together too? I have to study and I can't be alone anymore. Will you drunk study with me please?"

"I will drunk study your ass off," I said. I didn't want to be alone either.

"Okay." Abby nodded. She swallowed. She exhaled. She closed her robe around her and then sat on her hands. "Okay." She looked down at her lap. "Also, maybe we should try to have sex. I'm tired of Maddie and those girls calling me Virginia."

"They do that? Mean."

"Yeah," she said.

I nodded. I clapped my hands. "Yes!" I said. "Sex is a great idea!"

"Really?" Abby asked.

"Definitely. Know why? Ken and Barbie totally can't do it. They don't have the parts! They have nothing downstairs! Barbie has those big boobs but nothing going on in her…her undercarriage! Ken's wang area is flat as a pancake. We've got the parts to totally have sex all the time!"

"Yeah," Abby said. "Okay. Let's put that down on the to-do list."

"This is great! Do you have any paper?"

"I think I ate too much," Abby said. "I'm going to throw up."

• • •

Abby was asleep five minutes later. I rode my bike home and crashed twice, which hurt, and then slept on the couch in front of the TV. Around 3 a.m., I stumbled to the bathroom and tried to throw up. Somehow I got back to the couch. My head swam and my guts burned and I couldn't believe it was morning when morning happened because it seemed to happen a second after 3 a.m.

My alarm blared. I rolled and sat up.

The room spun for a minute. I had to meet Pig Boy. For the first time since Curtis. Monday morning meeting day.

Then I noticed a piece of paper. Lying on the floor next to the couch was a list I apparently wrote out before falling over when I got home.

Here's what it said:

1. Be mean to mean people to protect the weak.
2. Study while drunk a lot.
3. Have massive amounts of sex because Ken and Barbie don't have wangs.

The list made me laugh, which made my head pound and my stomach ache. I still found it funny.

Problem: I didn't love Abby in the morning like I did the night before. I don't know why. I didn't feel that thing, which made me feel bad for her.

CHAPTER 26
Pig Boy Needs Help

My body moved slowly. I pulled on my "I'm with Stupid" shirt for only the second time because I wanted to show Abby how serious I was about sticking it to the people who should be stuck. (I wanted to be on her team.) I planned to sit on the right side of Karpinski at lunch.

When I went upstairs for a bagel, Jerri materialized out of my haze and grabbed my arm.

"You unplugged the phones."

I nodded.

She squinted at me. "Good. I got into a screaming match with a man from Milwaukee on Saturday."

"Sorry."

She sniffed the air. "What time did you get home last night?" she asked.

"I don't know," I mumbled. "Midnight."

"That's too late on a school night, Felton. You're not an adult yet. Don't think I'm not watching."

"Okay, I won't think you're not watching." The room felt tilted toward the stairs. I worried I'd stumble a couple of steps and fall down them.

"You leaving this early?" she asked.

"Meeting. Freshman mentee."

"I won't be home for dinner. I've got class tonight and then I'm meeting with Terry."

"What's your definition of meeting?" I asked.

"Ha, ha," Jerri said.

"Terry's a bad person," I said.

Jerri paused. She shook her head. "You don't know anything, Felton. Divorces aren't pretty. Whatever that Abby is telling you isn't the whole truth."

"That Abby isn't telling me anything. I just don't like Terry."

"Mind your own business, Felton."

"You mind your own business," I said. "You're not watching me anyway."

Jerri stared at me.

"I have to go," I said.

• • •

When I got to school (after a frozen-face and gut-roasting bike ride), Pig Boy was already sitting in his homeroom. He had his notebook out and he was drawing. He looked up when I walked in.

"Nice shirt," he said.

"I'm with Stupid," I said.

"Did you wear that so I'd feel stupid?" he asked.

"No," I said. My guts bubbled and I had to reach out and steady myself on the dry-erase board, which erased something Mrs. Callahan had written on it. "Shit."

Tommy turned the page and began drawing another picture.

I sat down next to him. "You doing okay?" I asked.

"No," he said. "You smell like booze."

"I do? I showered. How do I smell like…" My heart began thumping.

"You drank it so it comes out your skin all day," Tommy said.

"Oh no."

"You need to shower your insides," Tommy said.

"I don't know how."

"You can't."

"What's wrong?" I mumbled.

Tommy thought I was asking him instead of asking myself. He answered. "My mom keeps showing up at my house and screaming at my dad that he killed Curtis, and Dad had to go to jail this weekend because he punched her arm."

I blinked. "What the hell, Tommy?"

"Good question," he said. "My grandma can't even cook toast anymore. She sits on the couch or shakes like she needs to sit on the couch. My brother's bed is just there in my room. I can't get it out by myself. I don't want to see that bed."

Then I thought of Dad hanging, twitching in the garage. "I'm so sorry, man."

"You're not. You won't email me back. I emailed you nine times and you won't talk to me."

"I wasn't in school because…because…and I can't check all my email," I said.

"Why not?"

"There's too much for me to read because…Wisconsin people want to beat me up."

"Oh yeah, I heard about that," Tommy said.

I took a deep breath. Tried to steady myself. "Okay…Okay… Who killed your brother?" I asked. "I saw that email before the shit storm."

"Confession!" Tommy said.

"What? No." I didn't want to hear that Tommy killed his brother.

"I did. I killed Curtis."

"No." I shook my head. It wasn't possible. The intercom called for Tommy when Curtis shot himself. "No, you didn't. You were at school."

"Yeah. But before school, I told him he should karate-chop Ryan Bennett…"

"Ryan Bennett!" I spat.

"Yeah. I told Curtis if he didn't fight Ryan, he didn't deserve to walk among the proud, didn't deserve life. Then he came home and died."

Tommy put down his pencil and put his face down on the notebook.

"Oh man."

He looked up. "My counselor lady that the school gave me says that's not my fault. She says kids just talk. She's wrong. I wanted Curtis to stand up like I stand up. They can hit me all they want. But I won't cry."

"Did Curtis cry at school?"

"I don't know. Probably," Tommy said.

"We have to fix this," I said.

"We can't. Curtis is six feet under."

I saw Dad in the ground. "You know my dad killed himself?" I said.

Tommy's mouth dropped open. "Really? What did you do with his bed?"

I paused. Stared at him. "I don't know. My mom might've burned it. She might still sleep in it though."

"I want to burn Curtis's bed," Tommy said. "I really, really don't like it being in my room." He blinked at me. Then Tommy started crying, then he started coughing, then he sneezed on the desk.

"That's what you want? To burn Curtis's bed?"

"Yeah," he wheezed.

That's what Jerri wanted to do. Burn Dad's stuff. She did too, out in the backyard of our house, while I cried and Andrew stared.

Snot poured down Tommy's face. I ran up to the teacher's desk and grabbed a bunch of Kleenex. "We better get cleaned up. School's going to start in a couple of minutes."

He tried to clean up. Didn't work that great.

"I'll help you get his bed out of your room," I said. "We can do that. No problem," I said.

Then the bell rang.

CHAPTER 27
I'm With Stupid

I didn't think about my dad or Badger fans the rest of the morning. I thought about poor Pig Boy lying awake at night staring at Curtis's empty bed.

I did sit next to Karpinski at lunch. I did make Abby laugh with my "I'm with Stupid" T-shirt, but I didn't care so much. Karpinski said, "Oh yeah, that's a really funny joke, Rein Stone" when I put my arm around him. "You're full of funny jokes. Wish I would've thought of grabbing the Wisconsin hat."

"You weren't recruited by Wisconsin though." I didn't actually say that to be mean, but it might've come across as mean.

Cody stared at me. "That's a dickhead shirt," he said.

"I know," I said.

"Whatever, Ken," Abby said. She walked over and hugged my head. Her chest pressed into my face and I could smell her skin and I thought I might love her for a moment.

"What do you mean, Ken?" Cody asked.

"Yeah?" Jess asked. "Ken?"

"Nothing. I have to go to the college for class," Abby said. "See you tonight, Felton."

"Yeah," I said. "Good." I imagined her sliding off that robe.

"What's up with you two?" Karpinski asked.

I got up and left for my locker. *Help Pig Boy. Have sex with Abby. That's all.*

Except it wasn't all. Mr. Linder was losing patience with me.

I'd failed to do any of the reading for AP English, and Mr. Linder called on me again and again because I didn't know crap about *The Dead* and Linder was tired of my weeks of nonresponse.

"Nothing, Felton? Ever hear of James Joyce?" he asked.

"Yes," I said, my face glowing red like a Chinese lantern.

"Who's with Stupid, Mr. Reinstein?"

"I am?" I asked.

"No," Linder said, shaking his head. "I am. Get it?"

The class sort of oohed. Gus stared at the side of my head, his mouth hanging open.

"I'm sorry," I said.

But *sex with Abby. Fuzzy navels.*

That's what I thought.

CHAPTER 28
Karpinski Mean

It's true. Abby is funny. She's really quick brained. She can be really mean. If you want someone to be mean to mean people, Abby's a good choice. She stung me so bad when I was a squirrel kid.

Abby got a funny idea when I put my arm around Karpinski in my "I'm with Stupid" shirt.

We sat next to each other on her bed. She drank a fuzzy navel. I drank a fake fuzzy navel—pretended to pour schnapps in my glass—because after school, I'd lifted weights but could only get through about half my reps because my muscles burned and fatigued and I worried that alcohol might be the problem. (I'm a genius!)

Abby talked fast. "The Karpinskis are hilarious, right? You know what would be hilarious? What if we made like a Karpinski family video? Or maybe just a video about Karpinski's dad? He's crazy. He horn-dogs on me all the time, like I'm some hot forty-year-old he might have a chance with."

"I've seen it," I nodded.

And, yeah, I'd seen it. Old Man Karpinski in action. Honestly, the Karpinskis are comedy gold.

The mom is sort of funny in that she dresses like a drunk, sexy country singer (short shorts and cowboy boots and really tight, sleeveless cowboy shirts all summer long), and she squawks like a chicken when she talks. *Bok.*

But the dad is the real prize.

Dave Karpinski looks like a 1980s porn star. He has a little mustache, and he clearly dyes his hair black and he wears it sort of long and combed straight back, so it always looks like he's walking into the wind, and he wears these giant wraparound sunglasses and too-tight polo shirts that totally hug his big gut, and he wears his own version of short shorts all summer long (just like his wife, except her legs are little super-tan chicken sticks and his legs are giant ham sandwiches), and he rides around on this tiny Honda scooter thing, sort of swooping around town for no apparent reason, just like he's a dumb high school kid with nothing better to do than drive circles, and he does tae kwon do and he speaks like he's a mixture of a movie karate sensei and a movie stoner.

During the football season, he'd see me running off steam on the weekends and swoop over and stop me and say, "Dude, you destroyed Lancaster Friday. Correct?"

"Yeah?" I'd say.

"Do you know why?"

"We scored more points?" I'd say.

"No, dude, no. You used both heart and talent. With great effort and great talent, championships are made. Am I right?"

"Yeah?" I'd say.

Then maybe some girl would walk by, and no matter what her state of dress or her size or her age or her hair color or anything,

Mr. Karpinski would lose his mind. "My lord, my lord," he'd say, shaking his head, his mouth hanging open. "Look at that pretty little lady. Legs up to here." He'd karate-chop himself right under his nipple.

I'd nod and he'd swoop off on his scooter and circle around her and chat her up, and the girl, whoever she might be, would totally laugh because I'm sure he made weird jokes and Dave Karpinski is funny, except he's not trying to be as funny as he actually is because he doesn't seem to know he's a cartoon character.

"We could make a video of you acting like him, right?" Abby said. "You could put on a fake mustache and sunglasses and ride around on Jess's scooter saying crazy things to girls."

"That's pretty funny," I nodded.

"I could be totally gross and in sweats, and you could circle around me and talk about how hot I am," Abby said. "Oh, sweet potato pie in a steaming dish of cream soup…stuff like that."

"Uh-huh. Yeah. Let's call Gus."

"Why?"

"He has a nice camera and he's funny as hell."

"He is?" Abby asked. "I thought he was just a nerd boy."

"Do you know Gus?"

"Not really," Abby said. "I've never hung out with him before last weekend."

I thought everyone knew how hilarious Gus was. I called him immediately. His response to the whole deal was a little weird.

"Tonight?" he asked.

"No, not tonight. This weekend if the weather isn't crappy."

"You want to make fun of Karpinski's dad?"

"Just have fun. Not make fun of. You know, just joke around."

"Seems kind of mean," Gus said.

Abby could hear him. She said, "Karpinski mooned you and gave you the finger, man. This is not a big deal."

"Okay," he said. "I guess. It's sort of funny. Email me some notes and I'll write up a script."

After I hung up, Abby said, "I don't think he has a sense of humor at all."

"No," I said. "He does. Just wait until Saturday. He'll totally crack you up."

"You want to email him the notes?" Abby asked.

"Yeah. Okay. Unless you do?"

"I'll write up the notes," Abby said.

She's funny. And mean.

Here's something weird, though, given that we'd decided massive amounts of sex were going to part of our anti–Ken and Barbie identities. I got up the guts to try to kiss her, and she fell straight back onto her bed and crossed her arms over her chest like she needed to protect herself and then said she had bed spins and might get sick and that we should have lots of sex another time.

"Okay," I said. I was a little embarrassed. Here's the truth though: Aleah and I were together for almost two years and we never did the whole thing. I was pure as the virgin snow. Real sex kind of scared me. (Not that I wasn't interested in giving it a shot.)

A few minutes later, Abby lolled out, drunk.

So I left.

• • •

On the way out of Abby's house, I ran into Nolan on the couch in the living room. He was shocked to see me. He stood up. "Why are you here?"

"I'm with Abby. Get used to it."

"Your mom is with my dad," he said.

"I guess," I said.

"You threatened my best friend."

"Who?"

"Ryan Bennett."

"I did?" I didn't remember actually threatening him, even though I'd thought about it.

"Maddie O'Neill told me that you're going to beat Ryan up and that he better watch his back."

"I never said that."

"Maddie said you did."

"Well, I'm sorry Ryan's such an idiot that he deserves to have his ass kicked. Maybe I will kick his ass."

I turned and headed toward the door. Nolan was right behind me. He followed me out to the front stoop.

"You stay away from my sister."

I spun around and faced him, stared down at him. He's a big kid, but I'm probably forty pounds heavier and a couple inches taller.

He tried to inflate himself, stood tall, widened his shoulders. "Jesus," I said shaking my head, "I know who you are. I know what you do. Don't you talk to me. Don't you ever say a word to me. Do you understand?"

He took a couple seconds trying to hold still, then nodded. I turned and walked down the step toward my bike.

"Felton," he said quietly. "What do you mean you know who I am?"

"You're a black hole who beats on weak kids to feel like you're something more. But you know you're nothing. Just empty space."

"Oh," he said. He put his head down and went back inside.

I shivered. I felt sick. I felt so off and terrible. This didn't feel like me. Not the me I'd write about in a college essay to justify my existence for sure. I turned around and walked up to the door. I wanted to apologize to Nolan.

Then I thought of Ryan punching Andrew. I thought of Nolan kicking Pig Boy.

Screw them, I thought.

• • •

Biking, I felt like shit. Nolan and leftover alcohol, I guess.

When I got home, I buried myself in blankets and shivered and felt the bubbles of poison in my legs and arms. I sort of cried. Around 2 a.m., I woke up because my phone buzzed. I was in the middle of a horror dream about my dad kicking at me while he hung. He was trying to kick my face. Andrew had sent several texts.

1: *You won't call me?*

2: *Hello????*

3: *Please call. Aleah's worried too. She called me.*

I probably would've called him if it weren't for the last text. What right did Aleah have acting like she was part of my family? Why wouldn't Andrew tell her to mind her own business?

Okay. Dudes use any excuse not to deal.

CHAPTER 29
I'm With Stupid, II

On Tuesday, I felt a little better, so after school, I lifted weights again. (You're not supposed to lift upper body two days in a row like that, but Monday had been such a waste.) Then I ran the stairs next to the gym for an hour. I felt a little stronger. No alcohol in my hammies. Usually, the basketball team has a game on Tuesday, but they were off. During a break from practice, Cody stood watching me run.

"Looking tough, man," he shouted.

I didn't answer right away. When I got back down the stairs, I said, "Whatever, Ken."

"What does that mean?" Cody spat.

I turned and ran back up the stairs, and Cody's practice began again. Between plays, he looked at me. My energy drained away. I stopped and went home.

After I showered, I saw that Cody had texted:

what up with you guys?

I didn't answer. I didn't really know what was up.

Abby texted a couple of times after that, but I just went to sleep in my sad bed.

CHAPTER 30
Mattress Kings

Wednesday was sunny and in the 40s right away in the morning. I'd slept terribly again, totally haunted by Dad and buzzed by pleading texts (Abby). Instead of opening my Facebook page to read what mean things Wisconsinites might have left for me overnight, I found Pig Boy's home phone number and, without allowing myself to think twice, called it.

The phone rang six times. No answering machine or voicemail picked up.

Then Pig Boy: "Hello?" He was breathless. Scared?

"Hey, Tommy. It's Felton."

"Hi!" he pretty much shouted. "Hi!" he said again.

"Hi. Hey. Do you have a bike?"

"Uh-huh," he said.

"Can you ride to school today? Let's ride back to your place this afternoon and take away Curtis's bed."

There was a pause. Then he whispered. "Okay. Okay. Good. Let's do this thing."

"Okay. We'll take care of it."

"See you later," he whispered.

When he hung up, I thought, *Good. Good. Good.*

Then I texted Abby: *sorry…so tired i fell asleep early and was dead to the world.*

She texted back: *thank you so much for msg i was scared you abandoned the team.*

I biked to school feeling cleaner. I could smell the soap on my body from my shower. *Disable your Facebook page.* I thought that as I biked in the spring-like air.

I cruised through the day with little incident. Even Mr. Linder decided not to call on me, which was good because I hadn't read whatever short story I was supposed to read. *Have to get on the reading!* I thought that. *Get back in the swing of things!*

After school, Pig Boy and I met by the bike racks and rode over to his house. Pig Boy's bike is exactly the same as Aleah's from the summer she was in town, except Aleah's was a brand-new crap bike (girl's) and Pig Boy's (also girl's) was two years old, super crappy, and rusting to hell. It creaked and groaned as he pedaled. I pretty much pedaled twice and coasted the rest of the way because he moved so slowly.

It took us twenty minutes to cover what usually takes me five. That's okay because Tommy wanted to talk.

"You ever dream you can fly?" he asked.

"No. I dream bad stuff. That's just me."

"My flying dreams are awesome because I can punch holes in clouds and that helps Curtis get to heaven."

"Hmm. Sounds sort of scary."

"No, it's great. It's really fun too. I'm a fast flyer."

"Cool," I said.

He was not, however, a fast biker.

Several decades later (so it felt), we arrived.

His house is on Fourth Street, a couple of blocks from where all the bars are in town. I think of this neighborhood as Dirty Town. There are lots of houses with old beer bottles and cans littering the yard. There are lots of old broken-down cars. The Dumpsters stink up the alleys. Tons of stray cats prowl around. It's a sad state of affairs.

The paint on Pig Boy's house was peeling. Three old cars—one without any wheels—sat in the driveway. I thought: If I ever criticize Jerri's maintenance of the yard again, please, somebody, punch me in the face.

We pulled between cars and he said, "Let me make sure Dad's not here."

I stood on the driveway and Pig Boy disappeared into the house. While he was gone, I watched some drunk college kids stumble by and saw two cats almost fight in the street until a speeding car caused them to run like lightning in opposite directions.

Tommy popped his head out of the front door. "He's down at the bar, but Grandma's home."

I was nervous going in. I didn't know what to expect. Here's what I got: the house smelled like Gus's old cigarettes mixed into Campbell's bean and ham soup. There were a couple of broken recliners in the living room and a long, plaid couch that sagged in the middle. His grandma sat on the right side of that and smoked a cigarette. She was watching *Ellen* on TV. She didn't look at me, say anything to me, nothing. She held that lit cigarette and stared at the box.

"This way," Tommy whispered.

I followed him into a dark hall. The doors were open to a couple bedrooms, but no lights were on and the shades were all pulled. Tommy's was at the end of the hall.

"Right here," he said. He flicked the light on.

I don't know what I was expecting to see. Blood maybe? Lots of trash? Not in Tommy's room. There were lots of Sharpie markers, which I assume Tommy took from school, and a big roll of butcher paper. (Andrew had a roll a couple of years ago that he used to collect quotes from great composers, so I knew what it was.) Most importantly, the room was just filled with pictures, drawings. Taped all over the walls. Giant pictures on that butcher paper. Good pictures. Superheroes and sidekicks. Action shots of cars speeding around corners. Muscle men in karate poses. Really, really good.

"Whoa. Nice," I said.

"Dad draws some too," Tommy told me.

I remembered Jerri asking, "What happens to people?"

"You're awesome, man. You do such good stuff."

"Can you lift that?" Tommy pointed down to the floor.

And there was the bed. Curtis's. Lonely little bed. Just a single mattress lying on the floor, no sheets or blankets on it.

Pushed against the opposite wall, Tommy's bed was made neatly, a Green Bay Packer bedspread over the top. Several stuffed animals sat at attention, leaning against the cracked paint. Two bears, a penguin, and a baby seal.

"Well," Tommy exhaled. "Let's move it, okay?"

I leaned over and picked up the mattress. It smelled like a kid, like Andrew. Tommy tried to help, but there wasn't really any point. The mattress was light. I balanced it on my shoulder and followed Tommy out into the hall. This got me: my shoulder sank into a depression, probably made by Curtis's body as he slept. This empty space made by that poor, dumb kid. I swallowed hard. We walked past a picture of Curtis in the hall.

"I'm sorry," I whispered. "I'm sorry."

In the living room, Grandma sprang to attention.

"What are you doing with that mattress?" she asked.

Tommy and I stopped. She took a drag on her cigarette and eyeballed us.

"Getting rid of it," Tommy said.

"Your daddy might want to sell it. You better ask him."

"No," Tommy said. "Just don't tell him. He won't notice. I look at it all night long. I don't want to look at it anymore."

She stared a moment longer, nodded slightly, then said, "Okay then. Go."

I followed Tommy out of the house and breathed deeply, like I'd been holding my breath underwater.

We walked behind the house and into the alley. A few houses up from Tommy's, there was a big green Dumpster. I followed Tommy over to it. The beer and puke smell was terrible. "College boy house," Tommy said. He pulled open the lid and I lifted the mattress high over my head and dropped it in. The Dumpster had been emptied recently because the mattress slid down to the bottom, nestled on top of empty bottles.

"You got a match?" Tommy asked.

"No," I said.

"Just kidding," he said.

"I don't have any bongo drums either," I said.

"What?" he asked.

"Nothing. My mom just…she wanted some drum thumping when she burned my dad's crap. She had a couple of friends hit drums."

"That's weird," Tommy said.

We walked back to his house.

He said, "Okay. Thanks. Bye."

I said, "No problem, man. Let me know if you…"

He walked up to the door, then turned and looked at me.

His big head sort of cracked me up. Gave me an idea. "Hey, you want to help make a comedy video on Saturday?" I asked.

"Really? I'm not funny," he said.

"Oh yeah." I smiled at him. "You're funny."

Pig Boy stared for a moment, then nodded, "Okay. I am pretty funny really." He smiled for maybe the second time ever.

During the day, Gus had forwarded me a Karpinski script he'd written based on the very mean notes Abby sent him. Funny though. And you know what? Pig Boy fit perfectly in it.

I biked home fast in that weird February warm air. I breathed deeply. I felt clean. Tommy wouldn't have to stare at Curtis's bed anymore.

CHAPTER 31
Love Birds

In Current Events the next day, Thursday, Karpinski glared at me. He shook his head at me. His mouth kept running, even though no sound came out. When the bell rang, he chased me and Abby out into the hall. He'd apparently just gotten devastating news.

His forehead was covered in little bullets of sweat. His cheeks burned. His eyes shifted back and forth between mine and Abby's. "What the hell? Are you messing with me? This is terrible. What the...What are you doing?"

"Uh...what?" I asked.

"You two? When did you two happen?" He turned to Abby. "Jess says you're with Felton? We're prom dates, for shit...you know you said..."

"Stop," Abby said.

"Me? You want me to..." Karpinski sputtered.

"Shut up," Abby said. "I am not going to another dance with you."

The air came out of Karpinski. He shook his head. "We said we'd go to prom together. We always said that senior year..."

"Stop," Abby said. "I'm tired of you people."

"Jesus Christ," Karpinski said. "You teach her this, Rein Stone? *You people?*" he spat. He spun and walked down the hall fast.

He sort of ran into, sort of elbowed this quiet kid, Erik Hallberg, on his way.

"*Hey!*" I shouted.

Karpinski flipped the bird over his head.

"Oh my God," Abby said. "How did I ever like him?"

Cody passed. He didn't look at me.

Jess said, "What's up with you two?"

"Karpinski's mad," Abby said.

"Yeah. He'll get over it," Jess said. She beamed at me. "Can't believe you're finally together. You getting a little action, Reinstein?"

"Ha, ha," I said. "Quite a bit. Sort of."

"Love. Birds," Jess said. "I knew this would happen."

Abby stared at the floor. "Whatever," she said.

"Whatever?" Jess asked.

Abby shuffled away. I could smell this sort of lip-gloss smell. I knew it was peach schnapps though, not lip gloss.

"We might have a problem," I whispered to Jess.

"Love. Birds," she said.

CHAPTER 32
I Will Not Leave You Alone, Ever

On Thursday night, I went over to Abby's and we drunk studied like we said we would. Go, team. Except I didn't drink. I faked it as best I could. (Abby poured me one fuzzy navel, which I had a sip of, then dumped in the toilet, then poured myself a glass of pure orange juice.) Then we "studied."

"Felton," Abby whispered. "I didn't go to cell biology at the college today."

"Did you drop it?" I asked. "Are you okay?" Her head wasn't holding up straight. Her eyes kept closing.

"No. Didn't drop it. I came home and did a few shots and then I broke two Van Halen vinyl records because they're Dad's."

"Oh. Then you came back for Current Events?"

"Uh-huh. I don't feel good. I'm going to sleep and then study. Is that okay?"

Before I could answer, she went to bed. I waited for twenty minutes. She didn't wake up. I ran through the house, hoping not to see Nolan. I rode my bike through a chill night.

At home, I pulled out my phone to see if Abby had called. She hadn't, but here's what I found—a text from Andrew saying:

I do not understand what you're hoping for, Felton, but I will wait. You can't shake me. I won't go away.

There was a text from Tovi too:

dude i won't leave you no matter what, ok?

These were weird messages, but they made me feel good. I have a pretty good family in some ways. I doubted anyone was treating Abby so well.

I texted Abby: *had to go sleep, but you're not alone, not ever, okay?*

I brushed my teeth and put on my sleeping shorts and tried to read this Hemingway story for Linder's class (couldn't concentrate), then texted Tovi and Andrew *thanks.*

Then I disabled my Facebook account (Crazy! What a relief!) and I went to bed without watching Homo Reinstein.

At 3 a.m., I woke up because my phone buzzed.

Abby wrote: *You are only one who cares. I am so lucky you are alive.*

CHAPTER 33
Team Eskimo Sexy Dance

Alcohol worries.

Before school Friday, I got up early and ran. Not bad. I ran the hill on the main road. My muscles were not heavy. Each time up, I imagined Roy Ngelale running next to me, trying to beat me. Good run.

While I stretched afterward, I looked at the track team manual from the year before because I was curious about when the indoor state meet would be held (the only time before the end of the year that I'd face Roy Ngelale), and in bold letters on the second page of the manual, it said: "Any violation of the Athletic Code will result in immediate suspension from the team for the duration of the season."

I'd already violated the code. Alcohol. Did Nolan Sauter know about Abby's drinking? *Oh shit...*

• • •

Then, at school on Friday morning, Abby slid up to me at my locker and whispered in my ear (in a way that made my heart go), "Let's go back out to Cal's barn tonight. Let's really tie one on. Let's let loose, man."

I turned to her and she kissed me right next to my mouth.

"Sound interesting?" she whispered.

"Yeah," I said. I breathed. "But let's talk later, okay? I want to make sure Gus is ready for filming tomorrow."

"We're gonna hang tonight though, right?" Abby said, back stiffening, her cheeks falling from a smile.

"Yeah. Yeah. For sure," I said.

She nodded. "Okay." She sort of zombie-walked down the hall.

Yikes.

Athletic Code.

I had to do something. In Current Events, I leaned over to Abby and whispered, "Gus has some work for us in the morning. We can't blow out tonight. Just come over to my house. I'll make you dinner."

There was no alcohol at my house. Jerri is generally the opposite of a drinker.

"You'll make me what?" Abby whispered. "Will Jerri be there?"

"Food. I don't know. Jerri might be there."

"Will my dad?"

Lightning bolts! "Uh. Maybe?" I said. Didn't want to bring Abby to hang with Terry and Jerri.

"Okay," Abby said. "Maybe just order a pizza? I'm not sure what you would cook."

"A sandwich," I said.

She nodded. "Pizza?"

• • •

At home, I slid around the basement clearing away my dirty clothes. (I did my own wash, which means there could be some exploding clothes hamper disasters from time to time.) Jerri wasn't home yet.

I ran up to the kitchen and loaded the dishwasher because the sink was totally full. I used 409 to spritz off all the counters. This action would've blown Jerri's mind.

Not that I wanted to see Jerri.

In fact, I felt serious relief when Jerri called at six and told me she'd be at Terry's for the night.

"Sounds great, Jerri!" I said.

Jerri paused. "Is something going on?" she asked.

"No! Why?" I shouted.

"You sound odd, Felton."

"I do? No! Just going to watch some TV or whatever!"

"Um. Okay. I might come home and check on you."

"Go ahead," I said. "Come by whenever." Jerri wouldn't follow through.

Then I called Abby. She was on her way. I ordered the pizza from Steve's.

Damn pirate Abby.

When she arrived, she held up two six-packs of this super-brown beer. "Look what Dad left in the fridge in the basement!"

"Oh. Awesome," I said. *Oh shit, oh shit, oh shit…*

"It's like specialty brown German beer," Abby said. "It's super expensive, I bet."

Did it occur to me that Abby believed her dad might show up at my house and we'd have that beer? Yes. Did I fear the slight possibility that Jerri would come to check on me? Yes. Did it even occur to me that Coach Knautz might swing by on a whim, just to say, "Hi!" and find me drinking so he'd have to kick me off the track team? Yes.

But I have problems, okay? I wanted to help Abby feel good! I wanted to feel good because beer fills me with that loving feeling.

And so…

Did I drink one of those weird, smelly brown beers when Abby pestered me to drink a beer? Yes. Did I fill up with the beautiful tears of a thousand crying angels? Yes.

Am I a danger to myself (and others)? Yes.

This beer was not Hamm's, like Gus bought. It was very strong or filled with cocaine or something. (I think more alcohol in it—that would make you stupid faster, right?)

By the time the Steve's dude delivered the pizza, Abby and I had already had a dance-off to that goofy song about what doesn't kill you makes you stronger and I'd put on a pair of Sorel snow boots and was stripped down to my boxers.

"Sexy Eskimo!" Abby shouted.

The doorbell rang.

I opened the door in my underpants.

It was my old friend Peter Yang's older brother, Carl, with the pizza. Carl's in college at the University of Wisconsin. He delivered pizzas when he was in high school. Sometimes, he'd bring a pizza home to me, Gus, and Peter when we'd stay there late to play *Dungeons and Dragons*.

"Reinstein," he clipped. "Looking pretty sexy." The Yangs show no emotions when they talk. They are intimidating.

"Uh…Aren't you in college?"

"Steve gives me a weekend shift when I need extra cash," Carl said. "So I come home."

"Cool?" I said.

"Sixteen-fifty," Carl said.

I had taken a twenty from Jerri's cash drawer (stole it—I had no cash). I handed it to Carl.

"You need change?" he asked.

"I don't think so," I said.

"Good," he said.

I nodded. Holy balls was I dizzy from the smelly German beer!

Then, for no reason, Carl said, "You're enemy number one up in Madison. Most hated man on campus. Can't believe you screwed around with the hat at your news conference. I wouldn't visit anytime soon."

Smelly beer buzzed in my veins (that and straight-up piss because of my generalized Wisconsin problem).

"Really?" I said. "I shouldn't visit?"

"They'd kick your ass if you did."

"Oh no," I said. "Would they kick my ass real bad, Carl?"

"Yes," he said.

"How bad?" I asked. I leaned toward him.

He backed up a step. "Shut up, man. You're wasted."

"I'm going to stick that change in your ass if you don't get the hell away from my house," I said.

"See you later, Reinstein."

"Yeah, take care, Yang."

He left.

I turned to Abby. She was lying on the floor.

"Give me another beer," I said.

"Awesome," Abby said.

"Let's go downstairs."

We half stumbled into the basement. Can't believe we didn't drop the pizza.

Bad.

• • •

We ate about half the pizza and drank like four beers each. I felt really full and mad about Wisconsin people.

And then my cell rang and it was Steve's Pizza's number. I picked it up.

"Yes?" I asked.

"This is Rick Heiser over at Steve's. I'm the manager."

"Yeah, I know."

"I just wanted to let you know we won't be making any more deliveries out to your place. You can't physically assault one of our drivers, okay? You can't do that. You're lucky we don't press charges, Mr. Reinstein."

"I didn't assault anyone…"

"Be that as it may…"

"Be what?"

"Be that as it may, no more delivery."

"Are you kidding me? Carl verbally assaulted…"

"That's all, sir."

He hung up.

"*Be that as it may?*" I shouted.

"What?" Abby asked.

"Jesus Christ. I just got banned from Steve's delivery." It's my favorite pizza of all time. "What the hell?"

"Why?" Abby asked.

"I physically assaulted Peter Yang's brother?"

"No, you didn't. I didn't see any physical beatings of any kind," Abby said.

"Why is everyone such a hater, baby?"

"Come here," Abby said.

I bent down and she kissed me. Tasted like sausage and that smelly beer.

"You better now?" she asked.

"Yeah. Sure," I said.

Abby popped another beer. She sat cross-legged on the floor. Her eyes were watery and she sort of swayed while she talked. I sat on the couch, and my gut just clenched. *Wisconsin people, oh yeah? Better not show up on campus, huh? You better not show up on my campus or my police force will engage in some police brutality, okay?*

"Don't you think it's dumb that Terry and Jerri's names rhyme?" Abby asked.

"I suppose." *Freaking Yangs should be spanked. All of them. One after the other. In a big line stretching down Yang Street.*

"It's really dumb. If your name was Gabby, I wouldn't date you. Abby and Gabby? Stupid."

"Do I look like a Gabby to you?" I barked.

"Flabby," Abby said.

"Flabby?"

"Not as muscley as you used to be," she said. "Not like before."

"Really?" That hurt my feelings. "I need to work out more, huh? What am I doing? This is stupid, Abby. I'm stupid."

"Terry and Jerri aren't coming here tonight, are they?"

"No." *Thank God. You stole Terry's beer.*

"We should break some of Jerri's stuff," Abby said.

"No. No. Why would we break Jerri's stuff?" I shouted.

"Okay. I didn't really mean that," Abby slurred. "Don't be mad at me please? I have problems."

"Yes!" I said. "What's wrong with you?"

She smiled. She said, "I love you, Felton."

Then she climbed up on the couch and we lay back and I turned on the TV, an NBA game.

"Look at that dude's beard," she said.

I think we were asleep in two minutes. Weird beer.

• • •

I woke up at about 2 a.m. Abby's sausage pizza, brown beer stanky breath assaulted my nostrils. I had to go into the bathroom and puke.

• • •

Then we both slept until 10 a.m., me on the floor, wrapped in my towel from the bathroom.

That's when Gus called. "Phone buzz," Abby mumbled.

I answered, super groggy. "Hey. What?"

"Where the hell are you guys?" he whispered. "Pig Boy's here. I don't know what to say to him. He's freaking me out."

"Oh yeah. Okay. We'll be there soon."

"Don't forget your costumes," he said.

The video. Pig Boy was already there.

"Abby," I said. "We're late."

"Oh my God. What's wrong with my head?" she whispered. "It really hurts."

Then Abby sort of cried. I slid onto the couch next to her and hugged her head. "We have to go," I said.

"I don't want to," Abby said.

Then I got a little pissed. "Jesus. Come on. Gus is sitting there with Pig Boy."

"What?" she mumbled.

"Please," I said.

"Just hold my head a few seconds longer," she said.

"Okay, okay…"

She breathed deep. "I might barf. I don't like Dad's beer. It almost killed us."

"Maybe he tried to kill us," I said. "Maybe he knew you'd steal it?"

"Probably," Abby said. "He wishes I was dead so he wouldn't have to pay for me."

CHAPTER 34
On the Set of the
Great Karpinski Masterpiece

It was foggy as hell. Clouds hung on the ground around my house. Wisconsin February should not be wet and 50 degrees. There should be ice balls and snow elves and crap. February is supposed to make you hate yourself.

Fog and mud. Moist.

Abby drove us to Gus's in the shit-bag Buick. When we got there, Pig Boy was sitting in the fog in the front yard on a lawn chair next to Maddie and Bony Emily (Andrew's old orchestra friend).

Pig Boy said, "You're late."

Maddie said, "Where's the scooter? We need a scooter." She glared at me.

Abby said, "Shit. I forgot." Abby turned and walked three steps. She called Jess, the owner of the scooter.

Pig Boy said, "What are we doing?"

Bony Emily slapped herself on the forehead. She said, "I've told you already three times, Tommy."

Pig Boy said, "I want to hear the king say it." He looked at me and nodded, his mouth open.

"I'm not the king," I said.

"He's not the king," Maddie said.

"Remember? We're making a funny video," I said. "Hopefully."

Gus poked his head out the front door. "Where the hell's the scooter?" he shouted.

Abby held up her phone. "Jess is bringing it over. She'll be here soon."

"Can't believe you'd forget the scooter," Maddie said.

"I brought my bikini. I'm not an idiot," Abby said.

"You are an idiot. Now Jess Withrow is coming over," Maddie said, shaking her head.

"What is your problem?" Abby spat.

"Jess is a bitch!" Maddie spat back.

"Jess is my best friend."

"Ooooh," Maddie said, waving her hands in the air, her eyes big. "Best friends!"

It didn't seem possible we could make a funny movie with so much pissy-ness floating around in the air.

"Everybody relax, okay?" I said.

"I'm going to wear a long blond wig," Pig Boy said.

"Yeah, I know," I said. "I invited you to this."

"Sorry," Pig Boy said. His face fell.

"No. I'm glad you're here," I said.

"Let's go inside and costume up," Gus said. "My parents are out at brunch. They'll go for a walk after. We've got like four hours. Go."

• • •

While Abby held her aching smelly beer head in the corner and Pig Boy stared at my ear (I'm serious, poor kid), Maddie pulled a black wig over my hair. It was a vampire wig from a 1970s costume and it smelled really bad. "Where did you get this?"

"Cal's basement. Cat probably pissed on it," Maddie said.

"Awesome."

"I got you a brand-new mustache though."

She glued on my mustache. It was slicked down, like a Latin lover kind of deal.

Then she gave me giant sunglasses her grandpa wore in the 1970s.

"Oh hell yeah. That's good." She laughed.

Abby looked up at me and giggled, nodding.

Outside, the sun began to burn off the fog. "We're getting good light," Gus said.

Then I went into the bathroom and pulled on a pair of gut-buster elastic band coaching shorts I bought when I thought that's what jocks wore (*just trying to fit in, homies!*…duh). Gus gave me a pillow from his room, and I stuck it in my too-tight white polo and pulled the shorts up and tucked in the shirt.

I walked back into the living room. Maddie, Abby, and Bony Emily blew a freaking gasket when they saw me. Abby seriously fell off her chair, laughing.

"Holy cow!" Bony Emily said.

I tried to do my best Mr. Karpinski imitation, "What are you ladies laughing at, heh? You get into the laughing gas over at the doctor's office? What makes a lady laugh? Gas. Am I right?"

"Holy shit! You have it down!" Abby said.

"Felton used to be hilarious all the time. Then he found sports," Gus said.

Just then, a scooter buzzed into the driveway. A couple seconds later, Jess Withrow knocked on the door. "Come in," Gus shouted.

Jess entered. She looked at me. She said, "Are you dressed up like Mr. Karpinski?"

I nodded. I tried not to laugh.

Jess smiled too, but she didn't laugh. "Wow. Cruel," she said.

"You would know," Maddie spat.

Jess blinked and looked at her. "Uh, okay?"

"Come on," Gus said. "Let's do this."

• • •

"Yes. Yes. Good light," Gus said. His hands were on his hips. He stared at the sky. (Back in the day of the wad, he'd have had to lift his hair to see up—I understood the advantage of the new 'do.). The sky held puffy clouds. The brown ground reflected an orange glow on everything.

Gus stood with his camera. (He has a Canon Rebel that takes awesome video.) I stood next to him fully dressed in Karpinski style.

Bony Emily wore really tight black clothes and sort of heavy black eye makeup. She stood next to me.

Pig Boy, in his Bully Me/Pig Boy T-shirt, wore a long blond Miss Piggy wig. He stood next to Emily.

Abby came out of the house in a robe because she had a bikini on and it was definitely not bikini warm.

Jess stayed and watched. "Karpinski's going to love it that you're making shit out of his dad," she told me.

"I'm not Mr. Karpinski, okay?" I said. "Call me Mr...Mr. Dickinski. I'm the Polish Fist."

"I don't know, Felton," Jess said. "Everybody's going to recognize you."

"I guess that's the point," I said.

A few minutes later, Gus started to film.

• • •

Gus, having learned what works from our pipe-fight video, shot a lot of me at low angles, karate chopping and kicking the air. He had me drive the scooter back and forth in front of his house, swooping across the street, doing little putt-putt loop de loops and crap. (At one point, some dude in a Ford SUV nearly smashed into me. He shouted at everyone and Abby gave him the finger, which made Gus tell her to chill.) Then Gus had Maddie hold a mic out while I first swooped around Bony Emily, she pouting, looking like an angry punk girl.

"Hey, baby doll. What you so angry about?" I asked (like Mr. Karpinski).

"Life is hell," Bony said. "My dad's a dick."

"Do you want to feel the thrill of victory?"

"Yes! Yes, I do!" she said.

In the next shot, "Mr. Karpinski" showed her how to punch-chop a man's neck so he'd die instantly.

Maddie filmed for a moment while Bony E punch-chopped Gus dressed like a dad and he died.

"Oh yes! Yes! Yes!" Bony cried. She kissed my cheek.

Then a close-up of me barking: "That's the Polish Fist!"

Bony said, "Sexy Victory!"

Gus stared through the lens. "That's seriously good. Seriously funny," he said.

It didn't really feel that funny. I just felt sort of dumb.

Then I hit on Pig Boy in the Piggy wig. I said a bunch of Karpinski crap. Using Karpinski ancient Polish-Chinese magic, I turned Pig Boy into Maddie. She pulled on his shirt and the wig and blinked sexy style at the camera. Poor Pig Boy sat there shirtless for ten minutes, covering his chest and nipples with his hands.

Then I swooped around and around Abby in her robe, whooping. Gus put the camera on a clip tripod on the front of the scooter and had me drive real slow and mumble super fast and over and over, "Legs up to here. What a filly. I'd ride that pony." (He also had me say that crap over and over into his iPhone so he had extra audio.)

Then I did some weird kung fu poses aimed at Abby and we used kite string tied on the back of her robe (and yanked) to make it look like a magic Karpinski wind blew it off. (Pig Boy actually screamed "Oh man! Oh!" when Abby's robe slid off).

Close-up. "You're a friend of my boy's up at the old high school, am I right?"

Abby, "Yessss…"

"Pretty, pretty, pretty, pretty, pretty," I mumbled. "Um-hmm. Sexy."

"Yes!" Abby cried.

"Would you like to be the new Mrs. Dickinski, baby doll? Would you like to hot-rod bikini style on the back of my motorbike?"

"Yes! Yes! Yes!" Abby cried.

Then me punching. Then a close-up. "That's the Polish Fist!"

Then Gus filmed Abby and me from ten different angles riding away, Abby on the back of the scooter, hugging me and laughing and oohing and crap.

"That should do it," Gus said. "I can make something pretty good out of what we've got."

"Freezing! Freaking ice cold!" Abby shouted, pulling the robe back over her.

"Jesus. I don't know," Jess said. "That's mean, Abby."

"So?"

"Don't you think rubbing Karpinski's face in…in the way his dad acts is pretty bad?" Jess asked.

"No," Abby said. "Not at all."

"Fine. Give me the keys, Felton."

I tossed Jess the keys to the scooter.

"I'm not going to tell Karpinski about this and I hope to God he never sees it. You're acting like a puke, Abby," Jess said.

"Up yours," Maddie said.

"Up yours, whoever you are," Jess spat. Then she took off.

Abby's face had gone totally pale.

"We don't have to make anything out of this," Gus said. "It was fun just filming. We should totally drop it."

"No," Abby said. "We shouldn't be afraid of what they think."

"They?" Maddie asked.

"Just make the stupid movie, Gus, okay?" Abby said.

"Okay," Gus said. "I don't care. They're not my friends."

I pulled off the wig and began to pull off the mustache, but it was glued pretty well. "Ouch. Mother mustache is stuck," I said.

Pig Boy came up to me and said, "That was the funnest day I ever had in my whole life. You are funny."

"Thanks, man."

"I'm going to make some cartoons of you being Dickinski solving crimes and helping kids."

"Okay," I said. "Sounds good."

I wasn't really paying attention to him though. I was worried about Jess and about Abby too.

Pig Boy grabbed my arm. "Really. It was really fun."

I squinted at Tommy. He nodded. He swallowed.

"I don't have much fun," he said.

"Okay, man. We'll do it again," I said. "We'll make some more fun stuff. That was awesome." I smiled big.

"Cool," Tommy said. "I'm going home."

He waddled to his dipshit bike and was gone.

"Pig Boy is one weird kid," Gus said.

"Felton, I need to get this swimsuit off," Abby said. "Can we go to my house?"

"Yeah," I said. Off we went to Abby's. I didn't want to go. I wanted to go home to sleep, but I meant it when I said I wouldn't leave her alone.

CHAPTER 35
No Cody

But Abby was a wreck at her house. She bitched about Jess. She bitched about Cody. She started crying but wouldn't say why. We ate spaghetti again (I thought I'd puke), and she didn't say a word for like a half hour.

Then she went to the bathroom for twenty minutes.

When she came back, she acted drunk again. She might've had some schnapps hidden in there. She tripped on crap on the floor. She swore really loud, "Bleep, bleep, bleep, Mom can't take care of bleep. What the bleep?" Etc.

My Mr. Karpinski shorts started feeling like they were strangling my business so I closed myself in her closet and changed back into jeans. I came out in time to see Abby pull off the bottom of her swimsuit. She stood straight up. "So. There. I'm naked. Are we going to do this?"

"What?"

"It," she said.

"We've barely even kissed."

"So?" she barked. "This is what you want, right? Come here."

Abby looks like a Russian tennis-playing *Sports Illustrated* swimsuit model, so I had to breathe really deeply a few times and blink. Then I shook my head. "No."

"No?" she asked.

"No," I said.

"Oh really?"

"Yeah. I don't know what's going on with…"

"Whatever. I have to go to sleep," she said. "I need to be alone."

"Okay?" I said.

Abby climbed in her bed and at least pretended to be asleep.

My stupid heart hurt. I waited for a while, then left her room.

I made it through the house without running into anybody. That was good. But not everything was good.

Big problem: I didn't have a bike or a car. I stood on the Sauter front lawn staring at the street leading toward my house, miles away.

In the past, when I found myself in this circumstance—without a car and far from home—I'd call Cody and he'd swing by in his truck and usually we'd get something to eat or whatever, then he'd drop me off.

I'd been rude to Cody. Stupid. I couldn't call him for help.

So I started hoofing it. The wind had shifted and it was cold.

I walked up Camp Street into growing darkness. An old car came rushing past. Someone yelled, "Homo Rein Stone," from the window. They took off up the street fast. It was a burner car, not a jock or whatever. It didn't make me mad. It just struck me as messed up. Why did these people who seemingly had no interest in sports otherwise care about Wisconsin Badger football? Lots of people care about the Badgers apparently.

Or maybe people just like to pile on when shit's bad? Could that be true?

I sort of hugged myself, mostly against that damn wind, and kept hoofing.

Twenty minutes later, about the time I hit Smith Park, my phone buzzed in my pants pocket. I worried about looking at it because I didn't want to turn around and walk all the way back to Abby's. But I wanted to be there if she needed me, so I did look.

The text was from Andrew. *Call me when you can, Felton. Serious.*

Andrew was really into checking on me. Good brother.

I thought, *You're not alone. Not like Abby.*

It began to snow.

By the time I got home, it was snowing pretty hard. I sort of liked it. When I got to the front door, I looked back from the house (the driveway light was on) and could see where I'd come from, my footprints in light snow going all the way down the drive, almost out to the main road before they disappeared in darkness.

You'll miss this in California.

I stood and watched the falling snow get thicker. Sweet. My stomach still hurt and I felt heavy. But the snow was pretty and I had Andrew and I took care of Pig Boy and I wouldn't leave Abby.

You're doing okay…You'll be okay.

I think I believed it.

Chickens Start
Landing

CHAPTER 36
Terry Sauter's Beer

When I entered the house, Jerri sat on the couch in the living room with only one lamp burning. She wasn't reading an accounting book or anything. She seemed to be sitting there in the gloom, just waiting for me to come in.

"Hi," I said.

"So you're a fan of German beer?" Jerri said.

"No." My heart accelerated. I mumbled, "Not a fan." My heart began thumping hard. Abby and I hadn't cleaned up the beer bottles. We'd left so fast in the morning that it hadn't even occurred to me.

"Are you a drinker?" she asked.

"Not really," I said.

"Is Abby Sauter?"

"Abby? How did you know about…"

"Terry saw the bottles and he swore the only way you'd have that kind of beer is if you took it from Abby's house. You can't buy it in town. You can't buy it in the U.S. Have you gone to Europe without me knowing?"

"I don't think so."

"Do you and Abby think it's funny to take people's prized possessions?"

"Terry's prized possession is beer?" I asked. "Really? You're okay with that?"

"You know what I mean."

"I do. Your boyfriend's prized possession is beer."

"Don't turn this back on me. You're stealing. You're drinking. I've given you room to be an adult and this is how you pay me back?" she snapped.

I paused for a second. I glared at Jerri ,who hadn't been a mother to me through the roughest of years. "You've *given* me room?" I spat.

"I've given you free rein…"

"This is your gift?" I shouted.

She sat forward in her chair. "What's going on, Felton?"

"Maybe I crashed a car. Maybe I beat up some kid. Maybe I got drunk by a Dumpster at Kwik Trip." I turned and walked out of the living room.

"You did what?"

"Up yours, Jerri," I called.

"You're grounded, Felton!" she shouted after me.

"You going to hang around to oversee that?" I shouted back.

She didn't answer, and I ran down the stairs.

I walked past the empty bottles and the half-eaten pizza on the floor. My head exploded. That German beer smell made me sick. My mouth dried like crackers. I flopped onto my bed. "Shit," I said. I thought about calling Abby to warn her of impending trouble. Then I thought, *That asshole Terry isn't going to call anyone…these people aren't even adults.*

However, Abby wasn't remotely fine at that moment.

CHAPTER 37
Dad Drank Alcohol

A few hours later, I woke to my phone buzzing again. I didn't get it because I couldn't find it in the dark. A few seconds later, a voicemail dropped and I saw the phone light up in my pants pocket.

It was Andrew. I listened to his message.

"He won't go to the doctor. Please call, Felton."

Who won't go? Grandpa?

I called Andrew's cell immediately. He answered.

"Where have you been? I texted five times today. I've called five times," Andrew said.

"I'm sorry. I thought you were calling to check on me," I mumbled.

"So you don't answer? God, you're dumb," Andrew said.

"What's going on? Is Grandpa sick?"

"Yes," Andrew said.

"How? Why? Is it bad? Should he go to the doctor? What's happening? Can he stand up? Is he in pain?" I assumed Grandpa Stan was at death's door. That's how things work in my family. Disaster.

"He's not acting like Grandpa. He won't play tennis and he groans when he drives. He can't walk very far and he gets out of breath," Andrew said. "He's obviously in pain. Like when he wasn't feeling good at Christmas—but worse."

"Should we call Tovi so she can talk to her mom about this?" I asked.

"I called Evith this morning. She said she'd talk to him, but she hasn't called yet."

Freaking adults! "What's he doing now?"

"Well, sleeping. It's night. But he spent the evening listening to Wagner music in his study," Andrew said. "You know Wagner didn't like Jews?"

"No."

"Grandpa Stan knows. I'm very worried, Felton."

"Okay," I mumbled, trying to think what I could do. Then my dry German beer throat cracked and I started coughing and my eyes watered and my head swam. I had to put a pillow on my head, just to have some pressure on my face, because my face pounded after I coughed and coughed. The stupid, stinky Sauter German beer blew up my sinuses.

What's with this stuff? Why does Terry love it more than Abby? Maybe a minute later, I got back on the phone, not even sure if Andrew would be there still.

He was. "What's wrong with you?" Andrew asked. "Are you dying? Answer me."

"No. I drank beer last night. Weird beer. Too much," I said.

"What?" Andrew snapped. "With who? Gus?"

"Abby," I said. "It's no big…"

"You jerk. You stupid ass face jerk!" Andrew shouted.

"What? Jesus, Andrew."

"Is that why you won't go to a therapist because you're worried he'll tell you that you can't drink beer? Is that it? Are you that stupid?"

"Calm down. I just had some beer with my girlfriend."

"Emily told me you're with Abby, and Abby is freaking out because of the divorce and you're mentally unhealthy, of course, and now it sounds like you've signed some kind of suicide pact. Are you going to buy a convertible and hold hands and drive off a cliff, Felton? Is that your plan? I am so mad I could…I could puke on your face!"

"Andrew!" I shouted. "Stop. Dude! I'm okay!"

"Our father had alcohol problems and now…"

"Wait."

"And now you're going to spend all your time with some kind of fallen Satan angel girl who wants the town to go up in a big nuclear…"

"Wait!"

"What?" Andrew spat.

"Dad had an alcohol problem?" I had this glimmer of recognition. I knew this. Grandma Berba had said something about this, but Jerri, in all of her wild inability to tell the whole truth, had never really talked to us about it, so what was I doing? Was I falling into my dad's trap? Thinking I was getting along fine because suddenly booze made me think I was in love with a Russian swimsuit model who pretended to want to have sex?

"He got drunk and did stupid, mean things to people and then he couldn't fix his problems when he wasn't drunk and then he died, you idiot!"

"Oh Jesus."

"Oh crap. Shh," Andrew said.

"What?"

"I woke up Grandpa. Apparently I'm screaming at you."

"You are."

"I have to go, dickhead," Andrew said. He hung up.

I sat stunned in the dark, my throat aching. A minute later, Andrew texted:

> You have a completely addictive personality. Look how you run
> in circles around the yard like a sheepdog. Around and around.
> Can't stop running. Idiot.

He was right.

I called Abby immediately. No answer. I left a sort of psycho voicemail. "I can't drink anymore. Alcoholism is a major factor in people hanging themselves in my garage. So stop it!"

I called Andrew back. He didn't answer. I left a message. I said, "Don't worry. I'm done. I won't drink. Not ever. We're good. Great. Gotta stay positive. About Grandpa too. He's going to be fine."

Oh holy balls, my sense of potential world peace (nice snow outside, no Facebook, taking care of Pig Boy) totally exploded and I was scared as hell and how could I not dream of my poor dad?

Terrible dreams. Dad was dead in the room with me. Dad was drinking German beer. Dad had sex with Abby. Then Grandpa died in a head-on car crash.

The dead don't stay buried. I have a very real, very big problem. That tweak in my stomach. I had that tweak.

CHAPTER 38
Jerri Denies There Are Chickens

I woke up at eleven on Sunday. Apparently I'd finally exhausted my ability to shoot adrenaline through my body, so my nightmares stopped waking me. When I woke, my phone was locked in my hand, like I'd been grabbing the stupid thing so I could call and stop shit from happening I didn't want to happen.

It was dead. Battery gone.

I pulled myself out of bed and went upstairs, where I found Jerri reading the paper. She was dressed for the day.

"Jerri," I said when I entered the living room.

"What?" she said.

"You can ground me if you want," I said. "I don't want to go out into the world and break anything."

She stared at me for a second, then said, "No. See that? You're mature enough to rein yourself in. You know what's what."

I shook my head at her. "No," I said. "Not true."

"Sure," she said.

"I'm younger than you when Dad got you pregnant," I said. "I'm not mature."

"Jesus. Where did that come from?"

"My gene pool. My terrible, alcoholic, suicidal genes."

Jerri squinted. She sighed. "More Dad stuff, huh?" Jerri said. "Come here."

I crossed the room and sat down next to her. She put her arm around my shoulder. She said, "You're not like your dad. He had these problems…but how many times do I have to tell you? You're sweet and gentle…"

"You didn't know Dad in high school," I said. "Maybe he was sweet."

"Not a chance. No way," Jerri said. "Never."

"How do you know?"

"He was born mean. Some people have a defect. It's hardwiring."

"Really?"

"Just relax, honey, okay? You're great."

I nodded.

"You better?" she asked.

"Uh-huh."

"Good. I have to go to the library. My professor wants two book sources in our midterm paper. I need to read some business books. Sounds great, huh?" She laughed like she was a mom on TV who'd just done her job.

"Probably does to you," I mumbled.

"Relax, Felton. Kids drink sometimes. I did in high school a little. It's not the end of the world. Just don't do it again, okay?"

"Okay," I said. "Thanks."

"You got it," she said.

Five minutes later, she was gone.

Thanks for nothing. Worst mother. I might as well be a crack baby.

CHAPTER 39
Cody and a Giant Chicken

Awhile later, while I ate cereal in the kitchen, I thought: You have to parent yourself. You are your own parent. You don't need any other parent. What would you tell you if you were your own kid?

Then I thought of Gus in the faculty bathroom back in the fall.

WHO. ARE. YOU?

Shit!

Loser.

Addictive personality running circles in the yard.

Don't answer Aleah's texts because you're a jerk.

Protect fallen Satan angel who wants to blow up town, wants you dead?

No. Abby's not a bad person. Abby has problems...You help people, right?

Breathe, dude. Breathe.

The doorbell rang, which caused me to jump because nobody rings our doorbell ever. I stood so I could see out the little slot windows in the door. Cody's red baseball cap (Wisconsin cap) bobbed in one of the glass panels.

Oh man, I was relieved to see him there. Cody is about the sanest person on the face of the planet.

"Come in," I called. He didn't come in.

I got up and went to the door. Opened it.

"Hey, man," I said.

Cody, in the bright, iced February air, shook his head at me, said, "Dude, I did everything I could to help you. Brought you into weights. Called you to meet for drills. Got you okay with the football team. Made it easy."

"Yeah," I nodded. "I know. Thanks so much, man. I wouldn't be anything...I wouldn't be okay without..."

He shook his head. "No. No, dude. If I had known you were such a low-class scumbag, I would never have done that crap..."

"What?" I said.

"Yesterday, Dad tells me you were drinking at Kwik Trip."

"Oh no." Cody's dad is a cop.

"This morning, I see a video where you totally destroy my friend."

"Dickinski. You saw it?"

"Reinstein..." Cody said. He actually had tears in his eyes. "I don't want the football season, the state trophy, all the time driving around..."

"Cody, man," I said.

"You're such a...such an asshole. You're the worst, Felton. I don't want any of that shit because...Screw you."

He turned and walked to his truck fast. I ran out in the new snow in my bare feet, which killed. I shouted, "I didn't mean it. I don't know what I'm...I didn't know alcohol turned me crazy. I didn't..."

Cody paused before he got in. He said, "No. No more excuses. Stay away from me."

I stood in that snow, my feet burning. Cody spun the truck back and took off down the drive. Then I ran swearing back into the house. I ran downstairs and plugged my phone into the wall. I turn it on and waited. I had to talk to Abby or somebody. Gus?

When my phone came on, I saw there were texts and voicemails not filled with hate from Wisconsin but laughing like crazy and all from Bluffton.

The first was from Gus from three in the morning:

It's too hilarious. I couldn't stop until I finished. Vid is up. I posted on Facebook and YouTube.

Then, beginning at 8 a.m., there were slews. Almost all said something like *hilarious vid man* or *you nailed karpinski's dad... awesome*.

People were watching "The Polish Fist" in droves.

CHAPTER 40
Hamlet Had Chickens

The rest of the day Sunday, I didn't move. It felt like I'd break the world if I moved at all. *Will Cody tell Coach Knautz? Don't move…*

I only turned on my phone once, to tell Andrew to leave me a message about Grandpa as soon as he heard anything. A text from Aleah came through while the phone was on. *Composing is what I want to do, Felton.*

Aleah! You are not part of my life!

What the hell did composing have to do with me? Really? I had tragedies unfolding all around.

Otherwise, the phone was off, the computer was off. I stayed in bed.

After staring at the ceiling for hours, I reached in my backpack and pulled out the Shakespeare book we were using in Linder's class. For the first time in weeks, I read our assignment. I read more than our assignment. I read two weeks in advance. All of *Hamlet*!

HAMLET? Story of a kid obsessed with avenging his father's death.

It was hard to read—but Jesus Christ. Suicidal thoughts? Bad choices? Trying so hard to sort it all out, to the point of driving himself crazy, harming those he loved, and then everybody dies in the end? This play spoke to me.

I read parts three times. I read one part four times. That "To be or not to be" part. I wasn't sure I got it completely. *This is suicide he's talking about, right?*

CHAPTER 41
Chickens Land on Abby

You turned off your phone?" Abby said. "Why?" We stood at my locker between first and second hour Monday morning. Her face was red and her eyes were sort of bloodshot. She looked haggard, worn out.

"I can't deal."

"With everybody loving that video?" she asked.

"In part."

"I know," she said. "It's so funny. It's mean though. It's really mean."

"Really," I said. "I don't want to watch it."

"I tried to call you over and over," Abby whispered. "I had a rough weekend." She exhaled hard and grabbed my hand. "And you left that message about alcohol…"

"Jerri found our beer bottles," I said.

"Yeah," Abby said. "Dad called me. He totally screamed at me. He talked to Mom last night. He screamed at her too."

"About the beer?"

"That and he got a progress report from the college Saturday that I'm flunking cell biology…he's paying, you know?"

"What are we doing?" I asked.

"Mom freaked at me and I called her a stupid bitch and she

slapped me and Nolan had to hold her arms so she wouldn't hit me more."

"Oh shit," I whispered. "Abby, I'm…"

"It's my fault," she said. "I've been a wreck for months. I've been a mess…Mom flipped. She broke every bottle of alcohol in the house. There's glass all over the back patio."

"Are you okay?"

"No. I need quiet. Things are…things are breaking…" She nodded.

"I know," I said.

"I have to stop. I'm going to stop. I'm not going to flunk that class, Felton."

"Okay," I said, nodding.

"Yeah," Abby said. "And you left that message about people who hang themselves and then I cried for five hours."

I nodded. "My dad. Alcohol. Andrew told me."

"Why does Andrew know everything?" Abby asked.

I shrugged.

Then something. Abby leaned her forehead toward me. She locked eyes with me. She said, "You will never fall. Not on my watch. I'm serious, Felton." She grabbed my shirt in her fist. "I'm going to protect you."

I almost cried for some reason.

Abby isn't a drunken Russian swimsuit model by nature. She's a really tough person.

CHAPTER 42
One Chicken Makes the Dipshits Happy

Something weird happened at school the next couple of days (not as weird as it would become).

The Dickinski effect…

In English on Monday, Gus, out of his mind excited, told me the Dickinski video had been viewed 1,100 times.

"Weird," I said.

"Yeah, whoa. My best YouTube video otherwise has nineteen views and probably seventeen are me." He tried high-fiving me, but I wasn't looking. "Dude, high five."

I looked at him and he was holding his hand up. Gus is not a natural high-fiver. "Oh. Okay," I said.

By the end of the day, I could totally feel it. That video totally changed the energy in the school. The orchestra geeks (Bony Emily's crew) and the general dipshits (the spattering of humanity represented by Pig Boy) walked the halls with their heads held a little higher. It was like: *Watch out. You can kick us in the ass. But we'll come back and crush your balls 1,100 times over!*

The masses of balloon heads who'd been whispering "traitor" and "homo" behind my back stopped. Instead, they said, "Hey, Felton. You were awesome in that video!"

I nodded. I've always wanted to be a comedian. People laughed at me a lot when I was young but not because I'd made any good jokes. (I flinched a lot and dropped my books and crap.) It felt sort of good to be recognized for being funny.

Did I feel bad for Karpinski? Yes and no. He wasn't in school. He stayed home. I felt bad about Cody. He avoided me like death, so I avoided him. He'd told me to stay away and I had to because what if he told Coach Knautz about the Kwik Trip Dumpster beer? I had to do what he said.

I didn't think I could make it through spring without track.

Monday night, I lifted weights and ran stairs. The basketball team practiced on the gym floor below me. Cody didn't look at me once. I mean, I could tell he was avoiding looking at me.

On Tuesday morning before school, I saw Pig Boy. He looked like a different person. He wasn't wobbling when he walked. He passed me in the hall near the choir room and offered his fist for a bump. "Dude," he said.

That was a kid feeling pretty good about himself. How could I feel bad for Karpinski? Hadn't Karpinski walked through school feeling awesome his whole spastic life? Shouldn't Pig Boy, who had suffered so much, get the chance?

By the end of the day, I saw why Tommy was feeling so good. Bony Emily wore a "Bully Me" shirt like Tommy's but with "Cello Girl" written underneath it. Tommy had drawn my number 34 on the back of her shirt too.

Not all chickens are bad. Good chickens you send out can make larger good chickens happen. Is that karma?

I don't know. Ask Andrew.

I felt good when I saw Bony Emily's new shirt. But then feeling good made me feel bad for Karpinski and about Cody. Then I got angry at Karpinski for being a dick. *Karpinski is an athlete, so people put up with him all these years! He should feel what it's like to live Pig Boy's existence!*

Then I felt bad for everybody.

Then I ate a monster cookie I bought from the band's bake sale and I forgot about everything until after school. It was a pretty good cookie.

CHAPTER 43
Hamlet and Mr. Linder

After school, instead of going to run right away, I visited Mr. Linder to talk about *Hamlet*.

Linder was a little surprised when I walked into his room.

I knocked on the doorframe and said, "Can I ask you some questions?"

"Reinstein? Really? I'm not a coach, you know. I can't help you with your footballs."

"I'm here about *Hamlet*. I've read it a couple of times."

"Well, I'll be damned. I thought you forgot how to read."

"No. I've read some parts like five or ten times."

"Okay. Sit down."

I sat at the desk in front of him. I squinted. I asked, "Is Hamlet talking about suicide in that 'to be or not to be' speech?"

"Sure."

"I thought so."

Linder cocked his head to the side. He nodded. "There's a larger context in the story though. Hamlet's revealing the kind of person he is in that speech. It's called a soliloquy, by the way."

"What kind of person is he?"

"He's depressive and dark—his dad is dead."

"Yeah, I get that. But…"

"But his big problem is the human condition, which is everybody's problem. It's the mortal coil. Remember that from the speech? The mortal coil?"

"Yeah. I picture a killer snake."

"Good enough. But the mortal coil is a symbol, okay?"

"Okay," I nodded.

"It represents the trouble of being human. Right?"

I paused. I nodded. "I really don't know," I said.

"What's the human condition?"

"Uh…We're hungry a lot? I mean, I am."

"Psychological, not biological, Felton."

"We're weak?"

"We think a lot," he said.

"Oh. Yeah. I do. Too damn much."

"But we can't be sure we know anything. We don't know if we're right. We don't know about the future. We're born into all these responsibilities and relationships and histories that are so complex."

"Oh," I said. I nodded.

"We're tiny, but we have to make decisions about big things."

"I know."

"Hamlet has a huge responsibility, right? Huge. He's the son of the king! He believes his father's been murdered! But he isn't exactly sure. Is his mind playing tricks on him?"

"My mind plays tricks on me. I picked up that Wisconsin hat," I said.

"No kidding, Felton. What a stir over nothing, huh?"

"I don't know."

"I don't care about that."

"Good," I nodded. "Thanks."

"What are Hamlet's choices? To act on his belief, to harm those he loves? To avenge the death of his dad when he's unsure and not naturally given to fighting? Or to die, let go, shuffle off the mortal coil? Just dump it all! Break away!"

"Shit," I said.

"But he's afraid of death too. Afraid of the unknown that death represents. What if he dies and spends an eternity dreaming of his failings?"

"Shit."

"Tortured guy, Prince Hamlet."

"Shit, shit," I mumbled.

"Shit?"

"Yeah," I said. "Not everybody has a mortal coil. My brother, Andrew, isn't like Hamlet. He doesn't worry about that kind of crap. He's all action."

"Everybody has a mortal coil. Some people are better at handling it."

"Right. Andrew."

"But…you're like Hamlet?" Linder asked.

"Maybe," I said.

"How so?" Linder leaned forward. He nodded slowly.

"My dad killed himself."

"I know. And you're some kind of prince, aren't you? The football hero."

"That's genetics from my dad."

"Prince isn't an elected position. It's passed from parent to child."

"Yeah. Of course. Right."

Linder smiled. "So…do you understand something about your own existence from reading about Hamlet's plight?" he asked.

"Definitely. I should hurry up and murder my mom and my uncle."

The smile dropped from Linder's face. He shook his head. "I don't think that's the message."

"I don't actually have an uncle, not a blood uncle. My aunt is married to this guy, David. I've never met him. He couldn't marry my mom because he's already married…"

"Stop joking," Mr. Linder said.

"Really?"

"Don't take the easy way out. You're in here for a reason, I assume."

I stood up. Linder winced. I didn't really mean to joke. It just happened because shit falls out of my mouth. "I'm not like Hamlet. I do act," I said. "I do great when I'm on a football field."

"That's easy. There's a specific goal and there are set rules."

"Perfect. I like that."

"But Hamlet isn't playing a game. He's dealing with real life where there aren't set rules. He has to make up his own rules and it's driving him crazy."

"He's crazy?" I asked.

"Do you think he's crazy?" Linder asked.

"If you make up your own rules, then there aren't any real rules, and if there aren't any real rules then…then…then it's chaos! Who wouldn't be crazy?"

"That's the mortal coil right there, my friend," Linder said, nodding.

"That sucks," I said. "Somebody should make some rules."

"Make your own. If Hamlet had considered his values instead of messing around, drinking beer at university, maybe he would've been decisive when the crisis came. He'd have had his rules. He could've avoided the whole mess."

I started sliding toward the door. "Why are you talking about beer?"

"I'm not," Linder said. "Are you leaving?"

"I have to go running," I said.

"Of course you do," Linder nodded.

"Plus, if he had his rules and was decisive, then the story would be too short and it wouldn't be a tragedy and nobody would care," I said.

"Hamlet had to have his problems or Shakespeare wouldn't have a play. You're right."

"Everybody dies. It's Hamlet's fault."

"That's the magic of fiction, Felton. You get to experience the crisis and the causes without actually living through them yourself. What did you learn from *Hamlet*?" .

"Uh…It's complicated."

"That's my Facebook relationship status," Mr. Linder said.

"Gross," I said.

"You can do better than Facebook, can't you? Think."

"I really have to go for a run," I said. I ran out the door.

"Nice seeing you!" he shouted behind me.

WTF? Why are you running? I was running down the hall.

Mr. Linder emailed me five minutes after I left and told me he'd walk me to the guidance counselor's office if I needed the help or we could talk more about Hamlet another time. I saw the message when I got home.

Before that, I ran sprints for an hour.

After I saw the message, I sat at my desk and thought. *You're not like Hamlet. You do stuff. You decide. You act. You make funny videos that make dipshits happy...* Then I was struck: *Holy balls. Hamlet made a play.*

Seriously, Hamlet makes a play in *Hamlet* to see how his mom and uncle would react. *That's like an old school video.*

Holy balls. You're Hamlet?

Thankfully, Abby called at that moment to make our evening plan.

CHAPTER 44
Chicken Launchers Head to Walmart

Abby's plan for clean living: we couldn't spend any time in our houses except to sleep. "I need to be some place where there are bright lights and normal people," she said.

There aren't a ton of good places to go in Bluffton. Walmart is huge, and it has a deli section where you can sit and drink pop for hours on end. So we decided to go there for the evening.

I only wanted to read *Hamlet*. While I paged through the play, Abby buried herself in a giant textbook. She looked like Jerri nosed into her accounting text.

"You know why people go crazy?" I asked.

She shushed me, which I kind of liked, because that's the way the old Abby would behave. You couldn't stop her from studying.

"Because they don't know what else to do," I said. "They don't see a good path."

"Felton," Abby said. "Shut up. Okay?"

"You got it," I nodded. "To be or not to be…talking. Not talking."

I looked around. Stared at the fluorescent lights and blinked. *You're not like Dad really.* That's what I thought. *He wanted to break the mold. Shuffle off that mortal coil. You just want to chill. Hamlet and Dad weren't alike. Dad's dad is still alive. Your dad is dead.*

You're like Hamlet, not Dad? Everybody dies. You're going to die. Abby will die. Everybody in this store will die and rot in the ground, and won't they be happy they don't have to shop at Walmart under these giant lights that pretty much burn out your soul... My heart was starting to accelerate. *Oh God. What's wrong with you?*

I stood up. I said, "I'm going to take a quick run around the store."

"What?" Abby asked, her eyebrows scrunched with concern.

Then Andrew called. I grabbed my phone from my pocket. "My brother," I said to Abby.

"Talk to him. Don't talk to me," Abby said.

I answered. "Hi."

"Saw your video. Very inventive. I didn't know you were such a good actor."

"Uh-huh. I act. How's Grandpa?" I asked.

"He has an ulcer from taking too much ibuprofen because he gave himself a hernia, which apparently hurts."

"Oh good." I nodded. "That doesn't sound life threatening. He's not going to die."

"No. He's going to have minor surgery when I'm out of school this summer. The doctor asked if he wore an athletic supporter when he played tennis. Grandpa said no because he likes his boys to be free."

I laughed.

There was silence.

"Andrew?" I asked.

Andrew exhaled. "Aleah demanded I call you," he said.

I looked at Abby. She was engrossed in cell biology.

"Why?" I whispered.

"She'd like to speak with you. She has something important to discuss. That's all, Felton. I'm angry because you won't go to the therapists I sent you and I'm angry at you for thinking beer is funny…"

"I never said beer is…"

"But I told Aleah I'd call you anyway, even though you probably wouldn't answer."

"I answered."

"Good work."

Andrew hung up.

My heart beat weird. *No, Aleah. Not again. Won't do it.*

I went to the pop machine and filled my blue Powerade, then came back to the table. A couple older ladies standing outside the seating area stared at Abby and me and whispered. I heard one say, "Cute couple."

Then a thought struck me. *Are you and Abby really a couple? Like boyfriend and girlfriend?* Just the mention of Aleah could send my heart into a weird rhythm—but Abby?

"Hey," I said.

"Please, Felton."

"Abby, are we boyfriend and girlfriend?"

Abby paused. "Everybody thinks we are," she said.

"So…?"

"Do you want to be?" Abby asked. "Like a romantic couple?"

"I don't…I don't know…Do you?"

"Do you?" she asked back.

"Um…I kind of think of you as my hot sister, except when we drink."

Abby blinked. She nodded. "I'm going to tell you a secret, Felton." Abby's face began heating up. "Sit down."

I sat back down.

"You can't tell anyone. You swear?" she said.

"I swear."

"Listen. I don't want to have sex."

"Yeah, I actually got that."

"Also, I don't want to kiss…people."

"Okay?"

"I don't understand why people would think having a tongue stuck in their mouth is fun, and I don't have any idea why they'd want your thing stuck in their vajayjay."

"My thing?"

"Any thing."

"That's…that's cool?" I said.

Abby started talking fast. "Except it's totally abnormal. You don't think I've googled this? Like I have no interest in sex when I'm eighteen years old? And these websites say I have hormone problems or I'm a lesbian or I'm, like, some kind of child abuse victim and I don't think I am, except maybe the hormone thing, but I don't exhibit any other symptom of that and I really, really, really want to be normal, but I'm not, so I don't really want a boyfriend, but I want you to…to be around with me…to stay together like a team because…"

Abby kept talking faster and faster, and I got it because I spin out so much sometimes. It's not easy to watch someone spin out. I decided to help.

"Stop," I said.

"Why? You don't want the team?" Abby swallowed.

"Will you go to prom with me?" I asked.

Abby shook her head. She stared. "Really?" she said.

"Tuxedos and crap," I said. "For real."

"I'm telling you that…"

"We aren't going to do it. We're not together like that. I won't even kiss your hand."

"I'm really like Barbie," Abby whispered. "Plastic."

"No," I said. "You're not."

"I am."

"You don't have a plastic convertible or a beach house. Your knees bend."

"I'm Barbie," Abby said.

"Then I'll be 'Prom Date' Ken."

Abby stared at me. "Oh my God," she said. "I really like you."

We stared at each other more. Abby's eyes were wet.

And then my phone buzzed in my pocket, which made me leap out of my chair.

"Chill, Felton. Why are you so jumpy?"

"Gus," I said.

One of our chickens had just gotten huge.

CHAPTER 45
The Borders of Bluffton
Don't Contain This Guy

When Abby drove me home, she said, "I think people were staring at us at Walmart. Am I totally paranoid?"

"They were staring. Old ladies."

She nodded.

When Abby dropped me off at my house, she said, "Please don't tell anyone what I told you."

"Of course not."

"Thanks, Felton. Call me after you talk to Gus."

When I'd answered the phone from Walmart, Gus had shouted, "We're going viral, man!" Then he'd asked me to call him back in a half hour. He had to get off the phone because he was clicking at his computer and sort of hyperventilating.

I went inside the house. Jerri wasn't there. I made myself dinner (stuffed bread in my mouth and then a whole package of Buddig ham), went downstairs, and called Gus back.

When he answered, he said, "Okay. Okay. Really, you're going viral."

"No. I'm here. I'm not viral," I said.

"Yeah, but somebody on YouTube figured out that you're the Polish Fist," Gus said.

"Everybody knows that's me. We weren't trying to hide it or anything."

"Not Bluffton, man. It can't go viral in Bluffton, right? If I'm tracking it correctly, an ESPN reporter is the one."

The word ESPN sent a shock up my spine. "The one who what?"

"The one who sent it out to like 200,000 Twitter followers, and a bunch of them retweeted that crap to a shit ton of other Twitter freaks. It's…man…it's everywhere! Just this afternoon and tonight! Everywhere, Felton. Because of you, do you get it? Jesus. Who have you become?"

"I don't know," I said.

"Felton Reinstein sells tickets! This is crazy!"

"Yeah. Can you take the video down?" I asked. "I don't want it blasting off all over."

"It wouldn't matter if I did take it down," Gus said. "It's been copied and reposted about thirty times today. People are titling it 'Reinstein Dickinski.' This is seriously amazing. I've never been part of…"

"But, Jesus, it's an inside joke about Karpinski's dad! Why do they care?"

"No. It's legitimately hilarious. Haven't you watched it?"

"No. And I'm not going to."

"You're going to see it. It's everywhere," Gus said.

"I'm not interested."

"This is not the response I expected, man. You're a comedy hit. That's what you used to want. Remember? Remember when you tried stand-up in seventh grade?"

Picture me in a cheap blue suit telling jokes while kids boo.

"I have to go," I said. "Need to sleep."

"Come on, Felton. This is cool."

"It's cool. Okay. Except maybe not for Karpinski."

"There are already Dickinski tribute videos going up."

"Okay," I said.

"Get ready, Felton. School's going to be crazy tomorrow."

He hung up.

I shook my head, tried to shake out the news. Tribute videos?

Yeah, I sort of felt like Karpinski had it coming in school. But I wasn't from Bluffton High anymore, was I? Bluffton didn't remotely contain me. People from everywhere knew me, and I was bringing the whole freaking world down on Karpinski?

Shit. He didn't deserve that.

Abby texted: *wow. we are everywhere.*

Poor Karpinski.

Hamlet kills his old friends, Rosencrantz and Guildenstern. Cody Frederick and Karpinski.

Fast Falling

CHAPTER 46
Dickinski Grows and Grows

I have serious problems and it's too easy to be me. I'm the worst off and the best. I'm hard luck and the top of the heap.

That split is super hard to reconcile.

Born lucky, Prince Hamlet was the son of a murdered dude.

• • •

Gus was right. The school was buzzing the next morning, Wednesday morning. They'd mentioned the Dickinski video on KLYV, the radio station in Dubuque, and on WSWW, the local news station, so moms knew about it. It flew through Facebook and Twitter.

Karpinski continued to stay out of school. Cody glared at me. Bony Emily, wearing her "Bully Me" shirt, ran up and hugged me around the neck. "My cousin in Kentucky saw the video. He was like 'Hot damn, that's Emily!'"

"Weird," I said.

Pig Boy shouted across the commons, "I'm a movie star!"

Abby said, "Jess won't even look at me." Her face was totally pale.

The volume kept going up.

In the middle of Linder's class, the school secretary came to the door and knocked. Linder was in the middle of a discussion about how Hamlet kills the crap out of Polonius (sort of his girlfriend's dad) and how that wasn't exactly a well-thought-out act. Linder wasn't remotely pleased to see Mrs. McGinn standing there.

"What?" he asked.

"Felton Reinstein has a phone call in the office," she said.

"Can he return the call later?" Linder asked. "What you're seeing here…" Linder waved his hand in front of all of us, "is an educational classroom."

Then Mrs. McGinn whispered (across the whole room), "It's from a Madison TV station. They need an interview ASAP."

Several people shouted, "Jesus!" and "Whoa!"

Mr. Linder said, "Good lord. Go on, Felton."

I said, "No thanks."

Gus tapped me on the shoulder. "Go. Mention my name. Come on."

I got up slowly and followed Mrs. McGinn out the door. We walked through the empty halls. Mrs. McGinn said, "I went to school with Dave Karpinski. You got him just right, Felton. He was just like that back in '86 too."

A week earlier, Mrs. McGinn, wearing a Wisconsin Badger sweater, gave me the evil eye. I'm serious.

• • •

The reporter wasn't on the phone. She'd been set up on Skype. McGinn sat me down at her computer. "Hi, this is Megan Hansen."

"Hi?" I said, staring at her blond head. I recognized her from TV.

"Do you mind if I record?" she asked.

"Video?" I asked.

"TV news," she said.

"No?" I said.

"Great. Fantastic." She smiled.

Then Megan Hansen congratulated me on accepting the scholarship to Stanford. I said, "Thanks." She asked about the video.

"You remind me of Bill Murray in it," she said. "Was he your inspiration?"

Bill Murray? Talk to my dad. He's dead but still owns a *Caddyshack* poster. I took a breath. *You think, Felton. No thoughtless chatter. Don't make this worse.* "No. My friends were," I said.

"Tell me about it."

I told her it was Abby's brainchild. "My friend, Abby, is funny." I told her Gus directed, filmed, and edited the thing, and it was really his genius. "He's been studying films forever. He's great." I didn't tell her I'd never watched it and didn't intend to or that Karpinski wasn't in school.

"How do you feel? First, you're a star athlete. Now you star in a viral video with a million views."

"A million?" I asked. I shook my head.

"And counting," she said.

"Holy balls." *Keep it together.*

"Ha, ha," she laughed. "There are dozens of copycat videos out there too."

"I've heard," I said.

"Have you watched them?"

"I'm pretty busy."

"Preparing for track, I bet."

"Yeah. Lots of running. I run like a sheepdog. Around and around the yard," I said. "I can't stop." *Keep it together, idiot!*

Megan Hansen laughed. "Nobody knew you were such a funny guy."

"True that," I said. "I better get back to class. My English teacher's pretty rough on us."

"Wait. Do you have time for one more question, Felton?" She sucked in her cheeks and squinted like this was really important.

"Sure. A quickie," I replied.

She laughed. I don't know why she laughed. Then she asked, "Does 'The Polish Fist' represent your reaction to the way Wisconsin has treated you since you made your Stanford announcement?"

"What do you mean?"

"Does Dickinski…you know his stupidity and bravado…does he represent Wisconsin?"

My first thought was to say, "Hell, yeah! Wisconsin is a doofus, turd-swallowing pervert with a fat gut and a love of any female with boobs." But instead, I took a deep breath and gathered my non-Hamlet thoughts. "No," I said. "I understand why people were so angry. It was really stupid to grab the Wisconsin hat. I love this state. It will always be home to me. I'm so sorry."

"Perfect, Felton. I have that on video," she said. "I'll use it."

Back in Linder's class, I was greeted as a hero (not by Linder himself). Then the bell rang.

• • •

The story ran at the end of the 5 p.m., 6 p.m., and 10 p.m. broadcasts. I watched it once with Abby. Even though my interview part was edited way down, the piece still mentioned her and Gus. I also got home in time to see it an hour later with Jerri, who said, "When did you make this video? Can I watch it?"

"No," I told her.

I didn't watch the segment at 10 p.m. I felt sick about Karpinski. I felt sick about Cody. And the story was really focused on that final thing I said, my big statement of love for Wisconsin, my apology. I looked really honest and sad when I said it. And then I had to turn my phone off because out of no place, I began getting texts of love from random people, texts forgiving me for what I'd done two weeks earlier, texts wishing me luck in my move to California.

It made me sick. I didn't deserve to be treated well.

I ran for an hour in the dark on the main road outside our house.

CHAPTER 47
Bust

During the fall, coaches kept pulling me out of classes for this or that. A recruiter called. A reporter wanted to talk. A buddy was in town and wanted to meet me. Most teachers just went for it. Mr. Linder, however, did not.

In October, he went off on Coach Knautz. He called him a bald-headed Neanderthal in front of the whole class and said he'd flunk me if I ever got pulled from class again (one of many reasons I didn't want to go with Mrs. McGinn the day before).

Apparently, Coach Knautz got the message about interrupting AP English because he didn't barge right in. With about five minutes left to go in the class that Thursday, I could see his round walnut of a head bobbing in the little glass window in the doorway.

"You got company," Gus whispered.

"Why me?"

"Who else would Knautz be here for?"

My heart began to pound.

"What's that, Gus?" Mr. Linder asked.

"Felton has an escort waiting at the door," Gus said.

"Business gets in the way of art again, huh?" Linder said. "You're walking on thin ice, my friend."

"I know," I said.

When the bell rang, I bolted for the door.

"Hey," I said to Knautz in the hall. I was breathing hard.

"A word. Now," Knautz said. He was sweating. He looked ill.

"What is it?" I asked. *I know. Cody told. He has no reason to protect you.*

"Get your ass to my office, Rein Stone."

Knautz plowed through the corridors, kids falling to the side in his wake. I scurried along behind him like a scared dog. He bowled through the commons and my stomach dropped and my heart ached and pain fired into my arms and legs. *This is it. This is it. This is happening.*

It felt like I was floating on the ceiling, looking down at my doomed body walking.

We arrived in his office and he held the door. When I walked in, he slammed it behind me. His lips quivered. His eyes were blood. He walked to the other side of his desk and slammed his palms onto the top.

I jumped.

"Sit down," he said.

I sat.

He leaned over the desk. He shook his head. "What have you been doing to prepare for the track season?" he hissed.

"I don't know. I...I've been running a lot. I've been doing stairs and..."

"You're in a fishbowl. You're a target. You can't screw up. *What have you been doing to prepare for the track season?*" he shouted.

"I…I've been training a ton. I can't stop running."

"I know. I know, Rein Stone. I heard about your workout."

"What?" I gulped for air.

"Getting wasted? Drinking yourself stupid?"

"No."

"Why would you do that? Why couldn't you wait?" he shouted. "*Answer me!*"

"I don't know," I whispered.

"You've got everything you want. You have your free ride and your football championship and your hot girlfriend. What about your teammates? What about your friends who have just one more shot at winning something big, at grabbing for something they'll remember for the rest of their lives? Do you think Karpinski is going to play college sports? Do you think Hinkins or Hoyme or Satish are ever going to have another shot at doing this?"

"No. I didn't think…"

"You didn't think."

"No," I whispered.

"Too damn bad."

"What?" I gulped for air.

"You just wrestled our shot at winning the team trophy away from all those guys who have busted their asses for years."

"No. Coach. I…I…"

"*You got drunk and you got stupid and you are done!*" he shouted.

"I can't…"

"Get out of my office, Reinstein." Big drops of sweat bubbled on his red face. He hissed, "I've wasted too much time on your prima-donna ass. Get out now!"

I stood. The room spun. I slid back down into the chair. My breath couldn't go into my lungs right.

He stared at me. "You better be the hell out when I get back."

And then, Coach Knautz, the guy who found me, who guided me onto the team as a sophomore, who protected me from the seniors that wanted to knock me down, tore out of his office. He slammed the door so hard, it bounced back open and crashed against the cinder block wall so that the whole room trembled.

Freshmen gym students came running to see what had happened. They stuck their heads in the door.

Me? I trembled.

CHAPTER 48
Run

I didn't go back to school. I left out the west doors of the gym and escaped into the parking lot.

Thank God it was warm enough.

Thank God my keys were in my jeans pocket.

Go.

I unlocked my bike and I tore out of the lot, accelerating, pedaling as hard as I could.

Instead of going back into town, I crushed the pedals, heading toward the big M, the hill east of town that has a giant M built from painted boulders on its side. (M because Bluffton had a mining college.)

I pressed.

I'd blown up my team. My friends.

My knees felt like they'd break. My triceps were pooled lava from holding myself up on the handlebars. Worse, my quads felt like they'd explode, but I pressed. I rolled into the park at the foot of the M. Let my bike drop. Stumbled to a picnic table and lay down on my back. Blinked at that weird, winter blue sky that was warm when it should be cold. *This is a bad world. Broken.* I sucked for air. My chest collapsed, inflated, collapsed. My lungs burned.

This has been my place, this M. My dad took me here when I was tiny. This is where I ran off Jerri's insanity when I was a fifteen-year-old squirrel. This is where I breathed, going up and down the thing, when college recruiting felt like it would crush me. Cody, Karpinski, Abby, Reese, and Jess—we'd come here on summer nights to watch the twinkling lights of our tiny hometown. But mostly, this was where I'd run and run and run.

I lay there on that picnic table, energy flowing out of me.

I couldn't run.

CHAPTER 49
Culture of Violence

I think I fell asleep on that picnic table. I sat up shivering, sweating in my coat. The sun was beginning to set over Bluffton.

I'd left my phone in my locker, so I wasn't getting texts telling me what a jerk I was for blowing up the track season. *Good one rein stone screwing it for everyone...*

I didn't want to go home, but I didn't have any place else to go, so I biked slow into town and up past the high school. There were a few cars in the parking lot. Basketball practice was going. Cody's truck was there.

I turned right at the edge of the high school grounds. I pedaled for a couple football fields on Highway 18 (semis passing me, blowing me sideways). When I hit Ridge Road, I took a left and biked along the south end of Legion Field and then I saw something in the long shadows of the baseball field's stands.

Tommy Bode.

He was in front of someone. He was screaming. Then he was scuffling with someone. *Who would beat up a kid who lost his brother?*

I pulled my wheel up over the curb and pressed hard, accelerating through mud and muck until I was up to them. I threw down my bike and leapt on top of the other kid, pulling him out of

Pig Boy's grip, lifting him up by his armpit and leg, whipping him to the side, his head cracking against the aluminum of the baseball stands. The kid started screaming. Blood poured from a gash above his eye.

Pig Boy—hot, red, sweating—cried, "What did you do?"

"No one can hurt you," I shouted.

"But I was winning! I was winning! I was killing him!"

I looked at the screaming kid. I recognized him. It was Ryan Bennett. He was not big.

"Oh shit! Oh shit!" Ryan screamed. Blood ran down his hand, which he used to cover his wound. "Leave me alone!" he screamed.

"Holy shit, Tommy," I said. "A little kid?"

Ryan started to run.

I ran after him. "Are you okay? Do you need help? Can I ride you to the hospital? Do you have a phone? I can call your mom."

"Leave me alone!" he screamed again.

He kept running. I stopped chasing. I stood there.

What next? Call police? Arrest yourself for criminal assault on a little kid?

I leaned over, hands on knees, trying to catch my breath. Nothing felt real.

I turned and stumbled back toward my bike. I had to swallow so I wouldn't throw up.

Pig Boy stood there.

"I was winning," Pig Boy said.

"Not now, okay?" I gulped.

"Why'd you do that?" he asked.

259

"I don't want you hurt."

"But you didn't have to do that. I chased him down on my bike. He tried to run."

I stood straight. I stared at Tommy. "You chased him. You wanted this?"

"I saw him walking and wanted to tell him that he was mean to Curtis. So I chased him and I pushed him and put him in a head-lock and we fell over and then you came and picked him up."

"Oh shit, Tommy," I said.

"You whipped him like a bag of potatoes."

"I don't know what I'm doing."

"I'll find him again and finish this," Tommy said.

"*No…No!*" I shouted.

"It's my job to fight evil," he said.

"No, you idiot. That kid…that kid isn't evil. He's a little puke piece of shit, but…" I caught my breath. I nodded. Talked fast. "We have to apologize. You want to come to Ryan's with me? We can explain about Curtis."

"No." Pig Boy shook his head. "My elbow hurts." Pig Boy climbed on his crap bike and rolled away.

I nodded. *Of course. Of course.*

It had been a dozen years since my dad killed himself and I was still freaking out. Curtis had died five weeks earlier. Tommy would be crazy forever. But Tommy had it worse. I never had an older kid in my ear, filling me with shit, saying I was his sidekick, agreeing to fight evil. What if I turned Pig Boy into a murderer?

Look at you. You set in motion the events to hurt everyone.

No. He needs to be powerful.

I don't know. Oh shit. Oh shit.

I got on my bike. I rolled home, snuck inside (Jerri was upstairs), and fell over into my bed, and after three hours of this sickness in my gut, loss of track, Pig Boy murderer, Karpinski gone from school, seeing no path out, no path, I thought: *what about a beer?*

CHAPTER 50
Me and Hamlet, Two Nuts in a Sack

Then all night. I couldn't sleep because my heart was racing.

No Andrew. No Aleah. No Gus. They didn't understand. They couldn't.

In this weird fever, I saw Dad's rope. I saw it in my hands. *Why?*

Abby. She understood the slings and arrows. The mortal coil. She'd kept the killer snake away with peach schnapps. *That's not rope.* She understood. At 4 a.m., I looked for my phone so I could call her. Couldn't find it. Turned over my bed. Did it slide against the wall? No.

Then I remembered. It was in my locker at school.

I tried to breathe. I put my bed together. I lay there staring at the ceiling.

Go to school. Face your shit so you can get your phone…no schnapps left at Abby's…her mom broke the booze…go in Abby's car to Cal's barn.

Maybe I slept for a few minutes? Not really.

At 7:30, I rolled out of bed. I didn't shower. I pulled on jeans and a sweatshirt, tried to keep breathing.

What would I face at school? I'd skipped the last couple hours. *Detention?* I'd been kicked off track, which made me want to break my own face. *They will scream at you? Hate you? You hate yourself!*

The town will know everything. I'd beaten up an eighth grader. He bled. *The cops will come. They should come for you.*

Jerri wasn't awake yet. I moved quietly through the house. Ate a piece of dry bread to stop my stomach from rotting, then went out through the garage, muscles trembling.

I rode to school slowly, sick but ready to face what was coming so I could get my phone and Abby.

Maybe not ready…

I locked my bike and sucked for air. *Find Abby. Keep it together. Find Abby.* I moved toward the doors. Bony Emily passed me on the way in.

"Hi, Felton!"

So did Kirk Johnson, who is on the 4x100 relay with me. "Hey, man," he said. He was carrying a dozen roses. I stared at the flowers. *Is this a dream?*

I followed him through the doors and into the chemical-smelling commons, where all the kids gather before the bell rings. Lots of people had flowers. Lots of people were eating from candy boxes. Valentine's Day. I was so checked out that I didn't even know.

And nobody glared at me. No one even looked?

I picked up speed and turned toward the hall where the senior lockers are.

Two seconds earlier, I'd just wanted to see Abby. Then I saw her and she smiled and she carried a white flower and I didn't want to see her. I wanted to look at my phone to see if the cops had called about Ryan Bennett because they should've called.

Abby: "There you are. You okay? Man, I was worried about you

263

last night. I tried to drive over, but the Buick bit it in front of Weber's! Dead! I wish Jerri would let you plug in your landline. It sucks when your phone is dead. What should I do about my car? We can't get to Walmart to study without it. Hey, I got this white flower from the student council for you!"

I kept walking while she talked. She grabbed my wrist and pulled.

"Whoa, dude. Slow down. What's up? What's wrong with your hair? You look like a homeless guy. What's going on?"

"I don't know. You didn't hear anything?"

"About what?" Abby asked. "Nolan told me Knautz got mad at you for not getting in shape. He yelled at you in the locker room? Is that what you're talking about? Did you run last night? Is that why you didn't call?"

"No…I…I forgot my phone here."

"You need to work out a lot before we hang tonight? I totally get it, Felton. We have to stay on top of…"

"No," I spat. "You don't get it."

Abby shook her head. Her eyes watered. "What is up, dude?"

"Nothing. Okay? Let's talk later, okay, Abby? I have to get to…"

"You are not okay," she whispered.

"Let's talk later."

"Felton?" she said.

"Later."

I turned a corner—not to my locker but to get away from Abby. I turned into some random hall filled with lockers (freshman lockers and kids with flowers). There was Nolan Sauter. *Jesus. Ryan told him. He had to. I know…*

"Hey, man," he said.

I nodded.

"Sorry Knautz yelled at you," he said.

Was he trying to be nice? Ryan Bennett didn't tell him I'd popped his freaking coconut? And why the hell didn't anyone know I was kicked off the freaking track team? This was huge news! I needed someone to come after me to make it real.

I buzzed around a corner and down a hall and around another and down another hall and no one said one bad word to me, but I deserved terrible words, brutal words—*You should go into Knautz's office so he can scream at you again*—and then the bell rang. I ran to my locker to get books.

In my locker? My phone. Other than three texts from Abby, there were no new messages, no voicemails. Nothing.

• • •

In class, people were chipper. "Hi!" It was a happy day. Valentine's Day. Everybody munched on candy.

Where's Knautz? Where are the cops? Where's Karpinski?

After class, I practically ran up to Cody when I saw him in the hall because I figured he'd know it all—because he knows everything terrible I do.

"Hey," I said. I nodded at him. He wore a red flower pinned on his shirt.

"What?" he asked.

"Where's Karpinski?" I asked.

"Gone."

"Why's he gone?" I asked.

"Embarrassed." Cody turned his back and opened his locker. I took off.

At lunch, I asked Abby, "Is Karpinski sick? Is he okay? Have you heard?"

"I don't know, man. Should I ask Jess? I'll ask her. Do you want me to call him?"

"Did he quit school?"

Abby furrowed her brow. She shook her head a little. "Felton. You are the opposite of calm, man," she said. "You have to tell me what's going on."

"Nothing," I said. *Shut up. Om shanti. Be quiet.* I tried to keep my mouth shut the rest of lunch.

"Om shanti" is the peace chant Jerri taught me when I was a kid and she was a serious freak. I'd say it out loud and people would kick my ass.

* * *

I got to Linder's, to AP English. Gus sat in the chair next to mine. He wore a black Valentine's flower. Maddie's joke. He said, "Hey, did you see the Dickinski video from that group of black dudes in Las Vegas?"

"What?"

"They did a really hilarious "Jamaican Fist" video. They blow magical ganja smoke on ladies. That's the best knockoff so far. You should check it out."

"Shut up," I said.

"What? Are you kidding?"

"No," I said. "Nothing personal."

"Yeah, right," Gus said.

Linder started class. More *Hamlet*. I didn't want to think about Hamlet. No slings and arrows of outrageous fortune. Wasn't living through this shit enough? We had to read about it too?

"Do crazy people know when they're crazy?" Linder asked.

Carrie Smith, this nerdy junior girl said, "No. They totally can't tell. My uncle Mark is schizoid and he thinks he's, like, the height of clear brained when he's totally, like, hearing ghost voices in his head. License plate numbers told him he was the reincarnation of Gandhi once."

"Tough," Linder said. "How about this? What if you're a little off, a little cloudy? Do you know something's wrong then?"

Several people raised their hands and nodded.

"I know when I'm not right with the world," said Kayla Zielsdorf. "I just feel confused and can't decide about anything, like what I'm going to wear or eat or whatever."

You don't know the meaning of off! I screamed in my brain.

"Was Hamlet crazy? Did he know his behavior was off? Was it all a plan?" Linder asked.

Then Mrs. McGinn knocked on the door.

"Oh my God. Now what?" Linder spat. "Interrupted three days in a row."

Oh this is it. The cops are here. This is the time when the cuffs come out and you get hauled down to the lockup for crushing a kid against a bleacher. Please. Yes. Bring it on…

Linder opened the door. "We don't want any," he said.

"Special delivery," Mrs. McGinn said. She handed Linder a box.

"Of course," he said, "Addressed to Prince Reinstein of Bluffton. Who else?"

"It's probably a bomb," I said.

Everyone laughed. I didn't laugh.

Linder handed it to me. "Go ahead. We're derailed already. Open it up."

Everybody stared and nodded and smiled. With a buzzing head and weak, shaking hands, I opened the box. There was a handwritten Stanford University note inside. It said, "Congratulations, Felton!" Then I pulled out the most amazing football jersey I'd ever seen up close. It was that new one: dark red with black numbers. There was a little Nike swish and a black Stanford S just under the neckline. My number 34, but on this beautiful Stanford jersey. On the back it said "REINSTEIN."

"Number 34!" Kayla said. (She wore a "Bully Me" shirt that Tommy had made.)

"Whoa," Gus said. "That is cool."

My AP English classmates applauded.

Me? My brain? *Where the hell are the cops?* Where was the hammer from the angry freaking god of track? *Stanford doesn't know my crimes.*

"Was Hamlet crazy? Did he know his behavior was off?" Linder asked.

Hamlet needs a beer. Hamlet needs to lie down.

My classmates applauded.

I stuffed the jersey in my backpack.

CHAPTER 51
Saving Ryan Bennett

After school, I biked in a cold rain. Hard. I shot around town, in between cars that honked (I flipped them off), up big hills. I didn't want to go home and sit there. (I might drink the kerosene Jerri kept for our camp stove, because kerosene smells sort of like alcohol.) I didn't want to go to Abby's and not tell her I'd been kicked off track. *She doesn't understand.*

Part of my brain was saying, *It didn't happen. That meeting with Knautz was a bad dream. You're still on track. Everyone would know!* The other half of my brain said, *You're such a crazy Hamlet loser. Of course it happened. Crazy.*

After biking several circles around all of rainy Bluffton, I just needed some confirmation that all the pain from the day before was real. I biked like dying lightning over to the neighborhood where I knew Ryan Bennett lived.

The cul de sac where I'd seen dudes from Andrew's grade and the grade below playing hoops last summer was on the south end of town, behind the combination KFC–Taco Bell. When I'd biked past back then, one of the dudes had shouted, "Rein Stone, play some ball with us!" I'd waved but hadn't pulled in. One of those little jock kids was Ryan. I knew that.

It took me ten minutes to get there and get up the hill to the new developments that stretch out into former farm fields toward Cuba City. My brain fried and sizzled the whole time. I kept repeating *Ryan Bennett will tell me if I bashed his head for real.*

On the street I thought might be his, the mailboxes are lined up together so the mailman doesn't have to go up to each of the houses individually. I scanned the mailboxes. Sure enough, 115 Adams Court had the name "Bennett" on it. I rolled four houses down, and it was the same white box of a house with the basketball hoop I'd seen from biking before.

When I got in front of it, my heart almost gave out. *What the hell are you doing? You're going to ask Ryan if you actually hurt him? You're going to turn yourself in to his parents? "Sorry, sir, I should be punished. I tried murdering your son."* I took a couple of breaths. Then thought *Yes.*

I set down my bike on the wet ground. Rain had soaked my jacket. My jeans were heavy and sopping blue. My homeless dude hair hung on my forehead. My backpack weighed a ton. I knocked on the door. Carly Bennett, his sophomore sister, answered.

"Uh, hi?" she said. Her face turned red. She sort of stuttered. "What are you doing here?"

"I know. I know," I said. "I shouldn't be here."

"Well, I don't mean…I don't mean that. I just don't know why you're here," Carly said.

"Get Ryan."

"You're not going to hurt him, are you?" she gulped. "Nolan said you…He already has stitches, okay?"

"He does? Okay. Just get him, okay? I don't want to hurt him. I didn't want to."

"Didn't want to what?"

"Hurt his head."

"He fell down. You didn't hurt his head."

"*Just get him!*" I shouted.

She looked like I'd slapped her. "Ryan," she called.

"What?" he shouted back from deep in the house.

"Felton Reinstein is here."

"Ohhh…" I heard him moan.

Carly kept standing there. Staring at me.

Ryan slinked up behind her. Yes, he looked like a jock (wore a Badgers hoops T-shirt). Yes, he still looked like a little kid (tiny shoulders, hairless face). And most important, yes, he had a bandage on his head where it had bounced off the back of the bleachers the day before.

"I did that to your head," I said.

"What? Why didn't you tell Dad?" Carly asked.

"Because," Ryan said.

"You can tell," I said. "You should tell your dad," I said.

"No," he said.

"It's okay," I said. "Your dad should know."

"No…" he gulped for air. "No."

"What is going on?" Carly whispered.

"I had it coming," Ryan wheezed.

"Had it coming?" I said. "Not from me."

"Tommy Bode," Ryan wheezed. "I waited for Tommy when I saw him. I wanted to say sorry."

"Tommy hunted you down."

"No," Ryan said. "I had to tell him…"

"What?" Carly said, swallowing.

"Oh Jesus. Jesus Christ. I pushed Curtis Bode into the bushes outside the middle school right before he…he…" Ryan's eyes filled. His mouth trembled. Snot began to pour out his nose.

"Jesus, Ryan," Carly said. "You pushed Curtis Bode?"

Ryan gulped for air. "I jammed him in this…this stupid bush."

"Dude," I whispered. "Oh man…"

"Why would you shoot yourself?" Ryan cried. "Why would someone? We were just messing around. Why would you…"

"What the hell's going on down there?" A man's voice came from upstairs. "Goddamn it. I told you kids to be quiet until five. Third goddamn shift. Do you understand what…"

A large dude with a big gut came walking down the stairs.

"Sorry, Dad," Carly said.

"Holy…Felton Reinstein? What are you doing here?" the man said.

Ryan looked at me. Tears poured down his face. He wiped his nose on his sleeve.

"Hey," I said. I saw his hand reach out. I thought about what Gus told me about handshakes. I shook hands with that big dad standing next to his son who was totally bawling. That dad didn't even notice.

"Looking forward to track? We sure enjoyed watching you play ball last fall, didn't we, Ryan?"

"Thanks," I breathed. "I…I just wanted to tell Ryan that…that there's nothing better than playing football at Bluffton. He's going to have the time of his life next year."

"Even a klutz like Ryan, huh? He busted his head open walking home yesterday."

"I hear he's great," I said. "He's a player."

"Hear that, buddy?" Ryan's dad said. He still didn't look at Ryan, only at me. "All that work we put in is giving you a name, son."

"I have to go," I said. Ryan was completely losing it while his dad stood there all psyched to see me. Ryan blinked. His face burned. I turned to go. Then stopped. "Wait."

"What?" the dad asked.

I pulled my backpack off and opened it up. I reached in and pulled out the Stanford jersey. I handed it to Ryan.

"Take care of this. Take good care of this," I said. "It's going to be okay."

"Wow!" the dad shouted. "Look at that!"

I pulled my bag back on and moved.

I rode up the street. At the corner, I looked back. Mr. Bennett was still standing in his rainy yard, a shit-eating grin on his face. Ryan stood in the door holding my jersey.

CHAPTER 52
Can't Pardon Me, Governor

M essed-up world.

When I got home, Jerri stood in the living room staring at a letter she'd just opened. She looked up at me. "You're totally soaked."

"I'm cold," I said.

"Uh-huh. This came for you this afternoon," she said. She held up the letter and scrunched her eyebrows.

It was a letter from the Governor of Wisconsin. She handed it to me.

The letter was printed on official Wisconsin letterhead with a big seal of the state on it. It was dated February 13—the day before.

It said:

On behalf of the State of Wisconsin, on this date, February 13, I, Scott K. Thompson, the Honorable Governor of the State of Wisconsin, hereby accept your apology to the people of the state.

All is forgiven, Mr. Reinstein. Best of luck at Stanford. We hope you will return to play for the Packers someday!

"What the hell, Jerri?" I asked.

"Why do people care so much about you?" she asked.

"Do you understand I won the genetic lottery?"

"Those aren't my genes."

"No shit," I said.

Jerri glared.

Then my phone buzzed. A call. I pulled it out of my pocket. A Madison number. "What's this?" I asked Jerri.

"I don't know," Jerri said. "Who?"

I answered. "Hello?"

"Hi, Felton, this is Megan Hansen from WISC-TV. We talked the other day."

"Yeah?"

"Hope you don't mind me reaching out to your cell number. I figured you were out of school by now and we'd like a comment for the 10 o'clock news."

"How'd you get this number?" I mumbled.

"Jay Haas, the sports guy."

I'd talked to him a few times in the fall. "Okay…"

"We received a press release from the governor's office with the text of a letter officially accepting your apology to the state. Did you get it?"

"Yes," I said.

"Pretty cute!" laughed Megan. "We taped a short interview with the governor's spokesman—it's a hoot—and thought it would be fun to get a quick response from you. Just audio. Do you mind?"

"I don't know. I don't think…"

"Nothing complicated. Just a quote."

"Okay. Okay. Fine," I said.

"I'm recording."

Here's what I wanted to say: I banged this dude's walnut against a metal bleacher yesterday. He bled. I shouldn't say "dude." He's a little kid. Scrappy little shit hole of a kid with a fat dad. I did it because my friend's little brother shot himself in the heart with a handgun. That's real. That happened. But you're interested in my response to a joke letter from the freaking governor? That's what you care about?

"What did you think when you got that letter, Felton?"

I took a breath. Concentrated. And here's what I actually said: "Pretty cool. Made me feel good. Thanks, Wisconsin. I hope I play for the Packers too."

"That's all we need. The spot will run tonight. Great talking to you again, Felton. Take care!"

"Bye," I said.

I hung up.

"What the hell?" Jerri asked. "Are you a political asset?"

"I don't know."

"So many people care about you…" Jerri's voice trailed off. Her ears turned red, which is a sign she's pretty fired up. "Call that woman back. You call her back and tell her you will not be pushed around. You will not be made to look like a…a…supporter of some politician. Even if you did support that man, no one should listen to you. No one! Because you're good at a sport, this is…this is…I'm really pissed!" she shouted.

"I don't care about this. Pig Boy wouldn't be forgiven."

"What?" Jerri shouted.

"I don't care about the governor." I stared out the picture window at the darkening sky. Escape. That's what I wanted. Shuffle off the mortal coil. Run farther than I can run. Fast. Instantaneously.

Jerri looked at the ceiling and shook her head. "I don't understand."

"No," I said.

"Oh shit," she sighed. "I used to get so pissed at reality, you know? So pissed about how things are."

"Yeah," I said. "I'm pissed, Jerri."

"Well, what are we going to do about it?" Jerri asked. "Who are we going to fight?" She inflated her cheeks and blew out slow.

"I don't know. Who?" *Tell me, Jerri. Who should we fight?*

"Never mind, right? Never mind. Who really cares, right?" she asked.

"I do," I said.

"Good for you," she said. "Somebody has to." The red bled from her ears. They turned the normal color again. She turned to walk into the kitchen. "You hungry?" she asked.

Help, Jerri.

She disappeared.

"Can I borrow your car?" I called after her.

"Oh, honey," Jerri said. "I've got an economics study group tonight…"

"It's Valentine's Day," I said.

"Terry might come over after," she said.

"Yeah. Good. That's perfect."

277

CHAPTER 53
The Bully Takes a Shower

I had to shower. The freezing February rain had soaked into my skin and I shivered. I peeled off my pants and shirt, which wasn't easy. They felt glued to my body. The cold reached deep into my muscles. I practically cramped up doing the job.

While in the shower, steam rising, I thought: You need to shuffle off the mortal coil. Just a couple of beers. Just fast and easy. Just have to get this shit out of your body. Forget track. Forget Cody and Karpinski. Forget Ryan. Forget Megan Hansen and the governor. Forget Pig Boy, who wants to be a bully, who needs to be a bully…

Wait.

You're the bully, right? Just for the geeks instead of the jocks. Drunk bully scaring Carl Yang…

You're one of them. Throwing weak kids against the bleachers, pinning necks against lockers. You're a dude at a party shoving people, spilling beer. Brutal by nature. Brutal people make for good football players…and bullies and…and…members of the CIA? Death squad commanders? Flat-out murderers? Favorite sons of the State of Wisconsin. Deadly Hamlet, Prince of Bluffton.

Oh shit…Oh no…There's something wrong with the world.

Don't want this world.

I stood there in the water freaking out. Naked as a baby, eyeballs darting around.

Run from this shit. Run. You don't want this.

I turned off the shower. *There's no place to run. Then what?*

Oh God. Oh shit. No. Please stop.

My brain saw that rope. Saw the mortal coil. *Stop. You have to stop. Please!*

But I couldn't stop. I couldn't stop. I couldn't stop.

Shuffle off this mortal coil...

CHAPTER 54
To Drink or Not to Drink,
That Is the Question

Out of the shower, I called Abby. "Can you come get me?" I asked.

"Can you borrow Jerri's car? The Buick is dead, remember?"

"Oh right. Shit," I said. "We need a car. Jerri's got a study group. What about your mom?"

"She left the house. Can you believe it? She went to Nolan's JV game."

"Awesome timing."

"I'm glad she left. Do you want to call Gus?" Abby asked.

"Maybe. I don't know. No." Gus would stop me. He knows me so well he'd see my crazy and stop me. Couldn't have that. I couldn't see a path out, and Gus would torture me.

"You're a serious train wreck, aren't you?" Abby whispered.

"Total and complete."

"Oh…" Abby paused. "Maybe I can borrow Dad's car," Abby said.

"You think?" I asked. *Fat chance.*

"Maybe," Abby said. "He probably feels guilty for screaming at me about the beer and…and for ignoring us. Mom asked him to go to a counselor with us and I…I…" Abby slowed down. Then she whispered, "I bet I can borrow his car."

"Okay," I said. "Try."

"Call you soon," Abby said.

Can you bike there? You can bike. It's raining. You'll wear rain gear. It's dark. Where's your flashlight?

I had a plan. Friday night bar plan. I couldn't see any other path to that beer. I had to go out to Maddie's brother's country shit-house, where I knew I could relax with music and that Love Sac, and the mortal coil could stop tightening around my freaking neck for a few hours. I needed to know those angels were still there.

Abby called me back five minutes later. She sounded somber, but she said, "I just have to pick it up. We have an extra set of keys over here still. Dad said okay."

"What? Are you kidding? He did?"

"Terry would be delighted to let us use the car for the night," Abby said.

Thank God.

• • •

Ten minutes later, Jerri came through the basement, where I sat on the couch staring at the wall.

"Sorry about the car, Felton. Maybe I should get a new car so you can use the Hyundai this summer?" she said.

"That'd be great," I said. *Fat freaking chance.* I stared at the wall across the basement, which was just chipped beige plaster. "We haven't painted this wall," I said.

Jerri stopped. "No?"

"Isn't it weird that it's the same surface as when Dad lived in here?"

"We can paint it."

"Doesn't matter," I said.

"Felton…Do you want to go for a walk in the morning?" she asked. "It's supposed to be wet but still warm. Remember we'd take those hikes when you were a kid? I thought maybe we could…"

"Sure. Talk to you in the morning. Go to your study group."

"Great." She smiled. "I won't be late," she said.

When Jerri left, I climbed the stairs and took forty dollars out of the cash drawer in her bedroom. *I will pay Cal. He won't be mad.*

After I stuffed the money in my pocket, I felt terrible for a second, then I felt mad as hell. *You should be a better mother and then I wouldn't take your money.*

CHAPTER 55
Leave Him

Ten minutes later, Abby showed. She texted from the driveway. I pulled on a thick Bluffton Football hoodie and left through the garage, leaving the garage door open. It was wet but wasn't raining anymore. I still felt cold.

I climbed into Terry Sauter's Cadillac Escalade.

"Can't believe Terry said yes."

"Yeah, me either," Abby said. "What are we doing then?"

"Living the dream," I mumbled.

"Dark, dude. Okay, I mean, what do you want to do?"

"Cal's. Please."

"Uh-huh." Abby turned the Escalade around and rolled down the drive. "I don't know, Felton. That's a bad idea."

"No. Why?"

"First, duh. Remember what Andrew said? Second, I'm not drinking anything because my mom caught me and she's snapping back into reality and I don't want to be any more out of control than I already am. Third, Cal doesn't want us out there. He told us not to show up or he'd shoot us."

"I'm Felton Reinstein. You're Abby Sauter. We can go wherever the hell we want."

"Felton, I don't think so."

"You don't have to drink. We don't have to. It's secluded out there and I would seriously like to hide for a couple of hours."

"Are you sure?" she asked.

"Yes. Please," I said.

Abby paused. She breathed deep. "If we go out there, will you please confess your trouble?"

"Yes," I said. "At Cal's."

"Oh shit," Abby said. "Okay. Fine."

Abby aimed the car at Cal's place and we rolled into the Wisconsin darkness in silence.

We didn't have a problem finding it. We rolled south toward Big Patch. We pulled onto the tiny gravel road down through a creek bottom with high bluffs around us and then onto the tiny gravel drive and up into the woods.

The Escalade's lights were so powerful that the valley of darkness was totally illuminated in front of us. We caught sight of the building. Cal's dumpy schoolhouse looked smaller than before (maybe because the Escalade is so huge).

"Hope he's not pissed," Abby said, turning off the car.

"It'll be fine," I said.

We climbed out and knocked on the door.

A little girl with tangled brown hair answered.

"Who are you?" she asked. Her big blue eyes were wide and her face pale. I could see a resemblance to Maddie.

"Are you Cal's daughter?" Abby asked.

"Uh-huh." She stood staring at us.

Then Cal opened the door wider behind the little girl. He flipped on the light above the door. "What the hell?" he said.

"Uh," I said.

"No," he said. "I've got my kids this weekend. Go home," he said.

"Please," I said.

Cal looked at me. "I suppose I should be honored, right? Dickhead football star and his prom queen show up at my house in the middle of the dark night."

"No. I don't want you to be honored. We just…we just have some problems that need to be sorted…We just need a place to hide out for a little bit," I said.

Cal squinted at Abby and me. Then he said, "Well, aren't we angsty this evening? What's up your hole, brother?"

"Long, ugly story."

"How long?" he asked.

"My whole life."

"Ha. Stanford, here we come, huh?"

"Yeah."

"Fine. Go on back. I might join you in a bit. Got to get the girls down to sleep first," he said.

I stepped toward the door.

"No," Cal said. "Go around. Go around."

Abby and I walked slowly and blindly around the pitch-dark side of the house, stumbling over metal baskets and bike frames. I tripped, cutting my shin, and almost fell.

"Whoa," Abby said.

I had to put my hands down to keep from planting my knees in the mud. From down near the ground, I saw something.

"Abby. Do you have a flashlight app on your phone?" I asked. My hands were caked in cold mud. I wiped them on my jeans.

"Oh, duh," she said.

A second later, she'd illuminated the area around me. Right in front of my face, lying on the ground, was a tall, blue bike frame, a Schwinn Varsity frame, the same bike my dad had, that I inherited and rode constantly for three years, even when it was way too big for me, a bike I crushed to pieces when I found out who my dad really was (tennis star who knocked up his student, not a short, fat, gentle dude like Jerri had always said—he was a man like me).

"Oh shit," I said. "My bike."

"Is that really yours?" Abby asked. "I remember that bike."

"Just like mine." I pulled it off the ground. It had handlebars and a fork and a chain wheel, crank and pedals but no wheels and no chain. "It's not really mine. I broke my front fork and killed the derailleur with a shovel." I carried the frame to the side of the barn and set it upright, leaned it against a wall.

"I always liked that bike," Abby said.

"Me too. I loved it. I killed it."

"Why?" Abby asked.

"It was my dad's bike." I turned away and entered the barn. *Stop.*

We had to turn the lights on in the barn, which was fine, except I couldn't figure out how to make the outlet with the Christmas lights work, so it didn't look like I wanted it to.

"Do you think Cal would mind if we drank something?" I asked.

"Felton, I said no. You just want to hide. You aren't drinking."

"No. I'm here to drink."

"Come on! Did you just flat-out lie to get me here? What about what Andrew said? What he told you about your dad?"

"I need to shuffle off my mortal coil."

"What?"

"Seriously, Abby, I feel like I'm going to burst."

"Why?" Abby asked. "It sort of seems like things are going great, Felton. Stanford and the video…"

"And the governor sent me a letter accepting my apology to the State of Wisconsin."

"What?"

"Seriously."

"So…" Abby stared at me for a second. "That's good. That's all good. Are you really worried about Karpinski? Cody is going to forgive you during track, you know? You're just not spending any time with those guys right now. You're just not together. It isn't that big a deal."

"Abby," I breathed deep. "Knautz kicked me off the track team."

"*What?*" she shouted. "When?"

"Yesterday. That's what he was shouting about in the locker room. Not about being out of shape."

"He can't just kick you off. Why would he do that?"

"Someone turned me in for drinking."

"Oh no," she said.

"Yeah," I said.

"Jesus. Cody." She shook her head. "How could he?"

"No," I said. "He can."

"He's such an arrogant jerk," Abby hissed.

"No," I said.

"He said my shit would put you in danger, Felton. He threatened me outside the school on Monday. I told him we'd stopped. I told him we were taking care of each other. And now you're kicked off track? Is this to get you back for Karpinski?"

"It doesn't matter. It's right. It's what I did. I broke the rules. I'm glad someone is making me pay for doing the wrong thing."

"No," Abby whispered.

"Yes," I said.

"No, dude. You've totally spent this whole year protecting Tommy Bode. You're the only one of our friends who…you wouldn't have sex with me, man. I would've done it and it might've sent me over the edge. You saw the truth and took care of me. You're such a good guy. Why should you pay? What do you need to pay for?"

"Can we please have a drink? I brought forty dollars. I'll leave it for Cal. Please?"

Abby paused. She shook her head. "No."

"Come on," I pleaded. "I'm off track. I have nothing to lose."

"Call Andrew."

"What?"

"Call Andrew. If he can't talk you out of it, I'm in, okay? We'll drink up."

"Abby," I whispered, "I cracked Ryan Bennett's head against a bleacher yesterday."

"Jesus, dude."

"Okay?"

Abby shook her head. "No. This is probably what happened to your dad. He probably couldn't deal with the whole thing. Call your brother or I'm leaving."

Can I tell you how much I hated Abby at that moment? My damn skin was screaming and there it was, all this beer and crap right there behind Cal's bar.

Please. Please. Please…

She reached out and grabbed my hand.

"Please, Abby?"

"Call Andrew," she said.

"Shit," I said. "You're killing me."

"No, I'm not," Abby said.

I shook loose of her hand, glared at her, then pulled my phone out and called Andrew. It took him four rings to pick up.

"Felton, I have a gig," he said. "Can I call you back in a couple hours?"

"He's busy," I said to Abby.

"Come on," she whispered.

"No," I said. "I guess I need you right now."

Andrew paused for a second. "What is it?" he asked. "Is this bad news? Do you want me to sit down on my butt so I'm safe from fainting?"

"No. Maybe." My voice wavered.

"Felton, what?"

"Okay…Please? Give me a good reason why I shouldn't have a

beer because I'm telling you, Andrew, I'm all wound weird and I'm not feeling good and I know from experience that beer helps."

"Uh-huh? No. Don't have a beer," he said.

"That's not good enough," I said.

"Are you at a senior party of some kind? Is there peer pressure involved?"

"No. You think I'd worry about pressure from a bunch of numb-nuts sitting in a damn cornfield with a keg of beer?"

"Anger, Felton," Andrew said.

"I know," I said.

"So you really want to drink a beer because you're mentally imbalanced and you think alcohol will make it better. You're self-medicating."

My head hurt. I squinted. "Self-medicating?" I asked.

Andrew paused again. "Have you asked Jerri about this?"

"Jerri told me that I'm not like Dad at all. So she's not worried, okay?"

"Oh really?" Andrew said. "She's stupid."

"Oh really?" I spat.

"Yes," Andrew said. "Grandpa's with me at the Shells. You have to talk to him now."

"No!" I shouted, but Andrew had already taken the phone away from his ear.

I glared at Abby. My heart dropped. Embarrassed. I swallowed. "Now my grandpa," I said.

She nodded.

And my stomach turned hard. The hole in my middle opened. I heard him breathe. I heard him.

"What's this?" Grandpa Stan said on the other end.

"It's nothing," I whispered.

"No, Felton," he said. Beach Boys music began playing in the background. "This is the beginning of the end for you."

"I don't know," I said.

"This is how your father gave up control, Felton. This is how he gave up. He didn't drink in high school and he was sad sometimes because he was wired sad. He always bounced back though," Grandpa said, speaking fast. "He never crashed through the floor. But in college, he found his drug. After he was done with tennis, he spent all his time with whisky in his hand. All the pictures of him in graduate school, he had whisky in his hand. And he went down, down, down. Nothing we could do to stop him. He knew it was terrible for him, but he couldn't stop…"

I knew it. *There's no path…no other way out.*

"Felton," Grandpa said, "you are like your father in every way I can tell."

"No," I said. "I don't want to die."

"He didn't want to, Felton. Not when he was your age. He was funny and sweet."

"Why hasn't anyone told me that?" I wheezed. Jerri called me sweet.

"He would hold hands with his mother, even in high school, Felton. They'd walk holding hands…"

The image of my young dad holding hands with my grandma opened in my chest.

"He was a good boy, Felton. And I yelled at him for no reason. Yelled about tennis."

I could tell my grandfather was sort of crying. "Okay," I said. "I'm sorry. But…"

Grandpa's voice got higher. Words caught in his throat. "Then the switch flipped. His brutality. He would destroy his opponents. There was no grace in this. He would make them lie down in front of him, like you did to those poor kids when I came up for your football game. It stopped being a game to him and it became destruction. A display of power. That's all.

"And that's why I told you to love what it feels like to play. Do you see? It's just a game. But after I saw you destroy on the field like your father, I told you to quit now, get away, before it becomes who you are. Go climb a mountain! Go be a swami! I saw him in you, Felton. I can see him! Please. Do you understand?"

"I know," I whispered.

"Because when he stopped playing, he started brutalizing everyone off the court. He brutalized himself with this alcohol. He brutalized me. He brutalized your mother. He brutalized everyone…"

"I got kicked off track."

"No. Felton. Please. No. You stop. Booze makes it easy for people like you to forget everyone and everything."

"That's what I want."

"It isn't. You don't want them to go away. You don't want to go away. You're kind. You're funny. You're sweet. That's who you are. You want people with you."

"I want them to go…I want him to go away." I started to lose it. I started to shake. I started to sob. "My dad did this to me, Grandpa.

My dad did this. I have a hard time being alive, Grandpa, because my dad…"

"I'd kill your father again if he ever hurt you…" Grandpa howled.

"I don't know what to do."

"You leave him. Only him. You tell him good-bye! You get the hell away from wherever you are! I'll be there tomorrow, Felton. I'm coming. *Now, Felton. Go!*" he shouted.

CHAPTER 56
I Am There for You

Abby followed me out of the barn. I stumbled into the dark and turned back to look at that Schwinn Varsity, that bike like Dad's. "No."

I turned away and saw the path past Cal's, back to the car. I saw it and I followed it.

"Where are we going?" Abby called behind me.

"Out of here, okay? Now," I said, shaking.

I climbed into the passenger seat. Abby climbed behind the wheel. "Back to town?"

"Home."

"What's going on?"

"I have to leave my dad behind. I have to. That's what Grandpa said. He'll be here tomorrow."

She nodded and spun the Escalade around. She tore onto the gravel road and we headed for town.

My muscles twitched. I sucked air.

My brain began to shut down. I swear. I only vaguely remember Abby getting calls. I vaguely remember her saying, "Uh-oh." I don't remember anything else until we hit the driveway to my house back in Bluffton.

When we got there, Abby said, "I…I don't think I can hang out for too long, okay? Dad wants his car back."

"Okay," I said.

Odd. My house was like a damn star. Every light burned bright. We pulled up the drive into the halo cast around the whole yard.

Abby parked the Escalade out front. Jerri stood in the picture window just like she did when I used to run and she'd watch me. She stared down at us.

"That's weird," I said. "Why is Jerri home?" I mumbled.

Abby breathed in.

As we came up the front walk, Jerri left the window. I opened the screen door. Abby followed. She was breathing in sighs.

"You okay?" I asked.

"I don't know. It's okay," Abby whispered.

I opened the inside door and entered the living room. Jerri stood next to the couch, her arms folded across her chest.

"I was just about to call you," Jerri said.

"Why are you here?" I mumbled. "Your study group?"

She stared at my forehead. Her face was red. Her ears were red. "What's your plan? Where you going?"

"Nowhere."

"Really, Felton?" Then Jerri focused on Abby. "Hi, Abby! How are you? Everything just great?" Jerri snapped.

"What are you doing?" I asked.

Just then, the toilet flushed back in the house.

"Uh-oh," Abby said.

Terry Sauter walked slowly down the hall and into the living room.

His face was burning red. He smiled his big, fake, asswipe smile. "Look who's here!" he said.

"Shit," Abby said under her breath. She turned almost purple. She stared at the wall to her right.

"Have a good time, pumpkin? You enjoy Daddy's car?"

"Yes," Abby said. "I enjoyed our car."

"Our car?" he said.

"I enjoyed driving our car," Abby said.

"That's not your car."

Abby turned to him. "No? Really?"

"I told you no," he hissed. "I told you…"

"So?" Abby said.

"So?" Terry shouted. "So?"

"So what?" Abby said. "That's the family car. That's not your car."

"Ask my lawyer. Ask him whose car that is," Terry spat.

"What's going on?" I asked.

"Your girlfriend stole Terry's car," Jerri said.

"You can't steal what's yours!" Abby shouted.

"You little shit," Terry said.

"Little shit?" I said. Adrenaline shot up inside me.

"No," Abby cried. "You're the bad guy. You're the thief."

"You little bitch," Terry said. He took a step toward her.

I took a step toward both of them.

"You're the one taking everything. You're the one stealing," Abby cried.

"That is not your car. I pay your mother so you don't drive that car. Do you understand? Give me the keys." He took another step and inflated, stood tall, pushed out his chest.

I felt a rush of color and light around me. This is how it feels.

Abby fumbled around. She pulled the keys out of her bag. She threw them on the floor and they slid ten feet.

Terry looked at them for a second. He shook his head. He hissed, "Just like your mother. Rude and nasty."

"Mom?" Abby shouted. "Rude? Are you kidding? She cowers around you!"

Terry started whining, mocking. "Why can't I drive the nice car? Why do you have to go to work so early? Why don't you take Nolan with you?"

"I hate you," Abby said.

"You people drive me crazy," Terry said.

"Asshole," Abby whimpered.

"You think you're owed just because you were born."

Abby started sobbing. I moved a step closer to Terry Sauter.

Terry didn't even look at me. "Ignorant bitch just like your…"

I slid toward Terry because I couldn't take it anymore.

"Thieving little bitch," he said.

"That's it," I mumbled.

"Get out of my house," Jerri said.

I stopped. We all looked over at her.

"Get the hell out of my house."

Terry looked stunned. "Me?"

"How can you speak to your own daughter like that? Get out right now or I'm going to let my son here tear you limb from limb. Do you understand?"

For the first time, Terry looked at me. I was close. He immediately deflated. He got tiny. "It's cool, buddy," he said, putting his hands up like I had a gun on him. "It's cool."

"Pick up your keys," I whispered. I was trembling.

Terry slid over to his keys. He kept his eyes on me. He bent and picked them up and jammed them in his pocket. He stood straight, exhaled, and looked at Jerri. "I'm sorry," he said. "I'm angry."

"Go," Jerri said.

Terry stood in front of us, shaking his head. "I'm sorry," he said. "Please."

I reached out and grabbed his wrist. I guided Terry to the door. "You can't be mean to people like that, okay?" I said.

He nodded. "I'll let myself out," he said.

I let go. He left. We stood in this pressure, in this silence.

Then Jerri wheezed, "Oh my God, I'm sorry." She turned to Abby. "I'm so sorry."

And then Abby Sauter fell apart. She cried almost all night.

If she hadn't, I would've. I kept it together to keep Abby safe. I held her on the couch in the basement.

Around 4 a.m., Abby finally fell asleep.

I'd heard Jerri pacing upstairs for hours. When it was quiet, she came down.

She whispered, "I got a message from your grandfather. He'll be here in the afternoon."

"Good," I whispered.

Jerri shook her head. "I didn't know this was happening to you."

"I know," I whispered. "I'm going to sleep now, Jerri."

She nodded and left the basement.

Spring

CHAPTER 57
I Could Tell You

I could tell you that Coach Knautz didn't tell me the whole truth. I could tell you that by rule because my infraction was out of season, I only received an eight-week suspension. Knautz was a wreck when he found out I'd been hospitalized for an anxiety disorder. He'd tried to scare me straight! Not the best approach for this student-athlete, Coach! I could tell you about the Internet rumors of my drug use (I didn't show up at early invitationals) or how I worked as the team manager until April.

I could tell you about how good it felt to run with the team when I could finally run. The act of running (not running away) is reason enough to live. I could tell you about winning the 200 meters and the long jump at State. That was cool. Or how the team won State because that was great. Or how I raced Roy Ngelale just once at the meet, in the 100 meters final, and how I beat him but was beaten myself by a skinny blond dude in purple shorts, Jonathan Schindler, a sophomore from Waunakee. The kid was stunned. He was like, "I'm sorry, man. I'm so sorry." He totally made me laugh. Where do all these dorky kids come from?

I could tell you about how I apologized to Karpinski and he said he had it coming and that his stupid dad actually loved the video because people talked about him in bars. I could tell you about

Ryan Bennett's email, where he said he'd protect all the weak kids. I could tell you that Cody apologized to me and I hugged him and told him not to be an idiot because he's the best.

I could tell you about Cody's dad crying when he said he'd been the one to turn to turn me in. He's a cop. Of course he had to turn me in. He said, "You've been on the wrong side of a stacked deck so much." I told him thanks, and I meant it because this shit was coming for me. This shit was going to happen sometime. I'm glad it happened while Abby was around, while Bluffton, Wisconsin, was there to pick me up.

Or I could tell you about Mercy Hospital in Dubuque and Grandpa and how we sat in the cafeteria one afternoon and he asked me to call him twice a week, minimum, to give him updates so he could monitor me and give perspective on my dad. He said I should never be ashamed. Once, he cried because his wife, my grandma, died before she could help me.

Or about how I have both a "potentiating" background and have exhibited multiple warning signs in "action" and "ideation" that made doctors call me a suicide risk. Isn't that weird? But I did have thoughts. But I don't want to die. Did Dad really want to? I won't ever know. That's okay.

Or about my psychiatrist, Dr. Green, who thought I should take meds to combat my problems. Andrew was with me on this one. We both said, "No way." If it ever happens again—a break like that—I'll consider medication, okay? But I feel like I learned something. That talk therapy can work. It has worked. I still go twice a week (as well as calling Grandpa).

I could tell you about the time I complained to Dr. Green that I'd made my Stanford decision when I was a dickweed who couldn't think straight and she asked me to bring in my reasons for choosing Stanford, so the next time I brought in the list I wrote for Gus in the fall, thinking she'd see how messed up I was.

1. Dude in dress served me iced tea.
2. Cute guide didn't try to grab my wang.
3. Library had leather couches.
4. Kicker discussed Louis C.K.
5. Frisbee players were very good.
6. Fog on mountains.

She laughed while reading. She smiled. "You knew yourself pretty well, didn't you?" she said.

"Really?" I asked.

"You were looking for something specific from a school: accepting, ethical, intellectual, physically active, and beautiful."

I thought for a moment. I said, "Yeah. That's right, I guess."

"You wrote all that in this list, you know?"

"I guess I did."

"Maybe those are your values?"

"Maybe?" I said.

"You're doing great," she said. "Trust yourself. I love this list."

I could tell you about the fire I had in May, when I asked Jerri to come out to the pit in our yard with me, where I intended to burn Dad's "I'm with Stupid" T-shirt. But she stopped me before I could do it. She said, "Haven't we made this mistake before?"

I looked at her, glowing orange in the same fire she'd made when I was little, in the fire Andrew used to burn his clothes a couple years back, and I nodded. "Holy balls, Jerri. We do this crap all the time, right?"

"We can't erase your dad. We can't fight him," Jerri said.

"We should let him go."

"Let him be a memory," Jerri said.

"I bet he'd want me to remember not to be like him."

"Right," Jerri said, "He had problems, but…" Jerri swallowed. "He loved you."

"I don't know, Jerri. That's okay."

I folded up the shirt, walked with Jerri into the house. I put it back in my drawer. A month later, I put it in a box that was shipped to Palo Alto.

I could tell you that my barber, Frank, refused to cut my hair because I'd apparently cut him off on my bike in February. I'd apparently flipped him the bird when he honked. My Jewfro is wicked right now. I've gone six months!

I could tell you that Gus decided to break up with Maddie. The next day, they got together again, then he left for college in Massachusetts.

I could tell you that Andrew quit his Beach Boys cover band because he wants to concentrate on Buddhist meditation and thinks performance serves his ego (weird kid).

I could tell you that Aleah will be in San Francisco. She'll study music composition at the conservatory there. That's why she wanted me to call her. She wanted to ask my permission to go to school near me. Crazy. Of course I want her to go to school near me. Now we've talked. We've held hands. Fifteen days ago, we walked a trail to the top of Buena Vista Park.

I could tell you that Abby kept her Regents Scholarship and she'll do great at Wisconsin next year, but I don't know if she'll do great. That hasn't happened yet. We text a lot. She left for Madison yesterday afternoon. She texted, *here I go…*

And here I am, sitting in my dorm room at Stanford. I'm eighteen years old. My roommate, T.J., a freshman linebacker from Idaho, is playing *Halo* on his Xbox. We've been in training camp for two weeks and it hurts. T.J. groans whenever he moves. It seems pretty clear that I'm going to play a lot this year, maybe be first team right from the start, play this hugely violent game because I love it (I do, Grandpa) and I'm good and I run plays half the time with the first team offense and that's great, fine, but what I really want to tell you is this:

We have problems, okay? We're also great. There aren't many rules and there are one million freaking hurdles for most of us. Do you know what I mean? Hamlet's mortal coil is real. It's tough. We can't run away. You are always with you. I'm always with me. We can't run away. But we're not written into a play, so we can choose how we act.

My grandma Berba came up for graduation. She bent me down and kissed my forehead. Grandpa Stan had early surgery on his hernia because it got bad, so he couldn't be there. I walked into the gym holding hands with my mom, Jerri. Andrew, my little brother, followed us in, shaking hands with everybody he saw (like a long-lost hero). Gus gave the valedictorian's speech. He played

"O-o-h Child" through the P.A. system. Everybody cheered for him, and he said, "I am gone."

After the ceremony, instead of going to the big M with our friends (we'd gone a bunch of times in late May, sat up there on the hill with them all, watching the twinkling lights of Bluffton come on), Abby sent a text to Cal, then we drove her crap Buick out to Cal's place one last time. She promised it wasn't for drinking. I believed her, of course. But I still felt nervous. (I still feel nervous a lot—but I'm better.) "It's okay, man. I have a graduation present for you. That's all," she said.

When we got there, we found Cal standing out in front of his little schoolhouse holding the bike, an exact replica of the Schwinn my dad had ridden in college, the bike I rode while I grew from squirrel nut to mammoth jock. He'd fixed it completely. Refurbished it. He'd even repainted the cursive "Varsity" on its side.

I walked up to it, my heart pumping.

"Fully operational, kick-ass bicycle," Cal said. "Your prom queen over there is a hell of a sweet girl."

I turned to Abby, my mouth hanging open. "Oh shit," I said.

"You like it?" she laughed.

"I love this bike so much," I whispered.

"Ride it home, Felton. I'll follow you," she said.

"Eighty fat ones, lady friend," Cal said.

"I've got fifty bucks," Abby said.

"Good enough."

And I was already on my dad's bike, the good bike. What do I know about my dad? Speed. The best thing my dad and I share? Speed.

There was no thought on that bike, and in the dying light of the Bluffton June, I rushed into the wind and the weeds in the ditches blurred as I rode my dad's Schwinn Varsity faster and faster, the pool of Abby's headlights encompassing me, down the side of those southwestern Wisconsin bluffs, faster, the rush, so fast, I was stunned to find I'd gotten back into town so soon.

Abby pulled up next to me. "Good?" she shouted.

"You're my sister. I love you!" I shouted back.

But that's not the end.

We have problems, but we're so lucky too. That's the mortal coil. It's the whole thing, all of it, and it's easy to hate that mess in yourself, fight it, hate those who seem to cause it. But whoever we sit next to in school is the same and whatever jerk you read about on ESPN is the same and whoever honks their horn at you at the intersection is the same. They struggle. Do you know what I mean? They suffer too. We aren't alone.

Dr. Green says this is my guiding principle, something I've known without knowing and now I need to trust it, and I agree with her. I said it to her. We can act. Maybe not fix anything. But we can make it better for those others and that makes it better for us. I see it. I've seen it. Good comes back around.

The morning after graduation, I walked into the garage. Below the beam where my dad ended himself, Andrew sat balanced on my racing bike. We'd put down the seat so it fit him okay.

"Ready?" he asked.

I climbed on the Schwinn Varsity. "You?" I asked.

"I'm not the greatest cyclist," he said. "Don't take off like a gorilla."

"Try not to." I smiled.

We pedaled down the hill and onto the main road that leads to our house. Golfers whacked balls at the country club above us. Bees hovered in the ditch on our right. Then we turned and headed into town.

We rode slowly because Andrew likes to talk. He played the remember game. "Remember when you buried yourself in leaves that one Halloween and Ken Johnson ran you over on his dirt bike?" Andrew asked.

"Yeah," I said. "Barely."

"You got a cut on your nose," Andrew said.

"Really?" I didn't remember.

"Jerri said it helped your costume look more authentic."

"What was I that year?" I asked.

"A turtle," Andrew said. "A turtle with a bloody nose."

It took us twenty minutes (Andrew screwing around) to get to Tommy Bode's house near downtown. There were no cars parked out front, so I was afraid we'd missed him.

But when I knocked, he came to the door. He wore the Bakugan T-shirt he had on the first day I met him. It wasn't so giant. He'd grown.

He looked right past me. "Hey!" he shouted. "Andrew Reinstein!" People love Andrew for some reason.

"Tommy," I said, "We want you to try out a bike."

"Why?" he asked.

"To see if you like it."

"Okay," he shrugged.

Andrew leaned and got off the bike. Tommy climbed on the thing.

It's a pretty sweet ride, a Cannondale. But I didn't really want two bikes at Stanford, and I wasn't going to give up the Schwinn ever again.

Tommy teetered a little, rolled.

"*Pedal the sucker,*" I shouted.

He pedaled and began to pick up speed on Fourth Street. I nodded at Andrew and took off after him.

We hit a stretch of five blocks with no stop signs. Tommy pedaled hard. "I've never gone so fast," Tommy shouted as I pedaled up next to him.

"You're moving, man," I said.

"I can go faster," he said and really went. I had to change gears to keep up.

"You like it?" I shouted, after I pulled next to him.

"Hell yeah," he cried.

"It's yours."

Tommy hit the brakes and stopped. I stopped just in front of him, turned back to look at him.

"Why are you giving me your bike?" Tommy asked, breathing hard.

"Because I want to. Plus you have to move from sidekick to superhero, so you need some kick-ass equipment."

"Dude," Tommy said, "I am fast on this bike."

I smiled so hard my ears hurt. "Dude, you are stupid fast on that bike."

"Makes sense," Tommy said. He cocked his head toward me. He nodded and, using his deep and gravelly superhero voice, growled, "I'm with Stupid."

He took off up Fourth Street. He totally whooped as he rode.

Acknowledgments

Thanks so much to Jim McCarthy, my great agent. To Leah Hultenschmidt, my editor, who I have called a swing doctor for books.

She said, "What does that mean?" I said, "I don't know, exactly, but it's a very good thing to be."

To Sourcebooks generally—I love working with all of you. Thanks to my excellent mom, my genius wife, Steph, and to all those kids we hang with: Leo, Mira, Christian, and Charlie. My family is inspiring in a million ways. Thanks to librarians and teachers who keep getting books in kids' hands.

Finally, thanks to Minnesota State, Mankato, and the Andreas Endowment for the wonderful support.

About the Author

Geoff Herbach is the author of the award-winning *Stupid Fast* YA series. His books have been given the 2011 Cybil Award for best YA novel, selected for the Junior Library Guild, and listed in the year's best by the American Library Association, the American Booksellers Association, and many state library associations. In the past, he wrote the literary novel *The Miracle Letters of T. Rimberg*, produced radio comedy shows, and toured rock clubs telling weird stories. Geoff teaches creative writing at Minnesota State, Mankato. He lives in a log cabin with his tall wife.